ANNE STUART

"...nsummate mistress of her craft, Stuart crafts a sophisticated romance that mirrors the rigours of the era and adds her own punch of passion and adventure so that her characters can have the time of their lives. It is pure pleasure to indulge in this part-lighthearted, part-deeply emotional and all-glorious story."
—*RT Book Reviews* on *The Devil's Waltz*

"This taut romantic suspense novel from RITA® Award winner Stuart delivers deliciously evil baddies and the type of disturbing male protagonist that only she can transform into a convincing love interest... Brilliant characterisations and a suitably moody ambience drive this dark tale of unlikely love."
—*Publishers Weekly* on *Black Ice*

"[A] sexy, edgy, exceptionally well-plotted tale."
—*Library Journal* on *Into the Fire*

"Before I read...[a] Stuart book I make sure my day is free... Once I start, she has me hooked."
—*New York Times* bestselling author Debbie Macomber

"A master at creating chilling atmosphere with a modern touch."
—*Library Journal*

ICE BLUE
ANNE STUART

MIRA

Author's Note

The True Realization Fellowship and its leader, the Shirosama, is very loosely inspired by the Aum Shinrikyo cult in Japan and their charismatic leader, Shoko Asahara. Most people remember the sarin gas attack on the Tokyo subways twelve years ago, when terrorist attacks were less common, and there's something about cults, Jonestown and the like, that are macabre and fascinating. Believe it or not, the real characters were just as badly behaved as my fictional ones—sometimes more so. I simply used Aum as a jumping-off point to create my own delusional madman.

For those who want to explore the story further, there are a number of excellent books, including *Destroying the World to Save It* by Robert Jay Lifton, *A Poisonous Cocktail?* by Ian Reader and *Underground: The Tokyo Gas Attack and the Japanese Psyche* by Haruki Murakami.

For the three great natural beauties of Japan—
Etushi Toyokawa, Yoshiki Hayashi and Gackt Camui.

With thanks to Karen Harbaugh for technical
advice, my daughter for the inspiration, and my
sister Taffy Todd, who complains that I never
dedicate a book to her. Here you go, Taffy.

1

Summer Hawthorne wasn't having a particularly good night, though she smiled and said all the right things to all the right people. Someone was watching her. She'd been feeling it all evening long, but she had absolutely no idea who it was. Or why.

The opening reception at the elegant Sansone Museum was small and exclusive—only the very rich and very powerful were invited to the tiny museum in the Santa Monica Mountains to view the collection of exquisite Japanese ceramics. And even if she wasn't particularly fond of one of those guests, he'd have no reason to watch her.

Her assistant, Micah Jones, resplendent in deep purple, sidled up to her. "I'm leaving you, my darling. This is winding down, and no one will miss me. I'm assuming everything's going well, and I've got an offer I can't refuse." He grinned.

Summer jumped, startled. "Evil man," she said

lightly. "Abandoning me in my time of need. Go ahead. I've got everything under control. Even his holiness."

Micah glanced at their guest of honor and shuddered dramatically. "I can stay and shield you…"

"Not on your life! The True Realization Fellowship and their slimy leader are just a bunch of harmless crackpots. Hollywood's religion du jour. Besides, you've been celibate for too long, or so you've been complaining."

"If you'd wear anything but black you might get lucky, too," Micah said, candid as ever. "Even so, you look marvelous."

"You lie," she said, ignoring her uneasiness. "But I love you, anyway. Despite the fact that you're ditching the reception early."

Micah smiled his dazzling smile. "True love waits for no man." He leaned down and gave her an exuberant kiss. "You know your room's ready for you if you need it. Just ignore any whoops of pleasure coming from my bedroom."

"You're a very bad man," she said affectionately. "I'm fine, I promise you. You can enjoy yourself in private."

He blew her a kiss, sauntering off through the crowd, and she watched him go, ignoring her sudden, irrational pang of unease. Feeling the eyes digging into her back once more.

She was half tempted to call Micah back, ask him to wait. The reception would be over in another half hour, and then she could follow him down from the museum, and this odd, tense feeling would vanish.

But she hadn't gotten this far in her life by giving in to irrational fears. It simply had to be because of their esteemed guest of honor, his holiness the Shirosama. He had a reason to watch her out of his colorless eyes—she was standing between him and the prize Summer's foolish mother, Lianne, had promised him. And the Shirosama had not gotten to where he was, as head of a worldwide spiritual movement, without knowing how to get what he wanted.

He wanted her Japanese bowl, probably as much as she didn't want him to have it—the bowl her Japanese nanny had given to her a short while before she'd been killed in a car accident. It was one more betrayal from her self-absorbed mother, something she was used to by now. Summer had loaned it to the exclusive museum where she worked, just to keep it away from the religious charlatan for as long as she could. But sooner or later the creepy, charming Shirosama was going to get it, and there wasn't a whole lot she could do about it. At least she'd put it off for the time being.

But it wasn't the Shirosama who was watching her, or any of his white-robed minions—not as far as she could tell. She could feel the eyes boring into her back, and she turned, trying to catch whoever it was. Certainly not the elderly Asian couple by the fourteenth century incense burners. Not the tall, slender man with the sunglasses, who seemed much more interested in the impressive cleavage of the blonde he was talking to than in the exhibit. Maybe she was imagining it.

She recognized only half of the elegantly dressed guests who filled the gallery for this private opening, and none would have any reason to be interested in the lowly junior curator at the Sansone Museum. Her connection to Lianne and Ralph Lovitz and their Hollywood lifestyle was generally unknown, and by southern California standards she was totally ordinary looking, something she did her best to cultivate.

"His holiness wishes to speak with you."

She was very good at hiding her emotions, and she turned to face the monk, if that's what he was. For a group of ascetics, the followers of the True Realization Fellowship tended to be particularly well fed, and the plump young man in front of her was no different. He had the same round face, shaved head and faintly sanctimonious look they all did, and it made her want to stomp on his sandaled feet.

She was being childish and she knew it. She could come up with an excuse, but the reception was drawing to a close, the trustees were seeing to the departing guests and she had no real reason to avoid their guest of honor.

"Of course," she said, trying to add a note of warmth to her voice. Someone had trashed her house three nights ago, taking nothing, but she'd known instinctively what they'd been looking for. The Japanese bowl they coveted was right in front of them now, guarded by an excellent security system.

She crossed the room, feeling like a prisoner on her way to execution. She could still feel those eyes boring into her back, but all the Shirosama's posse, including the man himself, were in front of her. She glanced behind, but there was no one except the blonde and her date. Summer decided she must be paranoid, looking behind her for trouble when it was right in front of her.

"Dr. Hawthorne," his holiness greeted her in his soft voice. "You do me honor."

It was the softest of barbs—he knew very well that he was the one conferring honor on the place, at least by conventional wisdom. The Shirosama was highly sought after; obtaining his presence at a social event was a great coup.

Unlike his followers, he hadn't shaved his head— his pure white hair was long and flowing to his shoulders, a perfect match to his paper-white skin and pale, pink eyes. His white robes draped his rounded body, and his hands were soft and plump. Charismatic to those easily swayed, like her ditzy mother. Harmless. Unless he was thwarted, and Summer was thwarting him.

But she knew how to play the game. "You honor *us,* your holiness." She didn't even trip over the words.

"And this is the bowl your mother spoke of?" he said softly. "I wonder that it has no provenance, and yet you still put it in the exhibit."

He knew as well as she did that she'd put it on display to keep it out of his hands. "We're researching its background, your holiness," she said, the absolute truth. "In the meantime a piece of such singular beauty deserves to be seen, and we were ready to open an exhibit of Japanese ceramics. It seemed only logical to show it."

"Only logical," he echoed. "I would be very interested in anything you might discover about the piece. I am somewhat an expert in ceramics, and I've never seen anything that particular shade of blue. Perhaps you might let me borrow it, examine it more closely, and I could help you with your research."

"You're very kind," she murmured. "But I'm certain the piece has little monetary worth—it was simply a gift from my nanny, and for that reason I cherish it. If in fact it does have considerable intrinsic value, then I would return it to the Japanese government."

There was no shadow in the Shirosama's benevolent smile. "You are as generous and honorable as your mother."

Summer resisted a snort. It wasn't enough that Lianne was funneling huge sums of money into the True Realization Fellowship, which seemed to have an insatiable need for cash. They weren't getting Summer's Japanese bowl, no matter how much they seemed to want it. She knew why Lianne wanted to get rid of it. Ralph had told her it was valuable, and Lianne had always been jealous of Summer's nanny. Hana-san had been the mother Lianne had never had time to be, loving Summer, protecting her, teaching her what she needed to know and listening to her. The bowl had been one of the keepsakes she'd given Summer when Lianne had finally managed to fire her and send Summer off to boarding school, and Summer had promised that she'd keep it safe until Hana came for it. But Hana had died, unexpectedly.

And shallow, beautiful Lianne wanted to hand it over to her current guru. Over Summer's dead body.

"Your mother has expressed great sorrow that you haven't been to see her recently," he added in his soft, rolling voice. "She wishes to make peace with you."

"How very kind," Summer murmured. Lianne Lovitz preferred her daughter to be as far away as possible—it was damn hard to convince the world you were in your early forties if you had a daughter in her late twenties hanging around. If the Shirosama wanted her to say anything more, she wasn't going to; her relationship with her mother was none of his business.

He turned to glance back at the ceramic bowl. "You know that she promised this to me?"

Nothing like coming straight to the point. "And you know it was not hers to promise, your holiness," Summer said with exquisite politeness.

"I see," the Shirosama murmured, though Summer had no doubt her mother had filled him in on all this. "But do you not think it should be returned to its rightful place in Japan? To the shrine where it belongs?"

"Almost everything in this room should be back in Japan," she said. *Including you,* she added silently. "Perhaps I should be in touch with the Ministry of Fine Arts and see if they're interested."

It was rare to see someone with no pigmentation in their skin turn paler still. "I doubt that's necessary. I will be returning to Japan in a short while—I can make inquiries for you if you wish."

She bowed as Hana had taught her. "That would be very kind of you," she replied with exquisite courtesy. She'd heard rumors that the Shirosama and his Fellowship were not particularly well thought of in Japan—probably a result of the distrust built up after the sarin-gas poisonings on the Tokyo subways more than a decade ago, perpetrated by a fringe cult of doomsday fanatics. The Japanese government tended to look on alternative religions with a wary eye, even one steeped in sugary goodwill like the True Realization Fellowship. But the Shirosama was good at what he did, and he could probably count government ministers among his deluded disciples. If she turned the bowl over it might very well just land back in his hands.

He gazed at the bowl, sitting in innocent beauty beneath the bright lights. "I promised your mother that we would bring you by this evening, after the reception," he said, changing the subject. "She is most eager to see you and to clear up any possible misunderstandings."

"I'm afraid that's impossible," Summer said. "I'm

much too busy tonight. I'll give her a call and see if we can meet for lunch in a few days."

"She wants to see you tonight. I cannot ignore my duty in reuniting an estranged mother and daughter." There was only the hint of an edge beneath his rich, sonorous voice. It was no wonder he managed to mesmerize thousands. But Summer Hawthorne was not easily mesmerized by slimy old men.

"I'm sorry," she said. "I'm busy." And before he could say another word she turned away, heading toward the dubious safety of the caterers, hiding behind them as the Shirosama made his slow, gliding way toward the exit, surrounded by his entourage.

She was tempted to start scooping up champagne glasses and taking them out to the kitchen area, anything to keep busy, but they had an army of waiters to handle that, and it would have looked odd. The museum guests had gone, including the tall man and his bimbo, and Summer no longer had that peculiar feeling in the middle of her shoulder blades. Now it was in the pit of her stomach, and she knew exactly who had been watching her with thinly veiled animosity. The Shirosama.

The caterers were damnably efficient, whisking everything away in record time, leaving Summer alone in the building a good half hour before the night security force was due to arrive. The reception had ended early, but the alarm system at the Sansone was excellent, and Summer had no concern for the safety of the priceless works of art. No concern for the ceramic jar that Hana-san had left in her care. The Shirosama knew where it was, and no one was going to be breaking into her house again and bothering her when they knew the bowl wasn't there. It had been a preemptive strike, putting the treasure on display, and a good one.

She switched off the last of the lights, turning on the alarm system with its infrared beams and heat sensors. Then kicking off the high heels she'd forced herself to wear, she padded barefoot through the vast, marble hallway of the faux Grecian villa that encompassed the front entryway. The moon was out, a thick crescent hanging over the mountains, and even with the light from the endless city around them it shone clear and bright. She stared up at it for a moment, breathing in the serene beauty. The day had been long and stressful, but it was almost over. All she had to do was climb into her old Volvo station wagon and drive home, where she could strip off her clothes, drink a glass of wine and soak in the wooden tub that had been her one extravagance.

Suddenly she wasn't alone. She could feel the eyes on her again, watching her, the intensity like a physical pull. She glanced around, as casually as she could, but there was no one in sight. The landscaping at the Sansone provided ample places to hide and watch—someone could be in the eighteenth century gazebo in the midst of the formal gardens on the right, or hiding behind the shrubbery on the left. She'd parked her car at the far end of the lot to leave room for the guests, and it was hidden in the shadows of overhanging trees. For a brief, cowardly moment she considered heading back into the museum, waiting until the security guards arrived.

But she was worn-out, and decided her imagination must be playing tricks on her. She'd been sleeping at Micah's since her house had been broken into, but the last thing she wanted to do was intrude on her best friend's newly resurrected love life. Besides, she missed her own bed.

The guards would be there soon enough, and if an army of cat burglars decided to show up there wasn't much she could do about it. If she waited that long she'd probably fall asleep at the wheel. No, she was being absurd, paranoid. No one was out to get her, not even the greedy Shirosama. He didn't want her. He wanted the bowl, though she had no idea why.

She started walking down the drive, the tiny white bits of gravel sharp under her bare soles, and she cursed beneath her breath. Nothing would make her cram her feet back into the high heels, but maybe she'd see if she could talk the board of directors into paving the parking lot instead of littering it with decorative little shards of stone.

Her car was too old to be equipped with power locks, and she'd shoved her key in the door to open it when she heard a noise, so small that she might have imagined it. She jerked her head up, peering into the darkness around her—she could feel those eyes again—when suddenly the door of her Volvo slammed open and someone leapt out at her, knocking her to the ground, the tiny stones digging into her back as cloth covered her face and she felt the smothering darkness close in.

2

She wasn't going down without a fight. She kicked out, hard, but bare feet weren't much of a defense, and whoever had been hiding in her car was strong, wrapping burly arms around her over the shroud and dragging her across the pebbles. She began to scream, loud cries for help, and something cuffed the side of her head. She could hear voices, low and muffled, and a moment later the unpleasant sound of a car trunk opening. She fought back, but another pair of hands joined in, and she was dumped into the trunk, the lid slamming down on her before she could stop them.

She shoved the thin blanket away from her and began kicking and pounding on the lid of the trunk. She was in some kind of luxury car—the space was huge and carpeted—and she had a pretty good idea who had done this. The True Realization Fellowship had a reputation for getting what it wanted, and no one wanted anything from her but the Shirosama.

She kicked again, screaming at her captors, until someone pounded back on the trunk, a loud thwack that would have dented the metal of a cheaper car.

And then a moment later the vehicle was moving, tearing down the long, curving driveway that led from the Sansone, moving at dangerous speeds, tossing her about in the trunk like a sack of potatoes. Summer's head slammed against the metal side and she braced herself, holding on. Screaming was a waste of time—no one would hear her over the noise of the road or through the soundproofing. She needed to save her energy to escape.

She could feel the car turning onto the main road—the vehicle leveled out, and whoever was driving was keeping a more sedate pace, clearly not wanting to draw any unwanted attention with a woman in the trunk. Summer tried to listen, to learn anything that would help her figure out what they wanted from her, where they were taking her, but there was absolute silence from the front of the car. She didn't even know for certain whether there was one or more of them. Two people had tossed her into the trunk, but that didn't mean both had gotten into the vehicle. If she had to deal with only one man, and she was prepared, then maybe she stood a fighting chance whenever he decided to stop and—

The car sped up suddenly, tossing her against the rear of the compartment, slamming her knee against the locking mechanism. She cried out, but the sound was muffled in the carpeted trunk.

"Calm down," she said out loud, her voice soft and eerie in the darkness. She took a deep, steady breath, and then another. She couldn't just let herself be tossed around indefinitely—she had to think of a way out.

Wouldn't they have a jack and tire iron in the trunk? Under the thick carpeting? She slid her fingers beneath the edge, to a latch, but when she tried to pull it up the weight of her body was in the way. She scrunched over to one side as far as she could go, managing to get the lid up far enough to reach under it, into the well of the car. There was a tire there, all right, and she could feel the scissor jack. There had to be a tire iron as well.

She almost missed the small leather bag of tools. Inside was a nice iron rod that could manage to break a few bones if properly applied. The very thought was nauseating, but not as bad as being kidnapped in the middle of the night. She dropped the lid back down, rolling over on it, and tucked the foot-long iron bar into her long, flowing sleeve. She could even jab someone in the eye with it, if necessary.

They were going faster now, faster than when they'd sped down the road from the museum, so fast that she could barely maintain her balance in the huge trunk. She felt the car skid as the driver took a corner too quickly, and when he straightened out he sped up even more. It wasn't until Summer heard the sound of another engine, much too close behind them, that she realized they were being chased.

Not by the police—there were no sirens blaring, just the roar of a vehicle far too near for her peace of mind.

The loud cracking noise was unmistakable, and she rolled facedown in the trunk, covering her head with her hands. Someone was shooting, and she sincerely doubted it was some white knight coming to her rescue. No one had been around to see her being hustled into the trunk of the car, and if anyone was trying to save her, he'd hardly be firing a gun and putting her in even greater danger.

She felt a jolt as the vehicle behind them smacked the rear of her prison, then everything happened at once. Time seemed suspended. The sound of gunfire, the crunch of metal on metal, the screech of tires as the driver fought to maintain control and the car began to slide to one side.

"Shit shit shit shit," Summer muttered under her breath, a prayer or an incantation, as she felt her entire world spin out. The car was tumbling down an embankment, finally coming to a stop against something immovable, throwing her against the front of the trunk, knocking the wind out of her. She lay there in stunned disbelief as all went very quiet around her, except for the sound of the engine. The car was probably going to burst into flames and explode, with her in it, but at the moment she didn't care. She just lay still, trying to catch her breath, waiting for the explosion.

Instead the engine died, and the sudden silence

was shocking. There were no voices, but, more unnerving, she could hear footsteps outside the car.

She tried to sit up, to reach for the tire iron, which
had been rolling around in the trunk. The car was partially on its side, and she felt as if she'd spent the last
half hour in a blender—she was a mass of pain and
bruises, and she wasn't safe yet. Whoever was prowling around the car had a gun, and there was no reason to think he wouldn't use it on her.

She groped about, still searching for the tire iron,
and found it under her back just as the trunk popped
open.

She couldn't see a thing. Someone was standing
there, but they seemed to be on a deserted road, and
the lights from the car that had pulled up behind
them threw everything into stark shadows. She
wouldn't have thought there were any roads this
empty so close to L.A., but the driver had somehow
managed to find one. Unable to get the tire iron out
from under her, she simply squeezed her eyes tightly
shut and waited for the bullet.

Instead she felt hands hauling her out of the ca-
vernous trunk into the cool night air, setting her on
unsteady feet, holding on to her until the trembling
stopped.

It was the man from the gallery, the tall man with
the sunglasses. He wasn't wearing them anymore,
and her panic increased as she realized he was at least
part Asian, like her nemesis the Shirosama. It
couldn't be a coincidence, could it?

Even in the shadows she could see that he was exquisitely beautiful with high, perfect cheekbones; exotic eyes of an indeterminate shade; narrow face and rich, full mouth… His hair was long and silky, black, and he towered over her. Another of the Shirosama's hit men? Because he did look like a hit man—that is, what she imagined one would look like.

"Are you all right?" He might as well be asking if she wanted sugar in her coffee. She tried to say something, but words failed her, and she simply stared up at him silently. "Get in the car," he said.

That was enough to stir her out of her momentary shock. She wasn't getting in anyone's car. "No."

"It's your choice. I can leave you here, but there's no guarantee who will find you first. If you don't show up at the Shirosama's headquarters, someone will come looking."

"Is that who tried to kidnap me?"

"Unless you have any other dire enemies, which I doubt. Get in the car."

It wasn't much of a choice, and she climbed the bank toward the waiting car, limping slightly. She stopped, turning back to glance at the vehicle she'd been trapped in. It was tilted on its side, and someone was slumped over the steering wheel. Someone in a white robe, with red staining the pristine cloth.

"Shouldn't we see if he's all right?" she said, hesitating.

"Do you care?"

"Of course I care. He may have wanted to hurt me, but he's a human being and—"

"He's dead."

"Oh."

She was very cold. It was a warm L.A. night and she was freezing. "Get in the car," the man said again, opening the passenger door like the perfect chauffeur.

She got in. The seats were leather, comfortable, and it took her a long time to get the seat belt fastened. Her hands were shaking, and she couldn't seem to make them stop. She ought to pay more attention to her surroundings, she told herself, so she could give a full report to the police, but she couldn't bring herself to care. She didn't know what kind of car this was, though she'd recognized the other vehicle as one of the Shirosama's well-known white limos.

"Was the driver the only one in the car?" she found herself asking in a quiet voice when the man got in beside her and started the engine. A low, sexy rumble…it must be some kind of sports car. She didn't notice any insignia inside, which didn't help. She was going to be a piss-poor witness when the police questioned her. Assuming she got to the police.

He put the car in reverse, backed up and then took off into the night, moving so fast the road was a blur, the crash site vanishing into the darkness. "You don't really want to know that," he said.

Maybe he was right. She leaned her head back

against the cushioned seat and closed her eyes, feeling dizzy. "Where are we going? Are you taking me to the police?"

"Now why would I do that?"

She turned horrified eyes on him. "To make a report. Some men tried to kidnap me. They shouldn't be allowed to get away with it."

"Actually, they didn't just try, they succeeded. And they didn't get away with it."

Immediately, she pictured the man slumped over the steering wheel, the bright red blood against the white linen. *Calm*, she told herself. *Deep, calming breaths. Think about more important things.*

"Did you shoot them? I heard gunshots." The question seemed almost surreal, but he simply shook his head.

"They were the ones shooting. They didn't like being run off the road."

She could have asked him about the blood, but suddenly she didn't want to know.

Fighting her panic, she forced herself to look at the driver's impassive profile. "And who exactly are you? Don't try to tell me you're a random passerby— I won't believe you."

"If I were a random passerby I wouldn't know about the Shirosama, would I?" he replied in a reasonable tone.

"You were at the reception. I saw you there."

"I was."

"Where's your girlfriend?"

"What girlfriend?"

"The blonde with the boobs. It was obvious you couldn't keep your eyes off her cleavage…except it was you watching me, wasn't it? I could feel someone staring at me, but every time I turned around I couldn't find anyone. It was you, right? Why?"

"Let's just say I expected something like this to go down. The Shirosama and his bunch were practically drooling over the Hayashi Urn, and you were keeping it from them. I'm guessing once his holiness was through with you they thought they could get you to open up the museum for them."

"I don't know what you're talking about. The Hayashi Urn? Do you mean my ceramic bowl?"

He shot a glance at her in the darkened interior of the car. He seemed perfectly comfortable at the immense speeds he was traveling. His hands were draped loosely on the steering wheel. Beautiful hands, with long, elegant fingers. All of them intact, which ruled out her sudden suspicion that he might be a member of the Japanese crime syndicate, the Yakuza. Most members of that organization were missing at least part of their fingers, a sign of atonement for mistakes made. Unless her rescuer never made mistakes.

"You have no idea what you have?" he asked. "Where it comes from, its history?"

"I know it's something that other people want and that I'm not about to give up. What's the Hayashi Urn?"

"A part of Japanese history that wouldn't matter to you."

"Since the bowl is mine, then it matters to me. I'd like to know why someone tried to kidnap me in order to get his hands on it."

"It doesn't make any difference—the urn won't be yours for much longer. And you needn't pretend you're surprised—you put it in the exhibit just to keep it out of reach of the Shirosama. You decided it was best to hide it in plain sight. Unfortunately, you underestimated your enemy. The Shirosama isn't quite the philanthropic spiritual leader he presents to the world. He has no problem killing for what he wants."

"Neither do you." She wasn't quite sure why she said it.

"When necessary," he said, unmoved by her accusation.

"So where are you taking me?"

His eyes were on the road. "I haven't decided yet."

There was something about the flat, emotionless tone that made her stomach knot even more intensely. "Just tell me one thing," she said. "Am I better off with you than I was with those men?"

For a moment he didn't answer, and she wondered whether he would. Finally he spoke, not even looking at her. "That's up to you."

And for the first time in that shocking, crazy night, Summer began to feel afraid.

Taka could see her hunch lower into the seat, and he couldn't blame her. He wasn't going to lie to her, not if he could help it. She'd somehow managed to get through being kidnapped and tossed in the trunk of a limo with nothing more than a few bruises. He'd thought he was going to have to deal with tears and hysterics. Instead she was shaken but calm enough, making things easier. Maybe.

She was a liability, and he'd learned long ago that you couldn't get sentimental over individual life when the stakes were so high. There was an old Zen koan—the needs of the many outweigh the needs of the few—and if he had to choose between mass destruction and the life of one spoiled California blonde, then he wouldn't hesitate.

Except she wasn't what he would have expected. He'd skimmed the intel he'd gotten on her—daughter of a Hollywood trophy wife, product of Eastern boarding schools and college, advanced degree in Asian art, with no scandals attached to her name. She'd lived a quiet enough life—maybe too quiet. It wasn't her fault she just happened to hold the key to something that could tear the entire world apart.

His old friend Peter would be mocking him, telling him it was his damn Asian inscrutability that kept him so cold-blooded. The thought amused him, because Peter Madsen had been the coldest person Takashi O'Brien had ever known. Until he ran into the wrong woman, the same one who'd almost brought an end to Takashi's life.

Taka wasn't going to make that mistake again. If

Summer Hawthorne had to die, he'd do it as quickly and as painlessly as he could manage, and with luck she'd never know what happened. It wasn't her fault that hidden somewhere in her memory was the location of an ancient Japanese shrine. Nor was it her fault that people would kill to discover it. And that he would kill to keep her from revealing it.

He could pull over to the side of the road, put a comforting hand on the back of her neck, and snap it. Her death would be instantaneous, and he could take her body and dump her into the white limo's trunk. The scandal attached to the Shirosama's deluded cult would be an added bonus.

Taka should never have taken her away from there in the first place—he should have just ended it then. If he hesitated much longer someone might discover the crashed vehicle with the two bodies in the front seat. As far as he could tell, Summer Hawthorne had no more value. Now that he knew where the urn was, retrieving it would be simple enough for anyone with his talents.

Keeping her alive would only make things more dangerous. She knew where the site of the temple ruins were. One valley girl who'd never traveled farther west than Hawaii held the key to a location so valuable that hundreds of thousands of lives could depend on it. Better she die and the secret with her, than risk Armageddon.

It was all made more complicated by the fact that she didn't know what she knew. Hana Hayashi had left the secret with her, but so well hidden that no one might find it, Summer included.

The Committee couldn't take that risk. Better to terminate her and all possibility of finding the hidden shrine, than let the Shirosama move ahead with his lethal, dangerous visions.

Taka didn't even need to pull off the freeway to do it, or even slow his speed from the seventy-five miles per hour he was traveling. The technique was simple and he'd done it too many times already. He needed to stop thinking about it and just do it.

But then, his reflexes were still off from his accident. His fuck-up, which had landed him in the hands of a sadist. There was no need to take chances, just to prove to himself he was still at the top of his game. Taka took the next exit off the freeway, heading west, while his passenger sat quietly in her seat, asking no questions, oblivious to the fact that she was about to die.

He drove onto a less crowded street, pulled over to the side of the road and turned to face her. She had blue eyes, and she was prettier than he'd realized. She didn't wear makeup, and she had a sprinkling of freckles across her nose. He'd never killed anyone with freckles before.

"So what happens next?" she said, looking at him, and he wondered if she knew.

He put his hand on the back of her neck, under the single thick braid that was starting to come undone from her active night. He could feel the nerves jumping through her skin, feel her pulses racing, though he didn't know whether it was in fear of him or remembered panic. There was something there, in her eyes, that he didn't understand, couldn't afford to think about. Her skin was soft and warm, and his large hand could span her neck quite easily.

"Are you going to kiss me?" she asked, sounding as if that would be a fate worse than death. "Because I know you saved my life and probably figure that, as a knight in shining armor, you're owed something. But I'd really rather you didn't. I'd like you to tell me why you were watching me, why you were following those men and what you intend to do about it."

"I wasn't planning on kissing you."

"That's a relief," she said, despite the faint stain of color beneath the freckles. "So who are you, and what do you want from me?"

It wouldn't take much pressure. He could even kiss her, if that's what she wanted, and by the time he lifted his mouth she'd be gone. So easy, all of it. So logical, sensible.

He didn't need her help in retrieving the Hayashi Urn from the museum—he was one of the Committee's acknowledged experts at breaking and entering. When she died she'd take her secrets with her, the safest option all around. As long as she lived there was a good chance the Shirosama would get his hands on her and the secrets she didn't know she carried. Once she was dead that danger was gone.

Taka tightened his grip on her neck, exerting just a tiny bit of pressure, and he saw the sudden doubt in her eyes. He needed to move fast, because he didn't want that doubt to increase, to turn into terror before it went blank, and hesitation would only hurt her.

"I'm guessing you're some kind of private security guard hired by my mother," she continued, when he didn't answer her questions. "She must have had second thoughts. She knows how determined her precious guru can be when he wants something, and maybe she thought I was in danger. Too bad. They just didn't realize how easy it would be to steal the bowl from the museum."

He loosened the pressure an infinitesimal amount. Nothing that she would notice. "What do you mean? The Sansone has state-of-the-art security."

"Well, you'd think they'd at least try to get it," she said. "Most of the security is focused on the more valuable pieces. It would have been a lot easier than they thought—I was counting on them going for it sooner or later."

"Counting on them to steal the urn?" He was totally confused by this point. "Why?"

"Because it's a fake," she said in that maddeningly calm voice. "The real one is hidden. Sorry, but I don't trust my mother not to sell me out. I'm really quite touched that she hired you—"

"I don't know your mother."

Her smile faded. "Then why were you watching me? Why did you come after me? Who are you?"

Your worst nightmare, he wanted to tell her. But the game wasn't played yet, and he still had a job to do.

He'd have to kill her later.

3

"Where is the Hayashi Urn?"

Summer glanced over at his cool, exquisite profile in the darkened car. Now that she was beginning to calm down from the adrenaline rush of her abduction, she was starting to see things a little more clearly. And she was beginning to have the extremely unhappy suspicion that her dangerous night was far from over. Why the hell had she told him the bowl in the museum was a fake?

"Someplace safe," she said. "I think you ought to take me home now."

"I don't think that's a good idea," he said, starting the car. "Unless the urn is hidden there, which means it's probably gone by now."

"I'm not an idiot. Someone already ransacked my place looking for it. It's hidden where no one can find it."

"Where?"

Right. She was up shit's creek, from the frying pan

into the fire, and she hadn't even realized it. He was driving fast again, and she couldn't very well unlatch the door and jump out, even if she'd seen it done in dozens of movies. She'd end up roadkill.... She was better off taking her chances with this elegant stranger. He was hardly the type to hurt her.

"Look, I don't know who you are or why you happened to be hanging around the museum if my mother didn't hire you, but I'm not about to tell you a damn thing. I've already said too much. Either take me home or drop me off on the next street corner, and I'll find my own way."

He said nothing, keeping his attention on the road in front of him. They were heading toward the freeway again, and once on it she'd be effectively trapped. Maybe she'd just end up with a few bruises if she tried the rolling-out-of-the-car trick. She slid her hand toward the seat belt clasp, but he moved so fast he scared her, clamping his hand down over hers and pulling it away.

"Don't even think about it," he said, speeding up even more.

He was holding her hand in an unbreakable grip. She probably ought to struggle, hit him, anything to distract him from the road. She'd survived one car crash tonight; she'd probably survive another if it happened before they were going too fast. She just didn't know which was the greater risk—careening off the road in this little car or staying with this man.

He wasn't going to hurt her, she told herself. He

wasn't going to touch her. He'd rescued her. She just needed to hold on to that belief and she wouldn't panic and make stupid mistakes.

"All right," she said, relaxing the fist she'd automatically formed, and after a moment he released her hand. She could see his profile in the flickering light of the oncoming cars, and she stared, fascinated. No one that beautiful could be a killer, could he?

She shook the distracting thought from her mind. "Where are you taking me?"

"You wanted to go home, didn't you?" He pulled onto the freeway, and Summer closed her eyes, certain she was going to die, after all. But a moment later they were speeding down the HOV lane, still in one piece, and she let out her pent-up breath. When she got home she was going to lock all her doors, strip off her clothes, climb into her tub and never come out.

She tended to drive her Volvo too fast, and if she'd been behind the wheel they would have reached her little bungalow in fifteen minutes. He made it in ten, pulling up outside the run-down cottage and leaving the car still running. She'd been desperately trying to think of ways to get rid of him once they got to her street, but it was turning into a non-issue, leaving Summer even more confused. She hadn't told him where she lived.

"We're here," he said, putting the car into Neutral. "I'd see you to your door, but I expect that would only make you more nervous."

. "You mean you're just going to let me go?" she said, disbelief warring with hope.

"It looks like it, doesn't it?"

"And you're not going to tell me who you are, or why you were following me? Or how you knew where I lived?"

He shook his head, saying nothing.

"I guess I should count my blessings then?" she asked, reaching for her seat belt. This time he didn't stop her, didn't move as she opened the door and slid out. Her legs were a little wobbly, but she managed to disguise it by clinging to the door for a moment. She still didn't recognize what kind of car it was—something low and sleek and fast, but she wasn't enough of a real Californian to care about cars. She was going to have to come up with something to tell the police, but right then her brain wasn't working on all cylinders.

Her mother hadn't taught her anything worth knowing in twenty-eight years, but Hana had instilled good manners no matter what the circumstances. Clinging to the door, Summer leaned over, peering into the darkened car. "Er…thank you for saving my life," she said lamely.

There was just the faint ghost of a smile on his rich, beautiful mouth. "It was nothing," he said, and the depressing truth of it was, he meant it. Her life was nothing to him. Not that it should matter, she reminded herself. She preferred being invisible.

She could feel his eyes watching her as she walked

up the narrow sidewalk to her front door. She was overcome by the same sense of intrusion, invasion, protection. It was a crazy combination of all three, though she wasn't quite sure where the protective aspect came from. Maybe simply because he'd saved her before scaring her.

She closed the front door behind her, triple locking it, and then leaned against it to catch her breath. She heard the sound of his car drive away, out of her life. The last ounce of tension finally drained from her body, her knees gave out and she sank down on the floor, leaning against the doorjamb and putting her head against her knees as she shook.

She had no idea how long she sat there, curled up in a kind of mindless panic, but at least she wasn't crying. She never cried—not since she'd been told of her Hana's death in a hit-and-run accident. Summer had been fifteen. That made a solid thirteen years without shedding a tear, and she intended to keep it that way.

And she'd cowered enough. She grabbed hold of the doorknob and pulled herself to her feet, steeling herself to ignore the faint tremor in her legs. She peered out the window, but there was no sign of the sleek, low-slung sports car and her nameless rescuer. He was gone. If only she could rid herself of the almost physical feel of his eyes on her, still watching her.

She switched on a light and winced in the blinding brightness. She'd be happier in shadows right now, but shadows could hide scary things, and she had no intention of being scared anymore. She'd fought that battle once before, and she wasn't going to let herself be vulnerable again.

Her feet hurt, and she realized belatedly that sometime during the night she'd lost her shoes. They were expensive, but uncomfortable, and good riddance. She was going to strip off her clothes and throw them out, too, get rid of anything that reminded her of this hideous night. But first she was going to eat something, anything, have a glass of wine and try to rid herself of the lingering touch of his eyes, watching her.

The Ben & Jerry's had ice crystals, the raspberry yogurt was past its due date, the cheese had mold. She couldn't find the wine opener, and the only beer she had in the fridge was Sapporo—no thank you. She didn't want to think about anything Japanese and she walked through her living room with eyes averted, pushing the shoji screen aside. There was nothing she wanted more than to strip off her clothes and climb into the hot tub, but Hana-san had trained her well. Summer's feet were grass-stained and bloody, and she wanted to get the feel of the night off her before she settled into the blessed warmth of the water. She showered quickly, then climbed into the big cedar tub just outside her bedroom.

It *was* a blessing. She closed her eyes and let the warm, healing water flow around her. For a few minutes she didn't have to think, didn't have to worry. For a few blessed moments of peace she could just be.

And try to rid herself of the irrational feeling that somewhere out there he was still watching her.

For a smart woman, Summer Hawthorne was annoyingly brainless, Taka thought as he skirted the back of her bungalow. He'd already checked it out several days ago and knew just how pathetic her security was. Her house had been broken into recently, and yet she'd taken no measures to fortify the place. All three locks on the back door were easy to pick, the chain would break with one good shove and she had no outdoor security, no sensors or alarms. He could slip behind the house, disappear into the overgrown shrubbery and no one would even notice.

Her curtains were pathetic, as well. The faux-Asian synthetic rice paper shades were practically useless. She'd left the lights on in her living room and kitchen when she'd disappeared into the bathroom, and she was soaking wet and naked when she reemerged and climbed into the wooden tub, closing her eyes in obvious bliss.

So he could safely assume that she hadn't been lying—the Hayashi Urn was nowhere near her. He'd done a fairly thorough search the last time he'd been there, though far more discreetly than the Shirosama's goons, and he doubted he'd have missed it, though at that point he hadn't been specifically looking for it. He'd thought it was already at the museum.

He'd been looking for any kind of clue that would lead him to the shrine. If they found it before the Shirosama managed to discover it, the Committee could stop the cult leader's plans cold. The Shirosama needed the sacred location for his crackpot rituals, and without it he and his followers would be too superstitious to move ahead with their plans. It was only a few days till the Lunar New Year, the date the Shirosama had decreed was the most auspicious for his mysterious ritual, and at least for this year his time was running out. If they could just stall long enough, keep Summer Hawthorne and the Hayashi Urn away from him for the next few days, they'd have an entire year to figure out how to stop him.

And then there would be no need to silence her before she spoke the truth she didn't know she had.

The urn in the museum was an excellent forgery—Taka had enough of a gift at ceramics to recognize the hand of a master. It had been an error on his part not to recognize that the ice blue glaze had been a little too uniform, but then, he'd been concentrating on other things.

Too bad he couldn't just let it go at this point. The Shirosama would steal the fake from the museum, never knowing the difference, but he still needed Summer Hawthorne. In truth, she might be the more valuable part of the equation, and Taka knew what his orders were. If necessary, he was to destroy a priceless piece of Japanese art, culture and history, and execute the woman who held the key to where it belonged. And he wasn't supposed to think twice about it.

It was the "if necessary" part that was the problem. The Committee, and the ruthlessly practical Madame Lambert, trusted him to make that judgment call. But he wasn't quite sure he could trust himself at this point.

Because he didn't want to kill Summer Hawthorne.

If she was found floating in her hot tub, the Shirosama would know there was nothing he could do, and he'd be stopped cold.

It was simple. Practical. Necessary. Except that this scenario meant the Hayashi Urn would stay lost.

The bowl would stay in one piece, however. And sooner or later, maybe decades from now, maybe after they were all long dead, it would reappear. That knowledge should be enough to satisfy the committee.

Taka took less than thirty seconds to pick the locks. He moved through the house in complete silence—he could come up on her, push her under the water, and she'd never have a chance.

Drowning wasn't a good choice. He wouldn't be able to make it look like an accident, it took too damn long and she'd be frightened. He didn't want to scare her if he could help it. He just wanted it over, if that's what had to be.

She was sitting in the tub, her back to him, her long hair loose, dark with water. She was humming, some tuneless little song that was making this whole fucking thing even harder, but he couldn't let himself hesitate. He moved so fast she didn't have time to turn around, to know he was there, sliding his hand under her thick veil of hair, finding the right spot and pressing, hard. She was unconscious in a matter of seconds, and he pushed her down on her back in the water, holding her there.

She lay still beneath his hands, her hair fanning out around her, her face still and peaceful and eerily beautiful; he knew she couldn't feel a thing.

But he couldn't do it.

He hauled her out of the tub, a naked, dripping deadweight, and threw her over his shoulder. He didn't know how much water she'd swallowed, only that it wasn't enough to kill her. He tossed her on the bed, rifled through her drawers and grabbed whatever clothes seemed suitable. All black—she didn't seem to own anything in color, including her underwear. He was about to dress her when he heard the noise outside. The Shirosama already knew he'd lost his quarry, and he'd sent new stooges after her.

Taka wrapped Summer's unconscious body in the bedspread, tossing the dark clothes into the cocoon before he lifted her again. She was damn heavy; American women, no matter how thin, always seemed to weigh more than other women. Maybe they simply had bigger bones. Not that Summer Hawthorne was a delicate flower. He'd been working, but an important part of his job was observation, and Summer Hawthorne naked had a soft, curvy body, not his usual type of woman.

He shifted the weight, tossing her over his shoulder again, and a moment later he was gone into the night, as the white-robed brethren broke in the front door.

Summer was cold, wet, miserable and totally disoriented. She was immobilized, moving fast and she felt like she was choking, coughing up water. When she could finally catch her breath she tried to push the wet hair out of her face, only to find her arms trapped at her sides. She shook her head, realizing in sudden horror that she was back in that damn car with that damn man, hurtling through the night once more.

"What the hell...?" she said weakly, struggling. She was wrapped in her bedspread, her arms at her sides, the seat belt strapped around her, and the man driving didn't even glance at her.

"You had some unwanted visitors. I figured you were better off with me than the holy brothers."

She tried to speak, coughing instead, the spasms racking her body. "They must have tried to kill me," she managed to choke out. "How did you know?"

"I was keeping an eye on things. I didn't think they'd give up that easily."

She was silent for a moment. "How many of them did you kill?"

He glanced over at her. "You think I'm a cold-blooded killer?"

"I have no idea who or what you are."

"Takashi O'Brien. I work for the Japanese Department of Antiquities. We've been looking for the Hayashi Urn for a long, long time."

She blinked. He didn't exactly fit her idea of a Japanese bureaucrat, but then, nothing was fitting her preconceived notions today. "Why didn't you just come to the Sansone and ask if we knew anything?"

"We had no interest in drawing the attention of the True Realization Fellowship. We needed to secure it before they could get their hands on it."

"Why?" Her teeth were chattering. He reached over and switched on the heat, and she glanced at the dashboard clock. It was just after 1:00 a.m. It had been less than three hours since she'd left the museum. Three hours to change a lifetime.

"You can worry about that later. In the meantime we need to get you someplace safe and warm."

"And dry," she said. "And dressed," she added in sudden horror. "I'm not wearing anything under this, am I?"

"Since you don't make it a habit to bathe in your clothes, then yes, you're naked. I grabbed some clothes for you when I got you out of there—they're tucked somewhere between you and the bedspread."

She wasn't cold now, she was hot. For reasons she didn't want to think about she tended to be extremely inhibited, more so since her mother had always made it a practice to prance her perfect body around the house in various stages of undress, particularly if there happened to be men around. And the thought of this exquisite, enigmatic man hauling her own wet, naked body around was enough to make Summer wish those monsters had ended up drowning her, after all.

Except then she would have been naked and floating in her tub. *Please, God, if I'm going to die, could I at least do it with my clothes on?* she begged. Particularly if the oddly named Takashi O'Brien was going to be there.

Though if he were around, chances were she wasn't going to die. He'd saved her twice. Whether he admitted it or not, he was her guardian angel, and she was going to have to get over the fact that he'd seen her naked.

"Okay," she said in a hollow voice. He was once more driving like a bat out of hell, and she had no choice but to hang on. "Where are we going?"

"My hotel."

He was protecting her, she reminded herself, squashing down the needless additional panic. "And I'm supposed to walk in wearing only a bedspread?" she said.

"I told you, I brought some clothes. You can get dressed while I drive."

She glanced behind her, but there was no back seat in this tiny sports car. "I don't think so," she said. "Take me outside the city and I'll go change in the bushes."

"I've already seen you, Summer," he said in a bored voice. Unfortunately, that didn't help.

"Then you know you're not being deprived of anything spectacular. Find me a darkened street and some bushes and I'll be fine."

He glanced over at her, and for a moment she thought he was about to argue. She was going to forestall him when she started coughing again, finally leaning back against the leather seat, exhausted.

"All right," he said. "I'll find you some bushes." She must have imagined the odd note of guilt in his soft, emotionless voice.

What did he have to feel guilty about? He'd saved her, again.

Hadn't he?

4

His holiness, the Shirosama of the True Realization Fellowship, sat in meditation, considering his options. His practice was a far cry from the traditional forms. When he freed his mind the visions would come, the plans would form and true enlightenment would beckon like a bright white light.

He knew what he had to do to attain that permanent state, and the thousands of faithful were well trained, well organized to follow in his ways. He had the best scientists, the best doctors, the best soldiers, and the supplies were stockpiled, ready to be used. Awaiting his signal.

The blindness was increasing, a sure sign that all would soon be ready. His eyes were a milky brown— he still needed the contact lenses, but not for long. His colorless skin had needed no ritual treatment, and he hadn't had to bleach his hair for months. It had stopped growing, and what remained was the pure white he'd managed to achieve. His transformation was almost complete.

It was really all very clear to him. A simple matter of various forces coming into play, and he had learned to be patient over the years.

He knew his destiny. Karma had brought him to this place and time. It was his task to reunite people with their lost souls, reintegrate them into a new life past pain, suffering and need. He would bring them all to that place of white-light purity, leading the way, a beacon of truth and retribution. The more they suffered in the task of being set free, the greater the reward, and flinching from what needed to be done was unacceptable.

Pain and death were merely transitory states, to be moved through with as little fuss as possible, and those who weren't willing to embrace the change would be helped along by his army of followers. The gift he offered was of immeasurable value—the gift of a cleansed soul and a new life in a new world.

His needs were simple, and had been met by divine providence. He needed followers, true believers who never questioned. He needed the strong and the young, the old and the wise. He needed disciples of unflinching character who would do what he asked, and never consider it morally repugnant. There were times when delivering death was the greatest gift of all, helping someone past his or her current state of greed and passion, into the next life of pure thought.

The Shirosama had the disciples. He had the tools, the toxins and the gases that would render the subway systems and train stations in every part of this world into instruments of disease and death. This method had been tried before and failed, due to the weakness of the followers, the lack of vision.

Or perhaps it would simply be his time. The others had tried, for all the wrong reasons, the wrong faith.

The hour was almost right. The Lunar New Year was fast approaching, and he knew that time was finally right. Year after year had passed, but now things were finally falling into place as it was ordained. He had the followers, the weapons, the plan.

All he needed now was the Hayashi Urn, the ice blue ceramic bowl that had been in the care of his family for hundreds of years. The urn that had once held the bones and ashes of his ancestor.

The year 1663 had been a time of upheaval in Edo period Japan. Amid the warring clans, the daimyos and their armies of samurai, and the battling priests, there had been one man, one god. The original Shiro-sama; the White Lord—the half-blind albino child of the Hayashi clan, first considered a demon and later recognized as a seer and a savior. He'd foretold the disasters that had befallen the modern world, the terrifying eclipse of power and the new worship of greed and possessions. But he had been too powerful, his vision too pure, and in the end he'd committed ritual suicide by order of the shogun. His body had been burned, his bones and ashes placed in the ice blue urn and set in the remains of his temple up in the mountains, guarded by members of the Hayashi clan.

The steps were clear, laid out by the original Shiro-sama in the scrolls kept hidden by his family. The bones and ashes would be reunited with the urn at the place of his death, and his spirit would enter a new vessel. His descendant.

And that would signal the conflagration that would cleanse the world. Armageddon, where only the pure souls would survive.

There were too many stumbling blocks. For years the present Shirosama had no idea what that crazy old woman had done with the family treasure, and once he found out that an American had it, it was proving almost impossible to get his hands on it.

He could blame the disastrous war that had rav-aged his country and his family. Only the oldest male member of the Hayashi family knew the location of the ancient temple, and he'd died without passing that knowledge on to anyone but his young daughter. In an effort to safeguard the treasure, the bones and ashes had been removed from the urn and hidden in the family home, and Hana Hayashi had been sent to the country of their enemies with the priceless urn and the location of the temple ruins.

He knew it was one last test to prove his worth, and he accepted it with humility. Once his followers were able to bring him the woman and the urn, there was still the problem of locating the ruins of the original shrine. At least he had the bones and ashes of his ancestor. For the last seven years he'd been mixing the ashes with his tea, to ensure his transformation, but the chunks of whitened bones were still complete, and when they were placed in the urn and set at the site of his ancestor's sacrifice, all would become as it should be. Even the original Shiro-sama had been a test run. It was his destiny to finish what his ancestor had started.

He sat, and let his let his eyes roll upward in his head, ignoring the scrape of the contact lenses against them. Soon.

In the end, Takashi O'Brien had settled for a small park in a run-down neighborhood, pulling the car off to the side of the road. There were probably addicts roaming around, looking for a score, and maybe gangbangers, but they'd be much more interested in his very expensive car than a woman sneaking off into the bushes. If by any chance they found Summer more interesting he could take care of that as well.

Because, of course, he watched. She shuffled into the bushes, the bedspread clutched around her, and made him solemnly promise not to look. Was she really that naive? So far she'd taken him at face value, and he could back up the Ministry of Antiquities story quite easily. He was very good at convincing people who and what he was—he often went undercover as Hispanic, Italian, Russian, Native American and any Asian background. Being a mongrel, or *ain-*

oko, as his grandfather would have termed him, gave Taka advantages. He looked different, but he could shift those differences to mirror any number of ethnic groups.

He was going to need to make a decision, fast, before the Fellowship made its move. Once he finished this job he could get the hell out of here, back to the tattered shreds of the normal life his interfering family was assembling for him. The proper Japanese bride, the proper future.

People who worked for the Committee didn't live a normal life, though he could hardly explain that to his disapproving grandfather. His mother's uncle, his mentor, had some idea that Takashi O'Brien's work entailed more than his involvement with the Yakuza, Japan's organized crime family, but he wisely never asked. As long as Taka completed the occasional duties assigned to him, no one asked questions, not even his crazy cousin Reno. Particularly when his great-uncle was head of one of the largest Yakuza families in Tokyo, a fact that filled his industrialist grandfather with horror.

Not that it mattered. Takashi could never find favor in his grandfather's eyes no matter what he did. His blood was tainted by his American father and the eventual suicide of his beautiful, self-absorbed mother, and Shintaro Oda would never look upon his only descendent with anything but contempt.

Summer Hawthorne was heading back toward the car, her long hair dripping wet on her shoulders. He

didn't want to think about why he didn't finish the job
he'd started. He had an instinctive revulsion for
drowning, even if she'd been unconscious at the time,
and it could have raised unpleasant attention. That
was the second tenet of working for the Committee.
Do what had to be done, without flinching, without
moral qualms or second-guessing. And do it discreetly.

She was shivering when she climbed back into the
car, the bedspread clutched in her hands. He should
have told her to toss it, but that might have given her
a clue that she wasn't going to be returning to her little bungalow anytime soon. If at all.

"I don't suppose you brought shoes," she said, not
looking at him as she began to braid her long wet
hair.

"Behind the seat."

She reached around for them, brushing against
him in the cramped front seat of the car, and something odd shivered through him. A tiny bit of aware-
ness, which was impossible. He liked statuesque
American women with endless legs, he liked delicate
Japanese women with tiny breasts, he liked athletic
English women and inventive French women. He
liked beauty, and the drowned rat sitting beside him,
even when she was done up for a museum reception,
was never going to be a classic beauty.

Besides, she was a job, and he was adept at com-
partmentalizing his life. He did what needed to be
done, and some of the things he'd had to do would

make her shrink in revulsion. And he would do those things again, without question. To her.

"What's next?" He could hear the strain in her voice, and he wondered when she'd break. He'd been expecting noisy tears anytime now, but she'd remained strangely stoic.

"My hotel in Little Tokyo, where you can sleep and I can decide what to do next."

"Little Tokyo? Isn't that the first place the Shirosama would be looking for you?"

"They're not looking for me. They don't know I exist."

"But you've rescued me twice…" Her voice trailed off, suddenly uneasy, and he realized he had to calm her fears.

"The two men in the limo died in the crash—they never saw me. And I got you out of your house without anyone noticing." That was highly unlikely if they'd been the ones who'd tried to drown her, but he was counting on her being too worn-out to put things together. By the time she was more rested he'd come up with a plausible answer. In the meantime he needed to stash her someplace safe where he didn't have to think about her, and the small bungalow he rented inside the grounds of the hotel was as good a place as any.

"Besides, Little Tokyo is much too obvious a place to hide someone with a connection to a Japanese cultural treasure. It's the last place they'd think to look, and no one's going to know you're there."

She said nothing, simply nodded and leaned back in the leather seat. He expected her passivity was only going to last so long. He'd better be ready to move when she started asking the unanswerable questions.

The Matsura Hotel was a Los Angeles landmark. The entry was through a security laden torii gate; the landscaping was minimalist and yet preserving of everyone's privacy. He made his unwitting hostage duck down when he drove past the security cameras, but once he'd parked the car behind the bungalow, no one had any chance of seeing her. He ushered her into the two-room building, trying not to think about how he was going to get her out again.

She stood in the middle of the living room, and he could see the raw edges of shock begin to close in on her. He wasn't in the mood for noisy tears or awkward questions, so he simply took her arm and led her into the bedroom, ignoring her panicked start when he touched her. "You need to sleep," he said.

She looked at him, the wary expression in her eyes like that of a cornered fox. Pretty blue eyes, he thought absently. She was past words, but he knew what she was thinking.

"I'll be in the living room. I can sleep on the couch, but I'll wake up if I hear even the slightest noise. You'll be safe." For now.

She still didn't move, and he took her shoulders and turned her toward the bed. He didn't want to start undressing her—she'd probably jump to the wrong conclusion and that would only make things more difficult. He had no interest in her soft, curvy body or her lush, vulnerable mouth. He just needed her to go to sleep and let him think.

"Yes," she said in a rusty voice, reaching for the hem of the black sweatshirt he'd grabbed for her. It was huge—he assumed it had probably belonged to a former boyfriend, even though their intel had only come up with one, years prior—and she started pulling it over her head. The T-shirt came with it, which was his signal to leave before she was standing there in her underwear, with that same dazed look on her face.

"Call me if you need anything," he said, getting the hell out of the room and closing the door before she could respond.

He stretched out on the sofa, closing his eyes and wishing to Christ he could afford to have something to drink. It had been a rough twenty-four hours, but he couldn't take even the slightest of chances, not when things were so fucked. When this was over he could down a whole bottle of single malt Scotch, his drug of choice. And he suspected that was exactly what he was going to want to do.

He was going to have to face Madame Lambert sooner or later. He'd been ignoring her messages on his übermobile phone, but he couldn't put it off for much longer. She was going to want to know why Summer Hawthorne wasn't dead yet, and she wasn't likely to accept any excuses. Nothing ever touched

Isobel Lambert, marred the perfection of her beautiful face or clear, emotionless eyes. She was the epitome of what they all strived for—ruthless practicality and no weakness. She would have put a samurai to shame.

Taka wasn't sure if it was wisdom or weakness that had stopped him tonight. He could hear Summer coughing behind the door to the bedroom. She'd swallowed more water in the hot tub than he'd thought, but he couldn't very well have taken the time to do mouth to mouth on her with the Shirosama's goons closing in. In the ordinary world he'd have taken her to a hospital, rather than risk a lung infection of some sort. In this world it was the best-case scenario—if she got some virulent pneumonia from her near drowning it would no longer be his job to…finish her.

Things were stable for the moment. The true Hayashi Urn was currently out of reach, though he was going to have to find out where, and damn soon. He had no idea how good a copy the urn at the Sansone was. If the brethren decided to go for it, then all hell might break loose.

Taka groaned, shoving a hand through his hair. They were going to want to know in London why he hadn't taken care of things, and he wasn't sure what he could give them for an answer when he didn't know himself. He closed his eyes, listening to the sounds around him, identifying and then dismissing each noise—the traffic beyond the thick vegetation that surrounded the hotel; the sound of her breathing behind the closed door, slow and steady as she slept; the murmur of the wind; the steady beat of his own heart. He lay perfectly still, aware of absolutely everything. And then he let go, for a brief moment of respite.

Isobel Lambert stood in the window of her office, staring out into the breaking sunrise over London, a cigarette in one hand, a cell phone in the other. It was going to be another bleak, gray day, with a cold, biting rain that stung the skin and felt like ice. She hated January. But then, right now she hated everything.

She hated the small, elegant office in Kensington that she'd coveted for so long. She hated the cigarette in her hand. She hated London, but most of all she hated the Committee and the choices she had to make.

For that matter, she hated Peter Madsen. Her second in command was home in bed with his wife. He had someone to turn to to help wash away the stench of death and merciless decisions. A wife who knew too damn much, but there was nothing to be done about that. If Isobel needed Madsen—and she did— then Genevieve Spenser came with the bargain. And if Peter had complete faith in her, then so did Isobel, because Peter had complete faith in very few things.

She turned and stubbed out her cigarette, then cracked the window to try to air out the office before Peter got there. She hated smoking, had tried to quit a hundred times, but days like yesterday would send her right back. It could be worse, she supposed. People she'd started out with had turned to drink or drugs, or the kind of soulless abuse of power that Harry Thomason had wielded. It was a good thing her soul ached. The feeling proved she was still human beneath the hard shell she'd perfected.

The bitter wind swirled through her office, and she shivered, but made no attempt to close the window. She was ice inside; the temperature made no difference.

They'd argued about the girl, she and Peter, but in the end they both knew there was no choice in the matter. The young woman in Los Angeles was a liability of catastrophic proportions, and when hard choices had to be made, Madame Lambert could make them. Summer Hawthorne had no idea why she was so dangerous, and she'd have no idea why she had to die. It wouldn't have made a bit of difference if she did.

Hana Hayashi had left the urn with her, and the knowledge of where the ancient ruins were located. The Shirosama needed both of those things to make his ritual complete. A crackpot ritual that would signal the onslaught of Armageddon, or as close to it as one powerful maniac and a hundred thousand followers could enact.

And history had already proved that that could be pretty bad.

They could trust Takashi O'Brien to do what needed to be done. He was just as much of a realist as the rest of them—you couldn't survive in the twi-

light world of the Committee without being able to
see things clearly, unemotionally, and make the hard
choices. Summer Hawthorne was just one more in a
history of hard choices, one that Taka would make
without blinking.

These things took their toll eventually. Peter could
no longer work in the field, while some operatives
got deliberately careless, stepping in the way of a
bullet. Others perfected their image as a cool, soulless automaton. No one—not even Peter Madsen—
knew what roiled inside Isobel herself.

She smoothed her pale blond hair back from her
perfect face. No one had any idea of her real age—
in their line of work they used the best plastic surgeons—and she knew the image she presented to the
outside world. A well-preserved beauty, anywhere
between thirty-five and sixty, with the best face
money could buy. If anyone saw her naked, her body
would prove the lie, but no one ever did.

Right now she felt as if she were ninety years old,
and as ugly as the turmoil inside her. She couldn't go
on like this. These decisions were part of her daily
life; she couldn't let them destroy her. Summer Hawthorne had to die—it was that simple.

Madame Isobel Lambert reached once more for
her cigarettes, dry-eyed, practical, cool-headed. And
if her hand shook slightly there was no one to see.

Summer never thought she would sleep, but she
had, soundly. She had no idea what time it was when

she woke up—her watch was somewhere back at her house and the darkened bedroom had no clock. Light was coming in from the clerestory windows overhead, muted, shadowy, and she didn't know whether that had to do with the weather or the time of day. Her sense of reality was astonishing. It could be any time from five in the morning to five at night, and her body was giving her no signals whatsoever.

She pushed the sheets aside and climbed out of bed. She'd slept in her underwear, which in retrospect seemed ridiculous. She should have just stayed in her clothes—the baggy black T-shirt and jeans he'd brought from her house. At least he'd brought the fat jeans. She kept three sizes: fat jeans, which were miles too big for her, regular jeans and skinny ones. If he'd brought the skinny ones she would have been miserable; she needed to be ten pounds lighter to even begin to be comfortable in them. The fat jeans were way too loose, but right now she liked the extra folds of fabric around her, and she could have slept in them quite comfortably.

She didn't remember when he'd left her in the room. Had he helped her get undressed? She didn't think so; she'd remember if he put his hands on her. She wasn't used to being touched by beautiful men. She wasn't used to being touched at all, and she preferred it that way. She could remember almost nothing. At one point she'd been in his car, wrapped in her bedspread, in the next she was lying in her underwear in his bed.

She couldn't say much for his taste in clothing, at least as far as she was concerned. While he was elegant bordering on fashion model, the clothes he'd brought her were baggy and too big, including the plain black granny panties and industrial bra circa the time she'd been on the pill and gone from a thirty-four C to a thirty-six D, thanks to hormones. He must have taken one look at her and decided she was a sloppy pudge. That shouldn't bother her at all, given the circumstances. But it did.

A far more overriding concern was how absolutely famished she was. She hadn't had time for dinner last night; she'd been too busy working on last-minute details for the museum reception. And during the party she'd been too caught up in circulating and trying to keep away from her mother's slimy guru to eat. And of course, things had gone to hell in a handbasket right afterward, and she had sincerely thought she would never want to eat again.

Now she was starving.

She pulled on the baggy clothes, looking around for her shoes, then remembered she'd taken them off outside the bungalow. She needed those shoes.

The more Summer thought about it, the more she knew that getting away from her companion was as important as getting away from the Shirosama and his followers. She had no reason to doubt that it was His Plumpness who was after her, but she didn't have any particular reason to trust her guardian angel, either. He might have snatched her from the jaws of death a couple of times, but she still couldn't bring herself to put her life in his hands. Why would a Japanese bureaucrat appear out of nowhere like James Bond and rescue a hapless museum curator? It didn't make sense.

The first thing she needed to do was get the hell away from him. But she couldn't go back to her house, and she couldn't turn to her beautiful, brainless mother, who'd probably just hand her over to her beloved master. Her stepfather, Ralph, let Lianne do whatever she wanted as long as it didn't interfere with Summer's half sister, Jilly. Summer had learned to take care of herself long before Lianne had met her third husband, and Summer's mother and stepfather were hardly people to depend on. The best place was the house on Bainbridge Island—she could probably hide out there without anyone noticing until the Fellowship either stole the fake urn and disappeared, or gave up. She really didn't care which, as long as the real ceramic bowl stayed hidden, out of greedy hands.

Summer had no purse, no identification, no money, which made escape a bit problematic. But not impossible. Once she got away from her rescuer there were a number of people she could contact. The head of the Sansone Museum, William Chatsworth, was a shameless glad-hander and publicity hound, but he would jump at the chance to get rid of her, including forking over money with no questions asked. And there was her assistant and best friend, Micah, who was more reliable. Her passport was in the desk drawer in her office, it was all the ID she'd need unless she wanted to rent a car.

If that failed, she could turn to her half sister, but that was a last resort. Sixteen-year-old Jilly Lovitz was a smart, cynical kid who loved her older sister unconditionally and harbored grave doubts about her mother's good sense, but Summer didn't want to put her in the middle of things or draw any attention to her. Last night with its danger and its violence didn't seem quite real, but it was, and dragging her baby sister into this mess was the last thing Summer wanted to do. No, there had to be some other way.

But Micah would help her with no questions asked. And she didn't need to worry about Jilly. Summer's stepfather paid little attention to his wife's enthusiasms, but he wouldn't let anything happen to his teenage daughter, and Lianne probably knew that. She could offer up Summer without a qualm, but Jilly would be untouchable, thank God. And that was the most important thing in the world because Jilly was all that mattered.

She needed answers. What was so damn important about her porcelain bowl that people were willing to kidnap and kill for it? What exactly was the Hayashi Urn? And what the hell was going on?

But given the choice between getting out of there and getting answers, escape seemed the wiser choice. She really didn't want to see her so-called rescuer again if she could help it. He stirred irrational things inside her, things she didn't want to think about. She needed to get lost, fast, because too many people were out to get her.

And she had no guarantees that Mr. Takashi O'Brien, if that was really his name, wasn't one of them.

5

His holiness tossed down the last of his Fresca, settled his white robes more sedately around his body and walked into the meeting room of the tabernacle on the edge of Little Tokyo, his head lowered in a prayerful attitude. The contact lenses were an annoyance—his eyes were dry and itchy, and all the artificial drops in the world didn't seem to help. It would have been easier if he had blue eyes—going from dull brown to a colorless pink shade was more stressful on the eyes—but it was a price he paid willingly.

It didn't matter; he didn't have to be able to see that well. As long as he was in control he had others to do the seeing for him. His vision was clear where it counted: his divine mission to cleanse the world.

The innermost circle was already in attendance, kneeling around the edges of the room, heads bowed so low they touched the floor as he made his stately entrance, his bare feet light on the straw mat. His followers were particularly penitent today, a good thing, since they'd failed him most dismally. Two of their brethren were dead, and if he had his way the other four would follow them.

He took his seat, folding gracefully into a kneeling position despite his weight, and lowered his head in corresponding respect, keeping his expression blank.

"Who wishes to tell me of the disasters that have passed this night?" he intoned.

The one known as Brother Heinrich spoke up. He was one of the Shirosama's favorites—a former East German gang member who'd found salvation in the True Realization Fellowship. He could be counted on to carry out the most ruthless of disciplinary actions, all without question, but this time even he had failed.

"We have no idea where she is, Master," Brother Heinrich said in a low voice. "The car was forced off the road and the two brothers were dead inside, and she was nowhere to be seen."

"How did Brother Samuel and Brother Kaga die?"

"They both had broken necks. Presumably from the force of the crash. They must have hit the windshield—there was blood everywhere."

"How convenient." He allowed some of his acidity to seep into his voice. "And the girl managed to get herself out of the trunk on her own? Do limousines come with an interior latch?"

Brother Heinrich looked confused. "I don't know…"

"They don't," the Shirosama informed his follower. "And the two brothers most certainly didn't die from the accident. Someone must have been following them, following the girl, when I told them to be extremely careful there were no witnesses."

Brother Heinrich lowered his head further in an attitude of abject shame. He was only twenty-two, and he'd managed to kill at least seven people in his short life, three of them in the service of the Shirosama. It would be a pity to dispense with his services; very few followers had the blind dedication combined with experience to meet such special needs.

"So we can only assume someone helped Miss Hawthorne to leave our protection," the Shirosama confirmed. "You went back to her house to see if she was there?"

"We did, your holiness," Brother Jaipur said, sounding equally miserable. He was more dispensable than Brother Heinrich, and this wasn't the first time he'd failed him. Maybe the Shirosama could make an example of him. "The house was empty, but clearly she'd just been there. There was water surrounding her bath and her bedroom was in shambles."

"If a woman is running from what she mistakenly perceives as danger, she doesn't stop to take a bath. Someone else must have been involved. I am afraid Dr. Hawthorne is in very grave peril. It is our solemn duty to find her and bring her under our protection," he intoned. "If any harm comes to her then we should bear the blame." He allowed his milky gaze to rest on the four miscreants, one by one, making it clear that the "we" was only a figure of speech.

Brother Jaipur was foolish enough to speak up. "Shouldn't we just retrieve the Hayashi Urn and let the girl fend for herself? Do we really need her?"

The Shirosama turned to look at him, his long, silent gaze a reproach that turned Brother Jaipur's dark complexion pale. "We must care for all those unfortunates who have not yet seen the light. We need to lead her to paradise any way we can. There are no accidents. She was placed as the caretaker of the Hayashi Urn for a reason, and we must honor that." He wasn't about to share why he needed to get her under his control—that knowledge was his alone. As far as his followers knew, the Shirosama's wisdom was infallible. The plan had indeed come to him in a vision, but that vision had left out a crucial element. Where the final ascendance was to take place.

But he knew who held the answer. And he would bleed and burn it out of her if he must, once he got his hands on her.

"Then her escape would have been preordained," Brother Jaipur said.

The Shirosama's pale, bleached hands were hidden beneath the folds of his white robe and no one could see his clenched fists. His expression remained serene. "Brother Jaipur, it was hardly an escape when we only meant to protect her," he chided him gently. Brother Heinrich could strangle him—he'd taught the young German that squeezing the traitorous breath from doubters was an act of generosity, helping them escape their karma and move on to the next level. And Brother Heinrich enjoyed using his hands. "We make no mistakes, but unworthy and incompetent followers can be deluded by the snares of evil and allow the forces of the unrighteous to triumph. And if that happens, we must redeem the unworthy."

All four of the fallen monks hung their heads in shame. They wouldn't resist their punishment; the quickest path to paradise was to be cleansed by the Shirosama's judgment. But while Brother Jaipur was dispensable, both Brother Sammo and Brother Telef were brilliant chemists with unquestioning devotion. The death of Jaipur would merely sharpen their focus.

"We must find the poor girl," the Shirosama murmured, using his most hypnotic voice. "Look for guidance—our way will be made clear. I will visit her mother and see if the girl has been in touch, and I will meet with the younger sister as well. She could prove helpful in persuading Dr. Hawthorne of our sincerity. In the meantime, the rest of you must find out who helped her and where she is hiding. We can't allow anything to come in the way of the True Ascension."

The men rose to their feet, and he could feel the palpable relief in the room as they began to back away from his presence in abject humility. He savored the moment, until his quarry had almost reached the door.

"Brother Jaipur," he said in the most gentle of voices. "You stay."

No one looked at the hapless Brother Jaipur as they shuffled out—he had already left them on his trip to paradise. Brother Heinrich, without a word or a sign, moved to one side, knowing he would be needed. No, the Shirosama couldn't dispense with Heinrich. Not yet. In his own way he was just as valuable as the chemists. Who would have thought the same calling would attract German street thugs and brilliant scientists? Once the Shirosama reached ascendancy all would be made clear. Until then he would simply have to make do.

The last acolyte closed the door, leaving the room silent, with only the Shirosama and his two followers inside.

"Brother Heinrich," he said gently.

Brother Jaipur didn't scream, accepting his fate, going to his heavenly reward with the blissful assurance that all was well, and the excruciating pain would cleanse him.

Brother Heinrich met his master's eyes over his brother's corpse, looking for approval like a stray dog. The Shirosama nodded benevolently.

"Find the girl, Brother Heinrich," he said. "Bring her to the loving safety of our community. And kill anyone with her."

"Yes, your holiness."

The Shirosama nudged Brother Jaipur's body with his bare foot. "And get some of the brothers to dispose of this mess, would you? His soul is already in paradise—get rid of the garbage left behind."

He was really quite cross, when he shouldn't allow himself to be. Now that they'd located the urn he was getting impatient. There were only a few short days until the onset of the Lunar New Year. He needed the girl as well, to complete the ritual and perform the ascendancy.

He was getting tired of waiting.

Summer opened the door to the bedroom very slowly, as silently as she could, not wanting to attract any attention in case her rescuer was asleep. The front room was empty; in fact, there was no sign of him anywhere. The pillows on the sofa looked untouched, so either he hadn't slept there or he was very neat. It was dark outside, with a light rain falling, and her best guess was that it was late afternoon, and Takashi O'Brien was nowhere to be found.

She didn't hesitate, sprinting across the living room in her bare feet and grabbing her shoes, which were set neatly by the door. His weren't there, which meant he was gone, or so she hoped. But how far away was he, and for how long?

She opened the front door, peering out into the rain. She had no earthly idea where she should go. She could always make it out onto the street and see if she could find a cop, though L.A.'s finest were never there when you needed them. She could try to hitchhike, but that might be even worse than getting kidnapped by the Shirosama. Maybe she could just walk until she found a pay phone that had survived urban blight. Better than trying to find the main building of this rambling hotel complex. She didn't want to risk running into Takashi O'Brien.

She hadn't spent much time in Little Tokyo, but if it was anything like Chinatown it would be relatively safe, well-lit and well-preserved. Unfortunately, the True Realization Fellowship had their headquarters somewhere within this relatively small neighborhood, and the last thing she wanted was to run into one of them.

But she couldn't stay here and do nothing. The more she thought about it the less likely her rescuer's story seemed. How had he found her in the first place? How had he managed to save her without being seen by the Shirosama's men? And why in the world would anybody want to harm her? While Lianne and Ralph Lovitz were about as powerful and wealthy as anyone in L.A. society, most people had no idea of her connection to them. She herself had nothing of value—apart from an obscure Japanese bowl that was now ostensibly out of her reach.

No, scratch that. She'd foolishly told her rescuer that it wasn't the real one. Which meant he needed her to find it, and chances were he could be just as lethal as her mother's guru. More so, in fact. The True Realization Fellowship simply wanted her; as far as she knew they didn't actually want to harm her. But her companion had killed. And he sounded as if he had no objection to killing again if need be.

She couldn't afford to hesitate. She took off down the winding drive, keeping as close to the carefully planted vegetation as she could, skirting the other bungalows until she made it to the front entrance, guarded by the bright red Japanese torii gate. The city traffic was heavy, as always, but she crossed at the first intersection, heading toward the row of tiny shops and restaurants. Someone would either let her use the house phone or tell her where a pay phone was.

The one asset she still had with her was her brain— she'd memorized her phone card numbers. She could call Micah at the museum—he was probably wondering where the hell she was—and get him to pick her up, bring her passport and even front her some money and drive her car over. She had a second set of keys in her desk, and with any luck the Volvo was still sitting in the parking lot up in the Santa Monica Mountains.

She had no luck until the third restaurant, a tiny noodle shop, and by that time she was thoroughly soaked. The woman at the counter didn't understand much English, but with a combination of pantomime and pleading Summer got what she wanted—a pay phone at the back of restaurant, just off the kitchen.

She was ready to faint with hunger—the smells were making her crazy—but she had no money. She'd simply have to wait. At least Micah answered his private phone line immediately, and after a few panicked questions he settled down to write a list, and promised to meet her as soon as he could get there, probably an hour, given that it was raining and rush hour. She had to be satisfied with that.

She didn't think she was going to be able to explain to the proprietor that in an hour she'd have more than enough money to buy everything on the menu; their initial exchange had been difficult enough and the old lady had been reluctant. Summer ducked back behind the wall, into the shadows. People were coming in and out of the shop, the flow of Japanese and English incomprehensible from her spot, the smell of the food a torment that she had no choice but to endure till rescue came. She was so busy concentrating on the front of the shop that she didn't hear the kitchen door open, and then it was too late.

"What's up?" The cook was no more than a teenager, with several piercings, bleached hair and a friendly expression on his face. He sounded as if he'd grown up in the Valley, so at least with him the language difference wouldn't be a factor.

"I'm waiting for someone," Summer said. "Do you mind if I stay back here?"

"My mom would bust a gut if she caught you," he said cheerfully, and Summer's growling stomach tightened. "But she stays out by the counter—she doesn't trust anyone except me, and that's only sometimes. Go on in the kitchen. You can wait there."

"Thank you!" Summer breathed. Being near all that food was going to be an even greater torment, but at least she'd be safely out of sight for the time being.

The kitchen, really nothing more than a prep table and a couple of huge stoves, was a mass of steam and smells, and Summer found a stool in a corner, as far away from temptation as she could manage. When the kid came back in he took one look at her, grinned and said, "You hungry?"

Pride demanded she say no, but after the last twenty-four hours pride had no place in her life. "Starving," she said. "I have no money, but my friend is coming and he'll pay..."

"No problem," the kid said, dishing up a simmering bowl of noodles and squid and handing it to her, plus a pair of chopsticks. Summer didn't hesitate. She'd spent her life trying to avoid tentacles, but at that moment she'd eat a live cow.

Her newest savior busied himself dishing up noodles, refilling her own bowl once she'd emptied it, this time with chicken, thank God. He made several trips in and out of the dining room, and Summer ate until she couldn't move, then leaned back against the kitchen wall, feeling more human and hopeful than she had since this whole nightmare had begun. It had been close to an hour since she'd called. Micah should be there anytime, and she needed to be on the lookout for him.

The kid came back into the kitchen with a tray full

of empty bowls, setting it by the sink, and she was just about to offer to work on the dishes when the door opened again.

"I'm sorry," the teen said, sounding truly regretful, as two white-robed brethren headed toward her.

Her first, instinctive thought was she shouldn't have eaten the squid—she wanted to throw it up right then and there. But that was only fleeting; she was learning to be fast on her feet, and she moved, heading toward the stove as the two men closed in on her.

There were two huge vats of boiling water on the burners, heavier than she'd expected, but she was desperate. Summer pulled them to the floor, jumping ahead of the scalding water, which hit her pursuers. She knocked the kid aside as she sprinted out of the kitchen, howls of pain following her.

It was full dark now, the rain still falling heavily, and she heard the woman behind the counter let loose a shrill string of invectives as Summer ran out onto the sidewalk. A little boiling water wouldn't slow the brethren down for long—she'd heard rumors of the kind of training they went through—and she knew she had to move fast. The streets were crowded with people, enough to slow her down, not enough to hide her, but she wove her way through them quickly, keeping her head down while she tried to look for the familiar shape of her old green Volvo. Micah should have been here by now. With any luck he'd show up in time for her to jump in the passenger's seat and take off. Micah drove so fast he'd lost his license three times; once he arrived, no one would be able to catch up with them. He just needed to get there.

She thought she saw a flash of white out of the corner of her eye, and she sped up, moving as fast as she could. People didn't tend to wear white in January, even in L.A., and there were at least three white-garbed forms behind her, closing in. She didn't dare take the time to look back, just kept heading blindly forward as they got closer. She could try running—she would if she had to—but she was already feeling sick to her stomach. They couldn't just snatch her in broad daylight, could they? Except that it wasn't broad daylight, it was dark and raining, and people in cities tended to mind their own business and ignore trouble. She could see an alley up ahead, and she had a split second to decide whether to risk it or not. With no Volvo in sight she was going to have to save herself, not count on Micah.

She darted into the alley, away from the muted streetlights, and she could hear her pursuers following her. She was screwed, she thought desperately, taking time to glance behind and see the three white-robed men with shaved heads moving into the shadows after her. There wasn't going to be anything she could do about it.

Summer slammed into him hard, too busy looking behind her to notice his sudden appearance in front of her. He caught her arms and shoved her out of the way, behind him, and she fell, momentarily dazed. She didn't need to look through the shadowed alleyway to know who had turned up at the last minute to save her. Summer scrambled back against the brick wall, watching through the pouring rain with frozen fear as the three burly men converged on slender, elegant Takashi O'Brien.

And then she closed her eyes, horrified. Violence was one thing on television and in the movies—it had nothing to do with real life. In person, the slow motion, macabre dance of it made her feel dizzy, and she couldn't, wouldn't watch. The sounds were bad enough.

If she had any sense, she would get up and run—there were three against one, and she only trusted the one slightly more than the very dangerous three. They would make short work of him, and she needed to use this chance to get away.

And then the noises stopped, leaving just the sounds of the heavy rain and traffic in the street beyond. She opened her eyes, to see Takashi O'Brien standing over her, and she glanced past him to discover two white-clad bodies lying in mud and rain and blood, and no sign of the third.

He held out his hand and she took it, letting him pull her to her feet. His cool, beautiful face was expressionless—no hint of censure or emotion at all. "Don't run away again," he said. "Or next time I'll let them have you."

And she didn't doubt him for a minute.

6

If there was any chance the Shirosama's goons would have simply killed her, then Takashi O'Brien would have let her go and good riddance. He was pissed. As far as she knew he'd nobly saved her life, twice, and she'd thanked him by taking off when his back was turned.

In fact it was himself he was mad at. Normally he wouldn't have made the mistake of leaving her long enough to switch cars. Normally he wouldn't have had to factor her in at all—she wouldn't be alive.

He couldn't afford to make mistakes, not if he wanted to live. And he did—he'd fought hard when that madman had finished with him, survived when other men wouldn't.

The icy Madame Lambert was probably wondering what the hell was going on. During the night Taka had come up with a simple enough plan— switch to a less conspicuous car, find out where Summer had stashed the real Hayashi Urn and retrieve that, and see if he could figure out exactly what else she knew.

That had been his original mission. Keep the urn out of the brethrens' hands, find the missing piece of the puzzle and then wipe out any trace of his presence. But Summer Hawthorne didn't appear to be any more forgetful than she was compliant, and she wasn't about to ignore the events of the last twenty-four hours. He had his orders about her, whether he liked them or not. He couldn't waste any more time trying to circumvent them—the Shirosama and his followers were upping the ante, the lunar year was approaching and a mistake could be disastrous.

He stared at her, not bothering to hide his annoyance. She looked like a drowned rat again, but he was getting used to it. He actually preferred her that way; he had an annoying weakness for blond hair, and when she was drenched her hair looked brown as it snaked over her shoulders in sopping tendrils, not its usual sunlit gold. Hair color aside, he'd never once been interested in a woman with freckles.

She wouldn't look at the men in the alleyway, which was probably just as well. One was already dead—from a broken neck when he'd thrown him against a wall, and the other would soon be gone, too, hemorrhaging from the knife he'd tried to draw on Taka. The third had gotten away, another mistake, because Taka had recognized him. Heinrich Muehler was one of the Shirosama's better known followers—and one of his most dangerous weapons. If Taka had recognized the murdering German punk in time he would have concentrated on taking him out first.

Except if he had, Summer Hawthorne would already be dead. Instead he'd gone for the one who'd been coming at her with a knife, and by the time Taka had gotten around to baby-faced Heinrich it was too late. Taka had acted on instinct, and by doing so complicated his life yet again.

He took her arm and started toward the back of the alley. It was a good thing for her she didn't say anything, not even when saw the huge black luxury SUV he'd traded for. She winced when she climbed up into the passenger's seat, and he wondered if he'd gotten to her before too much damage had been done. At least she was still in one piece…and any pain she was feeling was her own damn fault.

He pulled out into the rainy night, not looking at her, keeping his expression absolutely blank. He didn't often lose his temper, particularly in a situation like this one, but right now he was having a hard time not lashing out at her. He knew he was being ridiculous—no matter how polite he'd been, her instincts probably told her he was as dangerous as the men who were after her in the first place. He'd flat out told her as much.

And her instincts were right.

"Where are you taking me?" She was looking for something as they drove down the crowded street, far more alert than she had been before. "Are we going back to the hotel?"

"No. And don't think you can jump out the next time I come to a stop. You really wouldn't want to see me any angrier than I am already." His tone was calm, almost contemplative, but she had the sense to be afraid.

She hadn't fastened her seat belt, but at his pointed look she did, grimacing slightly. There were red splotches on her hands, and her pant legs were soaked by more than the rain. He couldn't deal with patching her up now. It was more important that they get as far away from Little Tokyo as they could.

"I don't see why you're angry," she said after a moment. "You aren't responsible for me. I can take care of myself…" Her voice trailed off as she realized how patently absurd that was. She tried again. "You could just drop me at a friend's house and not have to bother yourself—"

"I'm not dropping you anywhere. You'd just be drawing your friend into danger, too."

"I would?" She sounded distressed at the idea.

Shit. "What have you done?" Taka asked.

Summer was silent for a moment, and he wondered if he was going to have to hurt her. After a moment she spoke. "I asked my friend Micah to bring me my car and some things from my desk at work."

"Shit." He said it aloud this time.

"It's not like anyone could trace me. I used a public phone."

"And where was this friend supposed to meet you?"

"Outside the noodle shop."

"The same noodle shop where the True Realization Brotherhood found you? Don't you have any idea what kind of danger you're in? This isn't a movie, and it isn't a game. These people are dangerous, and they'll stop at nothing to get what they want."

She looked shaken. "I think you're exaggerating…"

"Did you see what just happened in the alley?"

"I didn't look."

He shook his head, giving up, and punched a few numbers into his mobile phone. He said nothing but a number to identify himself, and then listened to the message. He hung up, then clicked the phone off so no one could pick up his signal. He took a sharp left turn. "And what was Micah Jones bringing you besides your Volvo?"

"My passport, a lot of cash, a couple of credit cards…" Her voice trailed off. "How did you know his last name?"

"A dark green 1996 Volvo was just discovered at the bottom of a cliff near Santa Monica, and the driver, an African-American male with the name of Micah Jones, was found dead inside. He was forced off the road."

She started hyperventilating, and Taka cursed beneath his breath. She was either going to pass out or throw up, and since they were going to be stuck in this car for a while, neither option was appealing. He couldn't afford to slow down, either. He took the back of her neck and shoved her head down as far as he could with the seat belt holding her back. "Breathe slowly," he ordered, still driving fast. He could feel her pulse against his palm, the fluttering, racing throb of it, and he figured once she started crying she'd calm down. She kept trying to hold it in, but she was a civilian, unused to the horror that often made up his daily life. She needed the release of tears.

But she simply let him hold her down as she shook, and it wasn't until he had an unbidden, unwanted erotic thought about cradling her head at crotch level that he let go of her, almost as if he were burned.

She sank back against the seat, her eyes wide and staring. "I killed him," she said in a bleak voice. "I didn't realize…"

"No, you didn't realize," Taka said, trying to forget about the feel of the warm skin at the back of her neck. He didn't want to offer Summer any kind of comfort, but he couldn't keep himself from adding, "You're in the wrong place at the wrong time, and anyone else you involve is going to run the same kind of risks."

"I wasn't trying to involve anyone. I just needed to get away from here…"

"You're going to need me for that."

She turned to look at him. "Who the hell are you?"

Takashi wondered whether he should try the Ministry of Antiques story again, then discarded the idea.

They were long past that innocent lie. The next lie he told needed to be far more plausible and deadly, or she was going to run again.

And he couldn't afford to let that happen. At this point the only way she was going to get away from him was if she was equally safe from the brethren, and, right now, the only way that would happen was if she was dead.

"Someone who's not going to let the Shirosama get you," he said, which was nothing more than the truth. She just didn't know what lengths he'd go to ensure that.

She leaned back against the seat, her color pale in the reflected city light. She didn't ask where he was taking her, and he didn't volunteer the information. He drove fast and well, moving through the constant traffic with the ease of someone who'd learned to drive in one of the most congested cities in the world, and she said nothing, retreating in on herself.

He still couldn't figure out why she hadn't cried— not once in the time he'd been with her. She'd been through more than most American women would see in a lifetime, witnessed more violence, and yet through it all she'd remained shaken but dry-eyed. He wasn't used to it—there was something almost unnatural about her control. As long as she kept that eerie calm, she was capable of bolting, and he couldn't afford to let that happen.

She needed to break, completely. And if the events of the last twenty-four hours hadn't managed to do it, then he was going to have to finish the job. Until Summer Hawthorne was weeping and helpless, she was a liability.

He glanced at her pale, set profile. The lights from the oncoming cars prismed through the rain-splattered windshield, dancing across her face in shards of light and dark. Yes, he would have to break her. Or kill her.

Or maybe both.

Isobel Lambert stubbed out her cigarette, hating the taste in her mouth, the smell on her fingers, hating everything. She needed to go back to the doctor, see if there was something new she could try. She'd already gone through the patch, gum, nasal spray, hypnosis, cognitive therapy, clove cigarettes, and everything else under the sun, but nothing had stuck. She'd manage a day, a week, even three months one time, then something would happen and she'd pick them up again.

Her therapist had a glib explanation: her job. Her life was all about death. The giving of it, the ordering of it. By smoking she could atone by seeking her own death in a slower, more insidious way.

Just so much bullshit, Madame Lambert had told the good doctor. If smoking made it easier to accept the hard choices she had to make, then she'd go up to two or three packs a day. But it didn't. Smoking just kept her hands from shaking.

O'Brien hadn't done his job, and the bodies were

piling up. Some civilian had gone over a cliff in the girl's car, and Takashi had had to take out God knows how many of that sicko Shirosama's mindless goons. She'd asked Taka what the fuck he thought he was doing, but he'd been avoiding her messages, and in the end, it was up to him. He had experience and cool determination, and if he was keeping the girl alive there must be a good reason.

Maybe it had been too soon to put him out in the field again, but she hadn't had much choice. O'Brien was tailor-made for the job—he could speak and read Japanese, he had the connections, the culture. No one else even came close. His body had pretty much recovered from some of the most advanced torture the modern world could devise, and his sang-froid had never been an issue. So why didn't he finish the job? He must still think there was a way to salvage the situation, but from half a world away Isobel couldn't see many signs of hope. But strategy, she knew. And the only way to stop a deluded megalomaniac, if you couldn't get close enough to kill him, was to take away his toys.

Summer Hawthorne had no idea that's all she was. A toy, a pawn in the hands of some very dangerous people, and both sides were deadly, experienced and ready to kill her before the other could get their hands on her.

Takashi must be convinced there was something to be gained from keeping her alive, or the situation would be done with and Isobel could finish whatever open pack of cigarettes she was rationing, go back to her elegant apartment and break something.

She'd tried with cheap dishes, department store glasses. Those didn't work. To stop the pain she had to smash something of value, something of beauty, something irreplaceable. Like the human life she'd just ordered terminated.

And then she could calm down, pour herself a glass of wine, and no one would have any idea why there were tears streaming down her face. Because by the next day her perfect, flawless complexion would betray absolutely nothing. Only Peter, who knew her better than anyone else, would guess.

She picked up the mobile phone and pushed the buttons that would send her through a circuitous route to Takashi O'Brien's corresponding device. She didn't expect to reach him, but she had to try. She needed answers, any kind of update. The faint hope that things weren't totally fucked.

She left another message, trying to rid herself of the powerful sense of unease that tightened her shoulders beneath the pale silk of her suit. If an operative didn't check in there was usually a very good reason, and Isobel had learned to live with silence and unanswered questions until the time was right. For all she knew Summer Hawthorne was already gone—Taka could be very gentle and she'd never know it was happening. His ability to kill painlessly, and his experience with southern California, had been two other reasons he was perfect for the job.

The fact that the Shirosama and his doomsday cult would hit a little too close to home for him only made the stakes higher.

Too high, maybe. She could have sent someone else, someone without an emotional investment in the Armageddon the apocalyptic cult leader was planning to rain down on Tokyo and every other major city in the world.

But she was a woman who went with her instincts, and there'd never been any doubt. Takashi O'Brien was made for this mission, and the sooner Isobel stopped second-guessing herself the better off she'd be.

Until Taka called in to tell her Summer Hawthorne was dead, she had no choice but to sit in her office and smoke, watching the streets of London in the misty pre-light, and wishing to hell she'd gone into some other line of work. Like being a travel agent or an accountant. Anything that would allow her to sleep at night.

The state-of-the-art phone vibrated in her hand, and she jumped, stubbing out still another cigarette. Someone had left a message—a coded text message—and she knew from the channel used that it could only be Taka. All she had to do was set the device into its cradle to read the news. And then she could move on.

For a long time she didn't budge. She'd never been one to avoid unpleasant truths, and she wasn't about to start, but she needed to take a deep breath before she found out that one more necessary loss had been completed.

But right now she needed one more cigarette. One more cup of coffee. Before another part of her soul was burned away.

7

He had blood on his hands. He had the most exquisitely beautiful wrists, strong but delicate, and she stared at them as he drove through the busy nighttime streets of L.A., her eyes riveted to the drying blood on the back of his hand, on the long fingers holding the steering wheel far too casually, given the speeds they were driving.

Summer wanted to throw up, to scream and hit something. The only thing to hit was him, and that would likely send them crashing into another car. In this tank they'd probably bounce off anything but a Hummer, but she didn't want to risk it. Too many people had died already, including Micah. Sweet, charming Micah, who'd just been complaining about his love life and the price of gas and the weather. Micah, who would never mind any of those things again. All because he'd wanted to help her.

She was cold, her muscles clenched tight so that she wouldn't shake. She didn't want to draw Taka's attention any more than she had to, not when he was already angry with her. She wanted to disappear, to vanish into nothingness, and she let herself play with the fantasy that if she just didn't move, didn't speak, didn't breathe, she'd vaporize, and there'd be no more blood, no more pain, no more—

"Snap out of it!"

She let out her breath in a whoosh, her tense muscles loosening slightly. He had the heat on in the car, flooding it with warmth, and the hot air on her legs stung. She must have splashed some of the boiling water on herself as well as the men chasing her.

She looked down at her blotchy hands, then turned to look at her savior. "What do you mean?"

"Take deep, calm breaths and think about the ocean. I can't have you freaking out on me right now."

"I wasn't freaking out," she said in a flat voice. "I was just trying to decide what to do next."

"And what did you come up with?"

"Nothing."

He nodded, watching the rain-drenched street as he drove. "Since you weren't going to have any say in the matter, it's just as well."

"Are you going to tell me where you're taking me?"

"Maybe. I need to figure that out myself first."

"Great," she said bleakly. "My knight in shining armor doesn't even know where we're going."

"Not exactly."

"You know where we're going?"

"I'm not your knight in shining armor," he said in his deep, unemotional voice. "It would be a mistake for you to think so."

The rain was letting up, slowing to a drizzle, and the traffic was beginning to thin. With the total illogicality of nature, her stomach had stopped its nauseous roll and now she was hungry again. Starving. They were speeding by fast-food places, and Summer, who'd been flirting with whole grains and vegetarianism, started craving an In-N-Out Burger with a fiery passion. She said nothing, until he turned right, and then she forgot all about food.

As he turned the corner again she knew far too well his eventual destination.

"It's a waste of time taking me to my mother's house," she said. "The bowl isn't there."

"Where is it?"

Why the hell had she told him the one in the museum was a fake? If she hadn't volunteered that information he probably would have left her alone. Then again, he wouldn't have come after her when she was trapped in that alleyway, and God knows where she'd be right now. At the bottom of a cliff with poor Micah?

She couldn't think about that—it was too painful. "What's the big deal about the bowl? Granted, it's beautiful, and very old, but it's not worth killing for."

"That's a matter of opinion. Clearly a number of people disagree with you."

"Then maybe I should just hand it over to them and end this nightmare."

There was absolutely no change in his expression. "I can't let you do that."

"Why not? It's mine—my old nanny left it to me…"

"I believe Hana Hayashi left it in your care, not as a gift. It belongs to Japan, not some California gaijin who doesn't realize its value."

"You're obviously half-gaijin yourself, so there's no need to be snotty," she said. "And the urn is seventeenth century Edo period, probably made between 1620 and 1660. It should be worth anywhere between one hundred and fifty thousand to three hundred thousand on the open market—probably closer to three hundred thousand dollars because of the distinctive ice blue glaze. People don't murder for less than half a million dollars."

"How naive are you? In some parts of the world people will commit murder for a handful of coins. Just because you've lived a safe, insular life doesn't mean the rest of the world is so well protected." There was no emotion, not even condemnation in his cool, deep voice. Just a statement of fact.

Summer shivered. She couldn't help it—she'd done everything she could to put her life before Hana out of her mind, but every now and then it resurfaced, as it did now, in the words of an arrogant, disturbingly beautiful man.

"Not as safe and well protected as you might

think," she said finally, staring out at the rain as it ran down the smoked windows of the car. They were still heading toward her mother's house, and she didn't know how to stop him. Only that she had to.

"Apparently not," he said after a moment. The man was too damn observant. "Otherwise you'd be a basket case. I haven't see you cry—not over your friend, not out of fear. Very impressive."

His words were like a punch to the stomach. "I don't cry. No matter how bad things are, I never cry. It's a waste of time. Crying won't bring Micah back, crying won't change anything. Would you prefer I was sitting here blubbering?"

"Yes."

She stared at his elegant profile in the darkened interior of the car. "Why?"

"Because it's an anomaly, and I don't like anomalies."

"Tough shit."

She had to imagine the faint movement of his mouth, what in another man might have almost been the beginnings of a smile. And then the thought vanished as he turned down the broad street that led to her stepfather's gated mansion.

"No!" she said, her voice rising in panic. "It's not here."

"Then where is it?"

He pulled up to the security gate and put the car in Park, punching in a security code that he shouldn't have had before turning to look at her.

The gate began to slide open, and Summer's panic began to spike. "Listen, I told you, it's not here," she said for the thousandth time. "There's no reason for us to go up there. We don't need to involve my family in this mess—put them in danger."

"It was your mother who put you in danger in the first place, and they're already involved. Your idiot mother is one of the Shirosama's most devoted followers. If the Shirosama's men haven't already been here then they'll come soon."

"No!" Summer said in horror. "We can't...I'll give them the bowl..."

"What are you so afraid of? Don't tell me you're trying to protect your mother. She already fed you to the wolves, and I imagine she'd do so again."

Summer didn't bother denying it. "Then why give her the chance? Let's just get out of here."

"She's not here."

"She isn't?" Summer said warily.

"Your stepfather took her to Hawaii this morning to try to get her away from the Shirosama. Apparently he balked at spending fifty thousand dollars for her guru's bathwater."

"What?" Summer cried, horrified. "Why would she want his bathwater?"

"To drink it. It's part of the True Realization Fellowship's initiation. You drink the Shirosama's bathwater to absorb his consciousness. They sell his blood as well, but that's a bit pricier."

"I don't believe you," she said flatly, horrified.

"Don't you?" Taka leaned back, his hands loose on the steering wheel, and in the dim light he looked elegant and deadly. "The True Realization Fellowship has over a billion dollars in assets, and that amount is climbing daily. Selling the blood and the bathwater and the tapes and the literature is just a lucrative sideline—and they make most of their money through the donations of their renunciants. And they do their best to attract the wealthiest of the disaffected. They need the poor students for their scientific expertise and the grunt work, and they need the rich ones to turn over their wealth. It's been very effective so far—the True Realization Fellowship has grown from a handful of followers ten years ago into one of the most powerful of the new religions, as they like to call themselves."

"A religion that condones murder?"

"Most of them do, as long as they believe their cause is just. And they all believe that." Takashi started to open the car door, and she put her hand on his arm to stop him. It was a strange sensation—he'd touched her any number of times as he'd snatched her out of danger, but she couldn't remember ever reaching out to him.

His arm was hard and strong beneath his jacket, and he could pull away easily, but he stopped, looking at her in the darkened car.

"Please," she said in a low voice. "It's not my mother I'm worried about."

"Your little sister is gone."

Relief flooded Summer for a moment, then suspicion followed. "How did you know about my sister?"

"I know everything about you. Your sister is visiting friends in the country, and she won't be coming back anytime soon. At least, not until this is settled. We've made sure she can't be found easily, and she has no idea what's going on. You don't need to worry about her."

Summer stared at him. "'We made sure'?" she echoed. "Who the hell are you?"

He didn't answer, and she no longer expected him to. The only thing she knew for sure was that he was no Japanese bureaucrat.

And he was about to break into her stepfather's mansion, an act that would only bring unwanted attention to her baby sister. Protecting Jilly was the one thing even more important than Summer's promise to Hana, and she wasn't going to screw that up.

"It's at Micah's house," she blurted out.

Taka didn't seem particularly gratified by her sudden surge of honesty. "And why would it be there?"

"Because Micah was the one who made the... copy." Her hesitation was so slight he couldn't have noticed. The last thing he needed to know was that there was more than one forgery floating around.

"All right," he said, starting the car once more.

"We can't go there. Don't you think the police will be all over the place because of Micah's death? They're not going to let us waltz in and search for it. And his friends will probably be there as well—" Her voice broke. Not in tears, never in tears. But simply raw pain.

"His body hasn't been identified yet. When it is, someone will see to it that the police don't make it public until I give the word. No one will bother us." He pulled out into the street, heading west, toward Micah's run-down Spanish-style villa, with unerring certainty.

It took Summer a moment to gather her wits. "What do you mean, he hasn't been identified yet? You told me…"

"My people know. A lesson for you, Dr. Hawthorne. My people know everything."

"And your people have the power to control the LAPD?"

His half smile was the epitome of cynicism. "A lot of people do. How could you have lived twenty-eight years and still be so innocent?"

She was past being surprised that he knew her age—he was heading directly for Micah's house. What else did he know?

A cold sweat broke out. Did he really know everything, including the sordid details of her childhood? Was he privy to secrets buried so deeply that even she had managed to suppress them?

"I'm not innocent," she said in a tight voice.

Thank God he didn't look at her. "Maybe not. But you've lived a rarified life, safe in academia and then locked away in a museum, untouchable. And one short-term affair doesn't make for a raft of sexual experience."

Her sense of panic was growing worse and worse, and she knew she should change the subject, because if he knew, she wouldn't be able to bear it. But she couldn't stop. "Maybe I'm not looking for sexual experience," she said. "Maybe I'm looking for love."

His laugh was quick and sharp. "I don't think you believe in love. Your history doesn't suggest you've made any effort to find it."

What history? she thought, anguished. "I love my baby sister. I loved Hana."

"But we're not talking about that kind of love, are we? We're talking true love, sexual love, happy ever after."

"Happy ever after?" she echoed. "No, I don't believe in that." *What else?* she thought. *What else do you know?*

He stopped the car, and she was shocked to realize they were already there. Micah's tumbled-down villa was miles from Ralph Lovitz's Hollywood mansion. But the ride had been ridiculously short. Her companion's breakneck driving style could account for part of it. His ability to distract her with devastating questions took care of the rest.

Micah had bought the old villa for a pittance ten years ago, and in the intervening years he hadn't manage to make much of a dent in reversing its rapid decay. She knew from experience that the few lights on in the old place were set on timers. Micah hated darkness and the lack of light in the winter months, and when he was living alone he didn't want to come home to an unlit house. She could see one of his cats prowling around outside—usually he'd be home by now, and the three stray cats who had moved in would be feasting on gourmet cat food.

She was going to have to do something about the cats, she thought. Assuming she got out of this alive.

The man beside her wasn't going to be distracted. "I have a key," she volunteered. "I stay here sometimes."

"Convenient. I don't need one, but it makes things easier." He slid out of the car, waiting for her, and for a brief moment she wondered whether she could run for it. She didn't care if Takashi O'Brien found the urn—she was well rid of it, and as long she was away from him, her family, her sister, would be safe.

It would be the smart thing to do. She had no reason to trust him any more than she trusted the Shirosama, and no desire to find out what he planned to do with her once he had the urn. But when it came right down to it, he bothered her. Disturbed her, in ways she didn't want to think about. Half of what he'd told her was lies, and he'd told her very little.

"Don't even think about it."

He didn't need to say anything more. He seemed to know what she was thinking before she did, and she was no match for him. Two more reasons he bothered her. If she decided to run away she was going to have to come up with something a little better than a spur-of-the-moment dash.

Summer climbed out of the car, closing the heavy

door quietly. She had no idea why she was trying to be surreptitious—if the neighbors were alerted to a possible intruder they'd call the police, and that would be a good thing, wouldn't it?

Though if they looked out and saw her they'd know it was all right. She'd spent so much time here she even had her own room as well as her own key. And a change of clothes, she realized with belated relief.

"I'm not sure where it is," she said, truthful for once. "We'll need to look for it. Any chance I could change into some dry clothes? I keep some in my bedroom here."

His dark eyes flickered over her dismissingly. "You look like a drowned kitten."

"And how would you know? Drowned many kittens in your life, have you?"

"Not kittens."

His flat voice gave her shivers. "Well, at least you're just as good at saving people from drowning," she said.

"I have my talents. Go ahead and change, but don't take too long. Just tell me where to start looking."

"My best guess is Micah's studio at the back of the house. Either that, or his bedroom, the big one just off the kitchen. I know it's not in the room I use."

"Do you, now? And why do you keep a room here? You and he weren't lovers—he was gay."

She really wanted to slap this guy. There was nothing dismissive in his comment, but his cool omniscience was infuriating. "He occasionally slept with women, as well."

"But not with you." It wasn't a question, and it would have been a waste of time to deny it.

"I have...sleep issues. Night terrors, they call them. I love my little house, but there are times when I need to be near someone."

Taka looked at her for a long moment. "Now what would cause night terrors in such a conventional young woman? Maybe we missed something in your background."

They were moving up the overgrown walkway, and the darkness would have hidden her expression. She didn't need a mirror to know her face had turned white, her eyes stricken. At least he couldn't see.

She handed him the key.

He said nothing, and she wished she knew what he was thinking. Whatever it was, she bet it wasn't pleasant, for all the austere beauty in his exotic face.

"You've got ten minutes," he said. "And don't make the mistake of trying to run again."

And then he moved into the shadowy house, ignoring her.

She fed the cats first, her hands shaking. At least she had her priorities in order, and Phantom, Cello and Pooska showed their appreciation. Takashi was in Micah's bedroom, searching, but making no noise at all. She knew almost nothing about the man she'd spent the last twenty-four hours with, but she was certain there'd be no sign of his presence in Micah's house once he finished his business, unlike the time the brethren had tossed her place. She left him to his search, heading into the small bedroom that was hers, grabbing some black jeans and a T-shirt as she went into the bathroom. She could take lightning fast showers, and within three minutes she was toweling off, inspecting the reddened burns on her shins and hands. She hadn't even noticed when the boiling water had hit her. No wonder—she'd been running for her life.

She pulled on the plain black bra and panties, sat down on the closed toilet and reached for a tube of ointment that was unlikely to do much good, cursing underneath her breath. It hurt like the devil, and blisters were beginning to form. Even her loose jeans were going to rub painfully, but she had no choice.

She didn't notice when the locked door opened. Didn't notice anyone standing there, watching her out of dark, unreadable eyes, until he spoke.

"What the hell did you do to yourself?"

8

Summer shrieked, grabbing her discarded towel and wrapping it around her body. "Go away!"

"Don't be tiresome." He came into the room, caught the edge of the towel and yanked it from her, tossing it to one side. "How did you get hurt?"

"Give me my clothes—"

"I don't give a flying fuck what you're wearing," he said. "I need to check your injuries to make sure you're able to keep up with me."

She'd wrapped her arms around her torso in a futile effort to shield herself from his indifferent gaze. She knew her average-bordering-on-plump body would have held little interest for him. Or that, God forbid, she wanted it to. She just didn't want those flat, dark eyes seeing her so exposed.

But he was also stronger, more determined and very impatient, and the more she resisted the longer she'd be in this awkward situation. "I was in the kitchen of the noodle shop when the men came after me, and I tipped over a vat of boiling water to stop them. I must have gotten splashed myself, though I didn't notice at the time."

"Give me your hands."

If she did that she could no longer cover herself. Since it wasn't doing much good anyway, she sucked in her stomach and held out one palm.

"Both of them."

She stopped fighting him, at least for the moment, holding out her hands. They were mostly steady, a fact she could be proud of, considering she was sitting in her underwear in front of a strange man, a very handsome strange man, and people were trying to kill her.

He took them in his, turning them over to examine the red blotches. And the scars. There was nothing she could do or say—any fool would recognize the marks of a botched suicide attempt. But he made no comment. "When we get to where we're going I probably have something that will help."

"Where are we going?"

He ignored her, dropping her hands and squatting down to look at her ankles. It was all Summer could do not to squirm. Having a man on his knees in front of her was bringing all sorts of strange, uncomfortable thoughts—erotic ones—a kind she wasn't used to having—and she would have given ten years of her life if she just had one more layer of clothes on. She'd managed to live a carefully untouched existence. She knew she could have sex with a man without screaming; her three months with Scott had given her that much, if not an appreciation for the actual event, and she'd spent the last few years safe and un-interested. But for some totally insane reason this man was stirring feelings that were either long dead or had never existed. And she didn't like it.

He didn't seem to notice or care. "These are slightly worse, but they shouldn't slow you down." He looked up into her face, not moving from his po-sition, and his hands still cradled her ankles. And Summer couldn't let her mind go any further in that direction. "So tell me where the urn really is and we'll get the hell out of here before anyone shows up."

"I don't know."

His hand shot out, wrapping around her neck, and his strength was unnerving. "I don't want to hear that again," he said calmly. "No more lies."

"It's not a lie." Her voice was muffled from the pressure against her throat. "Micah made the copy for me in the first place. I thought he'd put the orig-inal back in the house somewhere."

Taka loosened his grip slightly. "He hasn't. Trust me, if the urn was here I would have found it. Where else would he have put it?"

"I don't…" His grip tightened, and she let the words trail off. She swallowed nervously, feeling his palm against her throat. "He could have given it to someone else to hide."

"He didn't."

"I'm having a hard time breathing," she said tightly.

"Maybe you gave it to your baby sister," Takashi said. "No one would think you'd put her in danger, but people can surprise you. Maybe you don't care as much about her as you think, particularly when there's three hundred thousand dollars on the line."

"You're disgusting," Summer said.

"Then tell me where it is. Or am I going to have to ask your sister?"

Her eyes met his. They were cold, dark, implacable, and she wondered why she'd ever thought he was any kind of savior. If she wasn't so tired and frightened—if she wasn't sitting here in her underwear—she might be able to fight him. Right now she was no match, and the most important thing was to keep her sister out of it, at all costs.

And why the hell was she fighting him, anyway? She'd lost, and the stakes were much higher than she thought. This wasn't just about preserving a simple bowl of almost unearthly beauty that was a gift from the person who'd loved and protected her most, but the safety of her baby sister. A thousand priceless porcelain bowls were nothing compared to something so precious.

"I can find it," she said in a whisper.

He immediately loosened the pressure on her throat, then dropped his hand. "Do it," he said.

"Can I get my clothes on first?"

He let his eyes drift down over her body. "If you wish."

Of course he wasn't going to leave her while she dressed. He wasn't going to take those dark, unreadable eyes off her. She reached for her jeans and pulled them on, biting her lip rather than crying out when the soft denim rubbed against her burns. She yanked the T-shirt over her head—it was going to be cold, and she needed something warmer, but one look at his implacable face and she wasn't going to ask.

He was blocking the doorway into her bedroom. Odd that a man so lean and elegant could take up so much space. "I need to get my shoes," she said.

"Sneakers. We may have to run. And get a sweater. It's cold outside."

He never failed to surprise her. She could still feel his hand on her throat—for a moment she'd thought he could easily strangle her, and would if she'd fought him. And now he was worried about her getting cold.

Takashi moved out of the way, and she nodded, heading for the closet. She knew he'd searched there as well, even if he hadn't left any sign. She grabbed an old pair of sneakers and a baggy sweater. Vanity, never one of her major character defects, had completely gone out the window. He'd already seen her in practically nothing and been totally unimpressed. Not that she would want to impress him—that was the last thing she needed. But it was disheartening to feel so awkward and plain when confronted with such beauty.

And he was beautiful. She hadn't really had time

to dwell on it while she'd been running for her life, but with his silky, straight black hair, his dark, unreadable eyes and full, luscious mouth, he was almost as gorgeous as the porcelain bowl he was so desperate to find. But there was something unsettling about his physical beauty. She'd been around Hollywood-handsome men for a great deal of her life, and good looks were nothing more than legal tender. Scott had been one of the best-looking men she'd ever met, and with her artist's eye she'd chosen him as the logical man to sleep with, to get over her fears.

That plan had backfired, of course. She'd used him, hoping she could fall in love, and in the end all she'd discovered was that consenting, adult sex was highly overrated, no matter how gentle the partner. She could happily do without.

So why did she look at Takashi O'Brien's starkly beautiful face and suddenly feel lost? In the end it didn't matter; once he got the bowl he'd leave—with any luck—grateful to be done with her. And she'd forget all about the irrational stirrings that she wouldn't have believed herself capable of.

She couldn't wait until that happened. "It's not in the house."

He'd flicked off the lights, plunging them into a darkness lit only by the faint glow from the hallway. "You wouldn't be thinking of a wild-goose chase, would you? It wouldn't be a very wise move on your part."

"I don't know how wise I am. What are you going to do when I find the bowl for you?"

"I told you, take it to Japan."

"And what are you going to do with me? Are you going to kill me?"

She'd managed to startle him. "Haven't I been doing my best to keep you alive for the last twenty-four hours? Despite your best efforts to get yourself killed?"

She couldn't argue with that. "I'm ready," she said.

"Let's go get your goddamn urn."

He was going to have to kill her, of course. He'd known it all along, but he didn't like the fact that she seemed to know it, too. He'd come close a couple of times, changing his mind at the last minute, but once he had his hands on the urn the safest thing to do would be to finish her. Quickly, painlessly, before she even knew what was happening.

Unfortunately, she already suspected him. Would she fight when the time came? He hoped not. Fighting would make it harder for her. She'd be better off just letting go. He could overpower her very easily—she was soft while he was hard and strong. He'd let himself get distracted in the bathroom for a moment, and he'd been a bit too rough because of it. He hadn't needed to grip her throat that tightly.

His powers of observation were well out of the ordinary, and he'd taken in every inch of her exposed skin in the brief glance he'd allowed himself. The scars on her wrists were no surprise—he knew she'd attempted suicide when she was a teenager, soon after Hana Hayashi was killed. He was more distracted by Summer's pale, creamy skin, smooth and soft. She had a mole above her left breast, and damn if he couldn't see part of a tattoo peeking up from beneath the black cotton underwear that covered her hips. He never would have thought she was the type for a tattoo, and he found himself wondering what it was. He could look, of course. After she was dead.

The thought made him feel slightly queasy, uncharacteristically so. He could blame the last mission for the fact that he was having a hard time making his move. Maybe coming so close to death himself had given him a new respect for it, a new fear of it.

No, that wasn't entirely true. He'd already killed four men in the last twenty-four hours, and they'd barely registered on what was left of his soul. He hadn't suddenly grown a conscience; they were dangerous animals who'd needed to die.

Summer Hawthorne was a different matter. She was dangerous, all right, but she had no notion why. No idea of the secret locked inside her head that could bring about the deaths of thousands of people. No idea that he simply couldn't afford to let her live.

He followed her through the house, turning off lights as they went, the shadows growing behind them.

It was after midnight. If she took him straight to the urn he could finish everything and be out on the first plane in the morning, making sure the Shirosama knew what Takashi was taking with him, and what he'd disposed of. Until this afternoon they would have had no idea who was helping their quarry, but now Heinrich Muehler would be able to describe him, and there were enough powerful people in the True Realization Fellowship to be able to put two and two together. There'd be people looking for him, even when he was traveling alone, and while he could easily transform himself into one of his alter egos, he'd still need to be very careful.

No, he couldn't afford to be sentimental over a soft little gaijin with more brains than common sense.

It was chilly in the night air, and Summer shivered when they stepped outside. He resisted the impulse to give her his jacket—he couldn't afford to risk getting blood on it. He asked no questions as she led him around the side of the house. With anyone else, he might wonder if he were being drawn into a trap, but with Summer he had no such fears. He was the danger in their relationship, not her.

Technically, they had no relationship, other than hunter and prey. Captor and quarry. Perp and vic, as they said on cop shows. Murderer and corpse.

They reached Micah's old garage, its tile roof partially gone. Whatever was inside would be exposed to the elements. Was she lying again?

There was only one car inside the structure, a large, anonymous shape covered by a tarp and a pile of dead leaves.

She headed straight for the hidden car and pulled the tarp off. For a moment he stood in awe. He had no particular reverence for cars, having always been more interested in performance than beauty, but he would have had to be a fool not to recognize the beast in front of him.

"This was here when Micah bought the house. It was just a pile of rust, but Micah worked on it for the past five years." Her voice cracked for a moment, but there were no tears. Only pain. "Poor Micah," she said in a whisper.

"You'd be better off worrying about yourself," Taka said.

It was a Duesenberg, circa 1935, perfectly preserved, the chrome shining, the body a dark, rich blue, the seats a matching leather. "Does it run?"

She opened the side door, not looking back at him. "Does it matter? We're not about to drive it, anyway. It probably goes fifty miles an hour if we're lucky." She disappeared into the back seat, her legs still sticking out, and he could see her butt wiggling as she searched around for something. And for some damn reason he got hard.

He leaned back against the wall behind him, waiting. It was a waste of time being angry with himself—he had a healthy appreciation of female flesh, and while he'd never considered himself much of a connoisseur of women's butts, there was no denying that hers was delectable, trapped in that pair of faded black jeans.

But getting hot for someone he was about to kill was someplace he didn't want to go. He'd known men, and women as well, who enjoyed sex and death, who got turned on by the thought of killing someone and would combine both acts. That kind of thinking, and reacting, was the first step toward a sickness of the soul that was terminal. Summer Hawthorne was a job, off-limits, and if she emerged from that behemoth of a car with the Hayashi Urn in her hand then she would then become a casualty of war.

And he could go out and see if he could find a deceptively fragile, blond gaijin with pale skin, freckles and a delectable butt, and get his rocks off that way. Saner, healthier, straightforward. He was, after all, a practical man.

She slid farther inside the car, thankfully, so he no longer had to watch her wiggling ass, and a moment later flipped over so that she was sitting on the floor inside. "Got it," she said.

He was not a happy man. They could have searched all night and he would have been content. They could have driven south and tracked down her sister. But push had come to shove, and he had no more reason for delaying. He had orders, a job to do, and he was going to do it.

He pushed away from the wall of the garage and approached the Duesenberg, filling the doorway, blocking out the light from outside. He could see two things inside the huge old car. She'd placed the long-lost Hayashi Urn on the leather seat beside her, and even in shadow it was beautiful. And then he looked at her, forgetting all about the ancient ceramic he'd been tracking for months, and other people had been tracking for centuries.

She had blue eyes, not quite the intense shade of the urn, but bright blue nevertheless, and her wet hair was beginning to dry. She sat there on the floor of the car, unmoving, as if she knew what was coming now that she'd finally given him what he wanted.

He had no choice. He climbed into the car as she tried to back up against the far door, and there was no missing the panic in her eyes. She knew.

And he couldn't let that stop him.

Jillian Marie Lovitz, only child of Raphael and Lianne Lovitz, stuck out her thumb. Her big sister would be horrified at the thought of Jilly hitchhiking, but beggars couldn't be choosers, and at the moment Jilly was most definitely a beggar, with exactly thirty-seven cents in her pocket.

Why anyone ever thought she'd just go off with the Petersens was something she couldn't quite fathom. Whoever came up with this little idea knew absolutely nothing about her.

Few people did know her, with the exception of her half sister, Summer. Her parents were blindly adoring, and she was very fond of them in a maternal way. Her mother had the intellect of a toaster oven, her father could only concentrate on making money, and both of them thought their little darling was an innocent princess.

Jilly hadn't been innocent since she was twelve years old and walked in on her mother doing the gardener. While her father watched.

Neither of them had seen her, thank heavens. And she'd reacted like a child, running away to stay with Summer until she could begin to see things clearly.

Summer had always been more like a mother to her, even though she was only twelve years older. Lianne tended to see her older daughter as a liability, disputing her own claims of youth, and her younger daughter as a fashion accessory. Ralph didn't pay much attention at all, except to give Jilly money.

Which was fine; they trusted her implicitly and gave her no trouble. She had her life carefully arranged. She was one of those freakishly smart kids, starting her second year of college at age sixteen, and she had every intention of moving into her own apartment in the next few months. Her only problem was getting her graduate student lab partner to seduce her, but she was working on that.

In the meantime she'd been pulled out of classes and sent south on the flimsiest of excuses. The Petersens were friends of her father's, though she couldn't remember ever meeting them before, and they were the least likely of people to show up to whisk her out of harm's way, particularly when that harm was a nebulous threat from some deranged stalker she'd never even heard of.

They hadn't given her much of a chance to protest, and they watched her like hawks once they got to the remote cabin out in the desert. She'd had to wait two days until they'd finally relaxed enough to think she believed them.

It had been tricky getting past the locked doors and the dogs without causing too much noise, hence she hadn't been able to rifle through Mildred's purse for some much-needed cash. Jilly's main goal was to get the hell out of there, back to L.A.

She figured as soon as she could get to a pay phone she could call her parents to find out what was happening. Even better, she could call Summer, who'd jump in her Volvo and come and get her, no questions asked. The Petersens only had cell phones, which they kept with them at all times, giving her no chance to call out. When she'd asked, they'd simply said "too dangerous" and offered her more chocolate.

It hadn't taken her long to realize the candy was drugged. The Petersens knew she had a weakness for Rollos, and she'd spent the first two days in a daze, waking long enough to eat more chocolate before her paranoia kicked in. Jilly had made a lot of sacrifices in her life, but spitting out the chocolate when they weren't looking had to be the hardest. When she got back, away from them, she was going to eat Rollos until she was sick, and then eat more.

But right now she was on a stretch of deserted highway in the middle of nowhere, freezing cold, hungry and pissed off. She refused to let herself be frightened; she didn't frighten easily, and if, when she finally got a ride out of this nowhere place, her driver had other ideas, she knew how to handle that. Summer had had self-defense training, though she'd never said why. It had something to do with Summer's childhood, Jilly expected, and her big sister would tell her when the time was right. In the meantime Jilly had learned from Summer—learned to disable a two hundred and fifty pound man in a matter of seconds.

There were headlights in the distance, coming down the straight, empty highway, and Jilly felt a wave of relief. Rescue was at hand, even if she ended up fighting for it. As the car drove closer her relief grew, and she dropped her thumb and waited until the white limo pulled up beside her, the driver lowered his window and his shaved head poked out. "His holiness has come for you, little one."

Jilly despised being called "little one," particularly since she was almost five-eleven, and she found the pasty white Shirosama revolting. But as she'd already decided, beggars could not be choosers.

"Thank God," she said. And she climbed into the back of the limo.

9

The interior of the old car was very dark as Taka crawled inside it. Summer tried to scoot away from him, but even in a huge touring car there was only so much room, and he caught her easily, pulling her under him, trapping her beneath his body.

She didn't fight him. Even in the shadows he could see her eyes, a clear blue, staring up at him, and he could see the fear she was trying to hide. The longer he drew this out the harder it would be for her, and he cradled her face in his hands, his thumbs brushing against her jaw, her throat, stroking, knowing he was going to have to exert pressure.

She was so soft beneath him. He liked hard bodies, slight women, thin and muscled. She was like nothing he'd ever looked at twice, and she was so deliciously soft.

He wanted to kiss her mouth, just to see if it was as soft as the rest of her. He could kiss her, and she wouldn't even know she was dying as he did it.

She knew what was coming, she had to, and she closed her eyes, shutting him out, lost, resigned, and he moved closer, resting his forehead against hers, breathing slowly. His fingers were cradling her neck, his thumbs stroking her throat. He thought about the scars on her wrists, the darkness in her eyes. Maybe he was giving her what she really wanted, maybe not. He only knew he had no choice. He wanted to tell her he was sorry, but that was absurd, when he'd never been sorry before.

She was utterly still beneath him, though he could feel the panicked fluttering of her heart, which would soon be stilled.

He'd touched her lips with his, a benediction and a farewell, his thumbs beginning to press, when the mobile in his pocket began to vibrate.

He pulled away from her quickly, as if her skin burned him, and climbed out of the car, flipping open the mobile phone that was like no ordinary communicator.

He had his back to her, and he half expected her to make a run for it. He didn't want to have to chase her down—it would only make things harder—but he needed to concentrate on the message. And maybe, just maybe he could let her go....

But then someone else would get her, hurt her a great deal more than he ever would, just to find the hidden shrine. She might not even know where it was located, and she would die in excruciating pain. Or she would tell them, the pain would be the same, even more people would die and all hell could break loose. Now wasn't the time for mercy—look where it had gotten him the last time.

Once he retrieved the message, he severed the connection, then turned back to the car. Summer was sitting in the open doorway, but in the shadows he couldn't read her face. Just as well. He didn't have time to consider what she was thinking, what she was feeling.

"Time to go," he said.

She stood up, bracing herself on the side of the car for a moment, then took a step forward. She was shaken, but still strong. At least she wouldn't hold him up.

He went to pick up the urn, and she moved out of his way, so he wouldn't brush against her. He grabbed the bowl and brought it out into the marginally better light.

He yanked off his jacket and wrapped it carefully round the bowl. Summer had made no effort to run, but stood waiting for him. He led her out of the garage, shutting the door behind them and listening to the locks reengage. Then he took her hand.

It was cold, she was cold, and she wouldn't look at him. It didn't matter, as long as she didn't resist. But of course she wouldn't. He was death and he suspected she'd been seeking him on and off for most of her life.

"Let's get the hell out of here," he said. And she let him lead her back to the car in silence.

* * *

Hell and damnation, Isobel Lambert thought. This was turning into one royal fuck-up, despite the Committee's best efforts. The Sansone Museum had been broken into, all right, but two guards had died in the process, and the faux urn had been smashed on the marble floor. There was no telling whether it had been a casualty of the botched robbery—nothing had been taken from the place—or whether it had been recognized as the forgery it was. If the latter was the case they were in very deep shit indeed.

She had to hand it to the Hawthorne woman— substituting a believable copy was a stroke of sheer genius. Maybe a bit too much for an innocent. If she truly had no notion of the urn's value, why would she have gone to so much trouble to safeguard it? A sentimental attachment to her nanny would take her only so far.

Originally, it hadn't mattered. Taka had orders to take her out before the True Realization Fellowship could get their hands on her, and what she did or didn't know would then become moot.

But he hadn't followed orders. There was no one Isobel could send after him right now, and he was one of the best she had. It was going to be up to him to sort this current mess out.

One innocent life, Summer Hawthorne's, was an acceptable loss, particularly when the knowledge she had concealed in her memory was so very dangerous. The loss of her friend and coworker was simply a reminder of the havoc that could follow if Summer was allowed to survive and the Shirosama got his hands on her.

But the sixteen-year-old girl was another matter entirely. There was only so much loss of life that Isobel could tolerate, and a young girl put that quota over the top. They needed to get her out, and fast, before the brethren could try any of their inventive brainwashing tricks that could leave her a broken shell. And if her sister knew she was being held hostage, she'd give everything she had to get her back.

Life would be so much simpler if Summer Hawthorne was already dead. The Shirosama would have to find the site of the ancient shrine on his own, something he'd tried and failed to do for more than ten years. If she were dead, then using Jilly Lovitz as a hostage would be worthless. Her mother was already willing to give the Shirosama anything he wanted, and her husband indulged her, no questions asked.

If Taka had only followed orders this would all be over, at least for this year. But right now the cult held a very dangerous bargaining chip, and they couldn't be allowed to get away with it.

Madame Lambert leaned back in her chair, closing her eyes. This was a hideous game of chess, using real people as pawns. It was bad enough when they were simply soldiers, killers, conscienceless warriors on the right and the left. Every now and then a pawn would have to be sacrificed, and she made those decisions with equanimity. But as she got older those choices were becoming harder.

There had to be someone she could send. Someone to back Takashi up, someone who could do what needed to be done if for some reason he wouldn't. She couldn't send Bastien—he'd been brought in once to help Peter Madsen, but he had a new life now, with a wife and children and a peaceful existence in the middle of nowhere. He'd done more than he should ever have had to do; it was time to let him be.

And Peter couldn't go—he was still using a cane, and he'd made promises to his wife and to himself. He was deskbound now, her second in command, more than capable of dealing with the hard decisions she made on a daily basis.

The others were scattered all over the world, most of them under deep cover. Which left only one person.

She shoved her perfectly manicured hands through her perfectly arranged hair. Shit. She hated to fly.

She hated the long hours craving a cigarette. She hated the closed-in air. But most of all she hated having someone else be in complete control of her life and her safety.

There was no choice. The girl would be one loss too many. Someone needed to get Jilly Lovitz away from the Shirosama before she was broken, before they could hurt her. Before Summer Hawthorne gave him everything he wanted for the onset of Armageddon.

And Isobel was the only one left.

She was so cold. Takashi O'Brien was holding her hand like a vise, taking her back to the huge black SUV he'd gotten from somewhere, and the tightness of his grip kept the shivers from washing over her body. He opened the passenger door for her, a perfect gentleman, and she wanted to laugh. But if she did she might start crying, and she couldn't remember the last time she'd cried. Years and years and years ago. Tears were not an option.

He went around to the back of the vehicle, carrying her bowl with extreme care, placing it on the back seat before he climbed in. He didn't look at her. "Fasten your seat belt," he said, turning the key. "We'll be driving fast."

"As opposed to the sedate speeds you were driving earlier?" Her voice was raw, but at least it worked, a miracle to her own ears.

He didn't answer, which was just as well. She didn't want to start a conversation with him. Not until she came to terms with what had just happened in the old touring car.

She had to be out of her mind. The man had shown up time and time again, snatching her from danger and death. She had no idea why, but he'd appointed himself her personal savior, and the fact that she was still in one piece was proof.

So what had happened on the floor of the car? His body had covered hers, hard and strong, half pinning her, and his beautiful hands had stroked her face, and she hadn't screamed, hadn't cried, hadn't frozen. Instead she'd looked into his dark, merciless eyes and known she was going to die. And she hadn't cared. She hadn't wanted to move, to run. She'd felt no fear. Only the pressure of his body against hers.

And then he'd kissed her. Just the soft pressure of his beautiful mouth against hers, not much more than a brush of his lips, and then it was over. Once he'd pulled away she'd started shaking, and she wasn't quite sure she could stop.

At least he hadn't noticed. He probably would have thought she was crazy. Hell, she *was* crazy, and no wonder. Kidnappings and death were not a normal part of her everyday world, and while he hadn't specifically said so, she knew she was on the run for her life, and he was the only thing that stood between her and oblivion.

He had the bowl, and he still had her with him. That must mean something, though she wasn't sure what. She had to be insane to think he wanted to hurt her.

He'd turned on the heat full blast as he pulled into the street. She allowed herself a brief glance at him. He'd left his jacket wrapped around the bowl, and was wearing only a thin dark shirt. He must be even colder than she was, though he seemed oblivious to it, while she was doing her best to control the tremors that were washing through her.

She closed her eyes. She was holding herself in so tightly that her skin ached, and she slowly, cautiously began to relax. The tremors had finally stopped, leaving only a stray shiver dancing across her back, and after a moment she let out her breath, leaning back against the leather seat as he sped through the night.

He was driving so fast. If they had any kind of accident they'd be dead, instantly. She didn't care. She didn't need to open her eyes to know he was watching her. She knew that feeling far too well. It was what had started the entire nightmare—his watching her at the museum reception. At this point all she wanted to do was make her mind a blank. What had he told her before—think about the ocean? The blue-green ocean rolling in waves onto the shore, even, steady, throughout eternity, never changing, the sound a rushing whisper of comfort in her ear.

The siren startled her out of her trance, and her eyes flew open. Taka's face was starkly beautiful in the reflection of the flashing lights, but there was no emotion as he pulled the SUV to the side of the road and cut the engine.

He kept his hands in sight on the steering wheel, clearly used to dealing with cops, and remained very still as two of L.A.'s finest loomed in front of the window.

"License and registration. Slowly."

He leaned over, past her, towards the glove compartment, and for a moment she was terrified that he was going to pull out a pistol. But there was nothing inside the space but papers, and he drew them out, handing them to the cop, who flashed a bright flashlight into the interior of the car, illuminating her face.

She must have looked like a deer caught in the headlights, she thought, trying to gather her scattered thoughts. Here was rescue, safety, and she opened her mouth to speak.

Takashi took her hand in his, in a gesture that would have looked reassuring to the police. Only she knew the warning implicit in his touch.

"You all right, miss?" one of them asked, as the other went to call in the license and registration. "You look upset."

Taka couldn't stop her from saying something, couldn't stop them from helping her if she asked for it. She shouldn't hesitate—she knew nothing about the man beside her except that he was very dangerous.

She opened her mouth. "I'm…I'm fine," she said, stumbling a bit beneath the warning pressure of his hand on hers. "My boyfriend was just taking me out for a drive and he goes a little too fast."

Jesus Fucking Christ, why had she said that? Why in God's name had she called him her boyfriend, of all things, as if they were high school students? Why had she claimed any kind of relationship with him at all? She looked at Taka, but his expression was still determinedly neutral, and then the other cop was back.

"He's clean," he told his partner, ignoring them.

"Diplomatic immunity. Cut 'em loose. We gotta get up to the Sansone Museum—there's been a break-in and a couple of guards have been killed."

They'd taken the flashlight off her face, so they didn't see her jerk in shock, didn't hear the noise of protest that escaped her before Taka's hand tightened again on hers.

"Drive slower, Mr. Ortiz," one of the officers said sternly. "You're a guest in this country, and you wouldn't want to wear out your welcome."

"I'll do my best. Thank you, Officer." His voice was smooth, liquid, tinged with a Spanish accent, and in the light Taka almost looked Hispanic. She stared at him in shock as the blue and red lights flashed across his face, then vanished as the police car pulled out into the road, lights still pulsing as it headed up toward the hills.

He released her hand, and she flexed her fingers instinctively. "Why didn't you ask them for help?"

"You didn't want me to, did you? I thought that death grip on my hand was telling me to keep quiet."

"I didn't necessarily think that would stop you."

"It wouldn't have." She wasn't quite sure why she said that. "Mr. Ortiz?"

"People see what they want to see," he replied. "Your boyfriend?"

She wasn't cold anymore, she was hot, embarrassed, which seemed a ridiculously banal emotion, given the last twenty-four hours. "I just said the first thing that came into my mind. What was that they said about the museum?"

"It's been broken into," Taka said. "I got word earlier."

"Do you know what they took?" The forged bowl was the least of her worries. The exquisite treasures that filled the halls of the Sansone were almost like her children; if anything happened to them she'd be heartbroken.

"Nothing."

"But…"

"The forged urn was smashed on the floor. Clearly that was all they were after, since the rest of the collection was untouched."

"Thank God," she breathed. "Then that must mean they've given up. They dropped the bowl and now they'll have to forget about it."

"Maybe," he said. "Or maybe they realized it was a fake the moment they got their hands on it. Which would make them more determined than ever to get their hands on you or anyone who could make you give them what you want."

"What do you mean by that?"

He glanced over at her. "Never underestimate a religious fanatic." And he pulled back onto the rain-wet street before she could say another word.

10

The hours passed in a blur as he drove north out of the city. She paid little attention to the road signs, little attention to anything. The warmth from the heater was sinking into her bones, the hum of the tires, the soft purr of the powerful engine all combined to lull her into a state of half-sleep. Anything was better than the sense of complete powerlessness that came with total waking. She had nothing but the clothes she was wearing—no cell phone, no money, no driver's license or credit cards. Even if she could get away from the man beside her, who could she call? Micah had already paid the price of being her friend, and now two guards were dead at the museum. Because of her? She knew most of the guards; they were good men, with families. Which of them had been murdered by this group of fanatics in search of some stupid piece of ceramic art?

The urn had been so important to her, a piece of her childhood and Hana-san, and now it seemed pointless. If Summer had just handed it over to her clueless mother, none of this would ever have happened. Micah would be alive, and Summer would be safely home in her own bed, feeling nothing more than the casual resentment she felt when her mother used her. She'd promised Hana she'd keep the urn safe, to never part with it until she herself asked for it back. But then, Hana hadn't expected to die. And she wouldn't have wanted anyone to be hurt.

Summer had held on to it, and her world had turned upside down, and she was adrift, with no anchor but the dangerous man beside her.

Except *adrift* was too casual a word for hurtling into the night at ninety miles an hour. "You're going to get a ticket if you get stopped again." Her voice was quiet in the darkened car.

"I thought you were asleep."

"No."

He glanced at her, his dark eyes flitting over her face. "I have diplomatic immunity."

"You're a diplomat?"

"No."

"Does Japan have some kind of secret service? Or are you even Japanese, Mr. Ortiz?"

"Half-gaijin," he said, and she thought she heard a faint note of contempt in his voice. "And most countries have some kind of covert operatives. However, I'm not one of them."

"Then what are you?"

"Your best chance at this point. That's all you need to know."

"My best chance at what?"

"Staying alive."

She remembered the feel of his hands stroking her throat, the touch of his mouth against hers, the weight of his body, pressing down, and she wasn't sure if she believed him.

"Where are we going?" She must have asked him this question a dozen times since she'd known Takashi O'Brien, and didn't necessarily expect an answer to this one, either. But he surprised her.

"Belmont Creek."

"Never heard of it."

"It's a tiny town in central California. We'll be safe there."

"You just plucked it out of the air?"

"It's a safe house."

"A safe house for whom? Are you the police?"

"Hardly."

She sank back in the seat, closing her eyes. He wasn't going to answer her questions, and she was going to stop asking. At least for now.

Summer awoke with a start, squinting at the digital clock on the dashboard. Three-thirteen. He'd pulled into the driveway of a house, and even in the darkness she could see the outlines of a prototypical suburban dwelling, where one had two point three children and fought with the neighbors about the state of the lawn. There were no neighbors close by—she could see identical houses farther down the road, lit by streetlamps, but this one was at the end of a cul-de-sac, far enough away to avoid prying eyes. It was surrounded by more houses in various stages of construction, all identical, huge and far too close together, but for now they would be alone, unobserved. And she wasn't sure if that was a good or bad thing.

She watched as Taka pointed his cell phone at the garage door, and it lifted silently. He drove inside and the door slid down behind them. The overhead light had come on automatically, and it looked like any residential garage, with a riding mower, storage boxes, garden implements. Even a chest freezer. Was he going to dump her in there?

"Are you sure this is the right place?"

"The garage door opened, didn't it?" he responded, climbing out of the car and going around the back. She thought he'd stop and get the bowl, but instead he came to her side of the car and opened the door. "Can you walk?"

Stupid question. Even if her knees were weak she wasn't about to let him see, and she braced herself on the car door as she got out, shooting him a rebellious look. He took a step back, letting her wobble on her own. He aimed the phone at the door to the house, and it clicked open, plunging the garage into darkness as the lights went on inside.

"What the hell kind of phone is that?"

"Multitasking," he said shortly, waiting for her.

There were a few steps up into the house, and she

stumbled slightly, but he was smart enough not to try to steady her. Maybe he knew she was at the very edge of self-control and if he touched her she might start screaming. Something she hadn't done in a very long time.

He followed her in, closing the door behind them. "There's food if you're hungry," he said. "The house is kept completely stocked."

She looked around her. The scene before her looked like the set of a perfect television show, with everything safe and ordinary and in its place. Normal, and yet absolutely artificial.

"Where is the Brady Bunch?" she muttered.

"Who?"

She glanced at him. For once he was totally clueless—hardly a cause for rejoicing when the only thing she had over him was knowledge of odd TV shows. "Never mind," she said. "Where do I sleep?"

"Any bedroom you want. Check the closets until you find clothes in your size. There should be a suitcase as well—pack enough clothes for a week."

"A week? We aren't staying here?"

"We aren't staying anyplace for long."

"Are you going to tell me where we're going?"

"Away."

She wanted to throw something at him. "And I'm just supposed to trust you?"

"You don't have much choice."

He was right about that. She didn't want to stay with him another hour, let alone a week. He confused and frightened and upset her. Not for the obvious reasons. Given the circumstances, it made perfect sense that she would be a basket case.

No, it was more than just the patently insane situation she'd found herself in. It was the man himself, dark, disturbing, eerily beautiful. Her stomach knotted every time he came near her. She'd never reacted to anyone as she reacted to Taka O'Brien, and her response was even more unsettling than the total upheaval of her life.

She didn't think she could survive another week.

"Why are you doing this?" she finally asked. "Why have you made it your mission to save my life?"

"I haven't. You're an assignment."

It was like a slap in the face, but she recovered quickly. "An assignment from whom?"

He hesitated a moment, the first time he'd ever seemed uncertain. "The Committee."

"What committee?"

"That's it. All you need to know. More than you need to know."

"Then why did you tell me?"

He had no answer.

She needed food even more than she needed the answers he refused to give her. She went straight to the refrigerator, opening the freezer compartment. "Ben & Jerry's ice cream," she breathed, leaning against the open door. "I may cry."

"You'd cry over ice cream and not over a friend being killed?"

He sounded no more than casually curious, and she shouldn't have felt the need to defend herself. "Tears don't help," she said tightly.

"True enough."

"Ice cream, on the other hand, does wonders." She reached for the container, pulled off the top and went searching for a spoon. Mission accomplished, she started to eat straight out of the container. She glanced up at him. "I'm not sharing," she said, sitting down at the perfect little table in the perfect little breakfast nook.

"I didn't think you were." He went over to the fridge, and emerged with a Sapporo beer and a small black platter. He sat down opposite her, like the perfect husband in the perfect house.

The black platter had sushi and a pair of chopsticks. She raised an eyebrow. "Don't you think you're taking a chance with raw fish? Who knows how long that's been in there."

"Less than six hours," he replied. "I'd offer you some but it doesn't go well with ice cream."

She wasn't about to tell him that she had an indecent craving for good sashimi, and she almost would have given up the ice cream for it. She didn't need anything that would bring her closer to him. "I don't suppose there's any Diet Coke in the fridge."

"Diet Coke with ice cream?"

She could be enigmatic as well. "Yes."

To her surprise he rose, went back to the refrigerator and emerged with a fuchsia-colored can. "No Diet Coke, but this looks close."

She dropped her spoon. Tab was almost impossible to find in southern California—she only knew of one place to buy her supply, and she was used to accepting Diet Coke as a substitute. On rare occasions she'd even tolerate Diet Pepsi.

No one could have gotten Tab by accident. Whoever had stocked this house knew exactly what she liked, down to something as minor as her favorite kind of ice cream and her preferred soft drink. She had no doubt at all there'd be a complete wardrobe in her size, all in black and white and gray, probably from the same stores she patronized. They seemed to know everything about her, whereas she didn't even know who "they" were.

Just the man sitting across from her, eating his nigiri with calm dedication, his distant, elegant face giving nothing away. She could thank him for the food and the clothes she knew she'd find. He would have told them.

She pushed back from the table, suddenly sick. "I'm going to bed," she said, putting the lid back on the half-eaten quart of ice cream.

"Aren't you going to eat anything else?"

She didn't want to ask what else there was. There would be her favorite foods, the kind of yogurt she liked, her favorite wine, all the arcane little peculiarities she'd developed over the years. She didn't want to see. They knew too much about her.

"I'm not hungry," she said, only half a lie. She wasn't too shaken to leave the Tab behind—right now she needed all the comfort and normalcy she could get. "Any bedroom?"

"Take your pick. Just don't lock the door."

"The doors have locks? I'm amazed. Are you planning on making a surprise visit?" She could have kicked herself. Why did she keep bringing up sex when that was the last thing she wanted to think about.

He just looked at her. "I'm trying to protect you," he said. "Not that you're making it any easier. Leave the door unlocked in case we have to get out of here quickly."

She was too exhausted to argue. She found the room with the right clothes, including duplicates of things she'd had in her own closet. The sky was starting to lighten, and she pulled the miniblinds, shutting out the deceptive ordinary world of the suburbs, stripped off her clothes, down to her underwear, and crawled into bed. She wasn't going to sleep in constricting clothes. There was also no way she could fall asleep naked—there probably wasn't any way she could fall asleep at all, and taking a gulp of cold, caffeinated soda wouldn't make the slightest bit of difference. She'd closed and locked the bedroom door, despite his warning. She knew he wasn't about to come into her room while she slept; despite the odd kiss, she knew he had absolutely no interest in her apart from keeping her alive.

The house was completely silent. No traffic noise, not even the sound of birds disturbed the stillness.

Another day was dawning in this strange, nightmare world she'd stumbled into. And she closed her eyes, rather than face it.

"The child is unhappy, your holiness." Brother Kenno's soft voice was hesitant.

The Shirosama opened his eyes, blinking rapidly. It was past time to change his contact lenses. Each time he remembered to change the extended-wear contact lenses, he expected his eyes to have changed as well. It was always a shock when his own brown ones looked back at him, bloodshot and bleary.

It was happening, he knew it was. His vision was getting milkier and harder to focus—it was all part of the preordained change that was coming. By the time of his ascension he would be complete: Shirosama in body, mind and spirit.

"Are not all children unhappy?" he replied. "Are not all people unhappy? It is the way of karma. Her soul is at war, and the more she fights the more unhappy she is. Have you done nothing for her?"

"Your holiness, she refuses. She kicked Brother Sammo, and she refuses to wear our robes or listen to your holy word. I've told her that the gift we offer her is invaluable, but she is stubborn. Should we have Brother Heinrich deal with her?"

The Shirosama shook his head, the white hair settling around his shoulders. "Not until she is ready to receive the gift of moving past her karma. For now simply keep her contained and quiet. She's still in the induction room?"

"Yes, your holiness. She tried to block the speakers but she was unable to reach them."

"Good. Sooner or later my words will penetrate her stubborn mind, moving past the veil of illusion that rules humankind. When she is ready she will listen."

Brother Kenno bowed. The Shirosama couldn't see his expression, but it didn't matter. Kenno had been with him for the last five years, and his devotion was absolute. "And then she will be blessed?"

"Then she will join her sister on the next level, and all her worldly cares will be done with. They will have ascended before Armageddon—a gift indeed."

"Indeed," Brother Kenno echoed solemnly. He backed out of the room, leaving the Shirosama to contemplate the bloody, glorious, necessary future.

And whether Jilly Lovitz would need to learn personal instruction from the Shirosama himself, before she accepted her preordained fate.

She wasn't quite a child, but she was young enough. She wouldn't fight, not once Brother Sammo made certain she ingested the proper combination of medicines necessary for true enlightenment.

The Shirosama couldn't afford to indulge the child's needs right now, not until he found out where her sister was, and let the woman know that Jilly was under his protection.

The news would finish any resistance, and Summer would come to him herself, bringing the bowl.

He would also mine the stories his aunt Hana had filled her head with. Before he'd killed her.

Part of his karma was to live with that miscalculation. He had let frustration and anger get the better of him thirteen years ago, and he had acted rashly. In truth there were no mistakes—everything happened as it was meant to happen, and he was preordained to kill that infuriating old woman who had stood between him and his destiny.

Just as it was his fate to labor onward, gathering the pieces of the puzzle, the pieces he needed in order for his ascension to become complete. In the past thirteen years he had amassed followers and wealth, power that should have been his by birth. They followed his vision—thousands of them, hundreds of thousands of them. His role was a gift and a burden he accepted gladly.

Now it was all coming to fruition. The New Year was at hand. He knew what he needed, and he had the bargaining chip to bring her to him.

The Shirosama closed his eyes once more in blissful meditation, the gilded future bright and terrible.

11

Summer had locked the door, of course. She had no idea how predictable she was, at least in certain matters. Taka picked the lock in silence, opening the door and looking in on her. She was sound asleep, her long hair loose around her head, the covers tossed off. He wasn't surprised to see she was sleeping in the underwear she'd been wearing earlier, though if she'd looked closer among the clothes she probably would have found a reasonable facsimile of what she usually slept in. The Committee was good about things like that.

He never would have thought black underwear could be so utilitarian. She wore a plain bra, no lace, and panties covered her generous butt and then some. He leaned against the doorway, picturing her in sexy underwear and a thong, and then pushed the thought away, disgusted with himself.

He closed the door silently. He could give her another few hours, though he didn't dare sleep himself.

He didn't trust her not to take off, and she seemed stubbornly unaware of just how dangerous a situation she was in.

He could go days without sleep—a real benefit at times such as this. They were in a holding pattern. Summer had received a last minute reprieve, for the kidnapping of her sister changed everything. He wasn't quite sure why…. In the old days Harry Thomason wouldn't have hesitated; any complication was dealt with quickly and ruthlessly. Back then, Thomason would have had him taken out, as well, for not getting the job done in a timely fashion.

Complications aside, Taka knew that the sister posed no particular danger. Summer didn't even understand the knowledge she possessed, so could have hardly passed it on to anyone. Jilly Lovitz could harm no one—her only value was as a hostage. They could leave her in the Shirosama's pudgy white hands. Hell, it would serve their ditzy mother right. As long as Summer didn't try to go after her.

He glanced at his mobile unit again. No message since the last, when Madame Lambert had instructed him to go to Belmont Creek and stay put.

She was a different kind of boss altogether. She liked alternatives. Death wasn't always the answer, and when it appeared as if that was the only choice for Summer Hawthorne, she hadn't liked it any more than Taka had. But she'd ordered it.

And now she'd told him to wait. Fine with him. Only the longer he kept Summer alive, kept her with him, the harder it would be to kill her. It made no sense that he was having second thoughts about Summer Hawthorne, and had been since he'd first hauled her out of that trunk.

God, he'd kissed her. For no other reason than he'd wanted to. He'd never gotten that close to someone he'd had to kill. He knew he could do it if he got the word—he was a machine, the King of Death. He just wasn't sure if this time he could live with himself.

He needed a shower and a change of clothes if he wasn't going to allow himself any sleep. They'd be off again in another four hours, heading God knew where.

But first he needed to make sure the bowl was securely packed. His orders were to leave it behind, and someone would pick it up—presumably the same person who'd brought the Sapporo and sashimi and his favorite dark roast Ethiopian coffee. He wasn't particularly happy about leaving the urn; he'd gone to so much trouble to find it that letting go wasn't easy, but so long as they had it the Shirosama could do nothing.

And then Taka took a good close look at the urn.

Most people wouldn't have known it was another fake, but most people didn't have his knowledge of ancient Japanese ceramics. He shouldn't have been surprised, he thought, setting it on the kitchen counter in the bright artificial light. If she'd managed to get one fake, she could easily procure two. This was a beautiful copy, but the glaze was just a bit too uniform, the lines too smooth, the deep blue color muddied.

Taka couldn't help himself—he laughed. She was a resourceful woman, and it was a good thing he hadn't followed orders, or right now they'd be up shit's creek without a paddle, especially with the Shirosama in possession of Summer's closest relative. To find the urn, they would cut her into little pieces if that were necessary.

He made himself a cup of coffee, using the grinder and the coffee press provided, as he considered the fake bowl. He decided to do as he'd been ordered, wrapping it as carefully as if it were the real thing. He needed to keep the Committee off his back for a few days, long enough to figure out what the hell he was going to do next. Long enough to get Summer Hawthorne to tell him where the true urn really was.

He'd always been able to compartmentalize his life and his work. Sex was an everyday part of his job, one he did with his usual skill. It was said he could seduce a seventy-year-old lesbian and make her like it, and he didn't doubt it for one moment. Everyone had skills. Peter was a sniper, a born assassin. Bastien Toussaint could be anyone he wanted, and he was lethal with a knife.

Taka knew how to fuck. He could get what he wanted from any woman, no matter what age or sexual orientation. He had skills that would have made Casanova blush. His body was his best weapon—he killed by hand, seduced and destroyed with merciless determination.

Summer Hawthorne would be child's play compared to some. He wasn't going to have any choice, and he accepted that fact with equanimity. Betrayal was the name of the game—to get what he'd have to use every weapon in his arsenal. She hadn't responded to threats, to last-minute rescues, to danger, and time was running out. He needed to find out where the goddamn urn was, and he'd let her get away with too many lies.

He could tell her the Shirosama had kidnapped her sister, but that would only send her into a panic, and women in a panic were unpredictable. On the other hand, Summer was already enough of an anomaly— she managed to keep her head in circumstances that would have most women weeping. He needed something failsafe.

Sex. He hadn't used sex with her, and he didn't know why he was so squeamish in this particular case. Why was he hesitating? He could picture her, pale and defiant, and thought about that plain black underwear beneath the baggy clothes. These would be duplicates from her closet, so clearly she never wore anything that showed her body—nothing fitted, nothing with any color, and he once again wondered why. She had a good body. He'd seen her naked in the tub, and his powers of observation were topnotch.

She had nothing to be ashamed of, no reason to

Anne Stuart

cover her figure in wads of dark clothing. Her hips
and butt were maybe too generous, and her flesh was
soft, rather than the tightly muscled buffness so in
vogue nowadays. She had a woman's body—round,
soft, comforting. The kind a man stayed with.

He'd seen that uneasy expression in her eyes when
she thought he wouldn't notice. She watched him,
and she was fascinated. Frightened. Attracted. And
she didn't want to be. If Taka's instincts were correct,
it would take very little to get her on her back. Very
little to get between her legs and find out what he
needed to know.

He had hoped he could do it some other way. If
he did end up having to hurt her it would be betrayal
enough. He didn't want to have to fuck the information out of her.

But he'd run out of options, and there was
nowhere else to go. He thought about her, pale and
defiant, and he released the tight hold he'd had over
his body. Looked at her and began to get hard.

What would she respond to? Strength? Being mas-
tered? Some women were turned on by that, and he
had no doubt that part of her fascination with him was
because he was like nothing else she'd ever known.
Hell, he was like nothing else most people had ever
known.

Or would she respond better to softness? Gentleness, even a touch of uncertainty to give her the illusion of control? He could make her think she was
doing this for him, nobly sacrificing her body for his

pleasure, and she wouldn't know otherwise until he had her shivering and climaxing beneath him.

Or maybe a combination of the two. She was smart—that was part of the problem. Too damn smart. She would see through any half-assed attempt at seduction. He had to pull out all the stops to get her where he wanted her.

And in the end, she probably would have preferred he'd just killed her.

It was no one's fault but her own. He'd tried everything, but she'd kept her secrets, and too many lives depended on finding out what those secrets were.

Perhaps her ability to bury secrets explained why the rest of her was much too easy to read. She was afraid of sex, totally turned off to it, and yet she couldn't stop looking at him. She probably didn't even know she wanted him. She'd be horrified if he told her, if he made a move.

He could have her eating out of his hand. He could have her down on her knees in front of him, doing anything he told her to, and she had no idea how vulnerable she really was. He could feel it, see it, sense it.

He was accustomed to women wanting him. What shocked him was the simple fact that he wanted her.

Not hot, energetic sex. Not a blow job from a novice. He wanted her with a perplexing intensity he hadn't felt in years. He was the King of Death, and she was his consort.

And no amount of common sense could distract him.

There was limitless hot water, and he stood in the shower a long time, letting it stream over his body. He wanted a traditional Japanese bath—to sit in the still, hot water and let everything fade away—but he wasn't going to have that indulgence until he got back to Japan, and that return would come with its own set of problems.

He toweled off, ignoring his reflection in the mirror. He was used to it—the combination of his mother's exquisite, Asian beauty mixed with his father's appeal. His mother had valued beauty above all things, and certainly would have chosen someone of comparable beauty to marry. Not that Takashi knew—he'd never even seen a photograph of his dead father. All he knew of the man was his last name and what was reflected in Taka's own face. That, and the fact that his grandfather had had him murdered.

Ancient history. Taka pulled on the jeans they'd left him, at his request, zipping but not buttoning them, and then looked up again. To see Summer Hawthorne's horrified reflection in the bathroom mirror as she stared at his back.

He whirled around, but it was too late. "How long have you…?" he began, but she'd already taken off.

He caught her before she reached the front door. His hand clamped down on her shoulder when she hit the landing, and she came flying backward, falling against him so that they were both on the stairs, his arms wrapped around her, imprisoning her struggling body.

She kicked at him, but she was barefoot and her efforts were a waste of time. His arms were like iron bands around her, and for all her struggles there was nothing she could do. After a moment she stilled, the tension draining from her body, but he didn't release her.

"There are a thousand watts of electricity going through the front door," he said in her ear. "If you'd passed through you'd be dead."

She shivered, and a moment later his arms loosened. He stood, pulling her upright, and she stared at him in the early morning light.

He was shirtless, wearing only a pair of jeans, and once more her stomach knotted. How could someone so dangerous be so enticing? He was thin, strong, with smooth, golden skin stretched tautly over bone and muscle. Leaving no clue to what was on his back.

"I saw your tattoos," she said.

"I know you did. So?"

"So I know what they mean."

"That I'm a Japanese biker?"

"That you're a gangster. A member of the Yakuza."

"Yakuza." He corrected her pronunciation. "You've seen too many movies."

"Maybe. But in the last twenty-four hours I've

seen dead people, been kidnapped, run for my life, had a good friend killed…sounds like organized crime to me, even if you do have all your fingers."

"Movies again," he said lightly. "Does it matter who I am, as long as I'm keeping you alive?"

"That depends."

"On what?"

"On how long you're planning to do that."

He was still touching her, his hand a manacle around her wrist so she couldn't run. Not that she would—if she had to take her chances between getting electrocuted and staying with this man, the choice was clear.

"At least long enough for you to tell me where the real urn is. Micah made more than one, didn't he?"

Damn. Maybe he really was with the Ministry of Antiquities—that forgery was top-notch. "And then you'll let me die? Not much incentive."

He released her wrist, and she wrapped her own fingers around the place he'd held her, absently rubbing, trying to erase the feel of him. "The doors and windows are armed, and if you try to get out without knowing the codes you'll die. Keep that in mind while I finish getting dressed."

She said nothing, trying to move as far from him as she could.

"On second thought, maybe you'd better come with me. I don't trust you."

"I don't—" He took her arm and hauled her back up the stairs with him, giving her a perfect view of his back as they headed toward the bedroom he'd used.

The design was complex and beautiful—an Asian dragon, long and lean, curled protectively around something small and vulnerable, with angel's wings etched on his shoulder blades. The tattoos went down the outside of his arms, down his back beyond the waist of his low-slung jeans, and she wondered where they stopped. And then she jerked her eyes above his waist, immediately feeling heat flood her face.

She must have stalled, because he yanked her forward, pushing her ahead of him into his bedroom and onto the bed. She sprang up immediately but he simply pushed her back down again.

"Don't jump to any conclusions," he said. "I just don't want to be running after you."

She said nothing, though her mind was going a mile a minute. Either he hadn't slept or he'd made the bed—the pillows and covers seemed untouched. He reached for a long-sleeved shirt and pulled it on, covering up the intricate tattoos that marked his body—him—as dangerous.

"I don't know why you're so shocked," he said, shoving a hand through his damp black hair. "Who did you think you were dealing with? Have I ever given you the impression that I wasn't a dangerous man?"

"No," she said in a small voice.

He hadn't buttoned his shirt, but he grabbed a

dark jacket that was lying on a chair and pulled it on. Black leather, and beautifully tailored. So well-tailored that it had to have been made just for him, and once more she wondered where the hell they were and who was supplying them. She'd found a duplicate of her favorite pair of black khakis, same size, same brand, plus matching or similar shirts. And they'd even brought the same three sizes of black jeans she kept.

At this rate she'd be back into the skinny ones soon enough; she couldn't remember when she'd last had a decent meal. And right now her stomach was churning too badly to even think about it.

"Look at it this way," he said, leaning against the dresser and watching her out of dark, impenetrable eyes. "If I have any connection to organized crime it can only work to your benefit. I don't need to worry about trifles like legalities if I want to keep you safe."

"And do you? Want to keep me safe, that is?"

She expected a fast answer, something noncommittal, but for a moment he said nothing. "I want the urn," he said finally. "I want to know where it came from in the first place. That's why the Shirosama is so determined to get his hands on you. If all he wanted was the urn he would have killed you and taken it from the museum. You're the only one who knows where the original shrine is."

"Don't be ridiculous. I don't know anything at all about a shrine, or even much about the urn. I used it to hold cookies, for God's sake. And why should the

Shirosama care where some mythical shrine is? He wants the urn because my mother promised it to him and it's worth a lot of money and I don't want him to have it. I'm just the means to an end. I know how ruthless he can be, and I figured I'd have copies made to confuse him. But I don't matter to him."

"You know more than you think. Hana Hayashi wouldn't have died without trying to pass on that information. And you're the only one she could turn to."

"She couldn't have known she'd be killed by a hit-and-run driver," Summer protested.

"A very conveniently timed hit-and-run driver. She knew." Taka pushed away from the dresser. "Where's the urn?"

"I don't—"

He moved so fast she had no time to brace herself. He slammed her down on the bed, leaning over her, vibrating with rage. "Don't say it," he warned her, his voice low and dangerous. "I'm not playing this game anymore. Tell me where the fucking urn is, or you're not going to like the way I make you."

His hands were on her shoulders, pinning her to the bed, and she felt panic rise inside her. It was nothing like before, so long ago—then it was sugary sweetness and presents and touches that hurt.

"Let go of me." She spoke in a whisper so quiet she thought he wouldn't hear. But he did. He stared down at her for a long, thoughtful moment.

And then he pulled back, moving away from her,

turning his back. She was shaking. Too hard, and she couldn't stop. It wasn't the same, it wasn't…

"What happened to you?"

His voice broke though her terrified mantra, startling her. He'd turned again, and in the early glow of daylight suddenly she was even more frightened.

But he wasn't the one who frightened her. What terrified her was her own incomprehensible longings.

"Answer me." His voice was short, sharp. "What happened to you? Did your lover rape you?"

"No!" she protested. "He loved me. He would never have hurt me."

"Then who did this to you?"

She didn't want to understand his question. "I don't know what you're talking about."

"Don't you ever tell the truth?" He sounded both annoyed and weary. "Someone hurt you."

"That was a long time ago. I don't even think about it anymore."

"Sure you do. Whether you know it or not, it's part of your life. Every day. Didn't Hana Hayashi protect you?"

"Of course she did!" Summer's defense was an immediate response. "It happened before…" The words trailed off.

"You were six years old when Hana started taking care of you."

"Yes." Summer waited for the pity and disgust to fill his face. She went on before he could say anything. "It's no great tragedy—young girls are molested all the time. I'm over it. And Hana made sure it never happened again."

"Who?"

She shook her head. "I don't even know. A friend of my mother's. I was supposed to call him Uncle Mark. He was old and hairy and smelled like cigar smoke. I don't like cigars." Her voice was almost eerily calm. She couldn't remember the last time she'd talked about this. Scott had never known the details, just that he needed to be very very gentle with her. Lianne didn't want to hear, despite her brave attempts to explain what happened in the best way a six-year-old could.

"No, I imagine you don't," he said.

"He brought me presents," she said. "Pretty pink dresses and colored balloons. And he hardly touched me. I just had to…watch him."

"Would you like me to kill your mother?" Taka might have been asking if she wanted milk in her coffee.

It was her turn to be shocked. "She doesn't know."

"Bullshit. She knew what she was doing, leaving you alone with him."

"Well, she's forgotten about it." Summer pulled the shreds of her self-control back around her. "And I told you, it was a long time ago. Hana made sure I was protected, and in turn I protected my little sister. I'm a normal, healthy woman."

"Who dresses in black and white and only had one unsatisfactory lover."

"He wasn't unsatisfactory!"

"If he was any good you would have had others."

"I told you I wasn't looking for love!"

"You told me you weren't looking for sex."

"Not that, either."

"Are you sure of that?" His calm question set off a new wave of reaction, something she couldn't hide.

"Don't do that!" she said, her voice low and fierce.

"Don't do what?"

"Just don't."

He crossed the room, shrugging out of his leather jacket. He still hadn't buttoned his shirt. The complex and beautiful tattoos were hidden. All she could see was his smooth, golden skin.

"Don't do what?" he said again, his voice low. Too close, he was standing too close, and she could feel the heat from his body like a physical touch.

"Don't do this," she said. "Maybe you think I just need sex from a good man to get over my hang-ups, but you're dead wrong."

He almost smiled. "I don't remember offering you sex, Summer. And I'm most definitely not a good man."

She was well past the point of being embarrassed. "That's a relief," she said, trying to sound brisk and practical. "It's not that I really thought you wanted me, but the topic of conversation is a little distracting."

"Oh, I want you," he said casually.

Her heart stopped beating for a long, endless moment. "No," she said. "I don't like you."

"You probably don't. But that doesn't mean you don't want me. I'm trained to be observant. You watch me when you think I'm not looking, you shiver when I touch you. I think right now you're probably terrified. And wet."

Her eyes widened in shock. "You're disgusting."

"Sex isn't for the fastidious. Haven't you learned at least that much from your lone, incompetent lover?"

"You're not having sex with me."

He sighed. "You're right, I'm not. You're the only one who's going to get off."

"Dream on. If you think you can seduce me into telling you where the urn is, you have far too high an opinion of your dubious charms."

This time he did smile, and a wicked light filled his eyes. "'Dubious charms'?" he echoed, amused. "You'll tell me where it is and then you'll have sex. Where is the urn?"

"I'm not going to tell you."

"Of course you are," he said, picking up her hand. She tried to pull away, but he wouldn't release her. "Tell me where the real urn is. I've played around for too long already, and I can't afford to waste any more time. I don't want to hurt you, but you need to tell me where the urn is."

"No."

The pain was sudden, swift and blinding, so sharp that she could barely muffle her instinctive cry and then it was over. He brushed the back of his hand

against her face, tenderly; there was no mistaking the
regret in his austere, beautiful face. "Don't make me
do it again, Summer. People's lives are at stake, and
I can't let sentiment get in my way. Where is the
urn?"

"I won't—" The words were cut off as she gasped
again in pain. Then he released the cruel grip on her
wrist, and his fingers were gently stroking the red
marks. "Where is the urn, Summer?"

She looked into his calm, implacable eyes. He
would do this. He would hurt her until she told him
what he wanted to know, whether he wanted to or not.

And more than anything in the world she needed him
to take his hands off her. Not the hands that hurt her.
The hands that touched and comforted. And she'd do
anything, tell him anything, to make him let go of her.

"It's in the Bainbridge house," she said, yanking
her hand away. Her wrist was numb, throbbing, and
she had no idea what he'd done to her. She only
knew he wouldn't have stopped.

"What Bainbridge house? In Washington state?
There's no record of you or your mother owning a
house up there."

"It's in my grandmother's name. My father's
mother. She didn't want Lianne to know she was
giving it to me. She didn't trust her."

"Imagine that," he said dryly.

Why didn't he button his shirt? Why didn't he turn
away from her, turn that beautiful, treacherous face
away?

"The real urn is on the shelf in my closet, along with the kimono and the book of haiku Hana left me."

He was very still. "She left you a book? What does it say?"

"It's in kanji. I have no idea—just some hand-written haiku. I kept it because it was hers."

He nodded, and Summer almost thought she could see him process the information. He was no longer thinking about her, thank God. "And a kimono? What kind?"

"Two kimono," she corrected him, using the proper plural. "One is very old, a relic. The other is just an ordinary cheap dressing gown. Not important."

"Everything's important," he said absently.

She wasn't going to fight him. He could take anything he wanted from her, anything Hana gave her, as long as he left her alone.

"Then you can go and get it," she said brightly, feeling momentarily safe. He'd forgotten all about her. "I'll give you directions. And you don't need to worry that I'm lying to you again. This time it's the truth."

"I know it is," he said. "Now take off your shirt. I don't like you in black."

She stared at him, uncomprehending. "What? I told you where it was."

"And I told you that you would tell me. And then you'll have sex. Take off your shirt."

12

Summer didn't move. She sat there, frozen, as if he'd told her to turn into a pumpkin. Poor baby. She had no idea who or what she was up against.

She made one last, pitiful protest. "I don't want you touching me."

"Yes," he said, "you do."

"I'm going back to my room, locking the door and you're going to keep the hell away from me. I've given you what you want."

"Not entirely," he said. "But go ahead and try."

She did, of course, making it easier for him. He didn't want to get her on the bed—he'd been nothing but honest when he said she was the only one who was going to have sex. If he got on the bed with her he'd have a harder time keeping himself in check. He could, of course. But it would be much easier this way.

He caught her before she reached the door, hauling her back against his body. She didn't struggle. He wrapped one arm around her waist, holding her still, and she couldn't break free, even if she wanted to.

He knew women very well. He even knew this woman, different though she was. She was terrified of sex, terrified of giving herself away—so bound up in her fear that she was unpredictable. He needed to break through that, so he could control her. Simply because he wanted to.

He put his other hand on the front of her shirt and began unbuttoning it as he moved her closer to the wall. She was going to need something to lean against. At this point her arms were at her sides, and she wasn't fighting him, but that might change. For now she just let him hold her against his body, and he knew she could feel his heat sinking into her.

He pulled the shirt free from her pants, then reached up and covered her breast with his palm. She made a strangled sound in the back of her throat, but her nipple hardened beneath his touch.

He shouldn't have felt the slick surge of satisfaction—he was never wrong about these things, and he'd known she wanted him. But the physical proof was an added pleasure. The only pleasure he was going to allow himself to take.

She'd changed bras. This one was black, too, but it was skimpier and fastened in the front. He flicked it open, and her sweet, full breasts spilled out.

He would have given anything to turn her in his arms, to put his mouth against her nipple and suck on it, hard. But not now. Not this time.

Her breasts were exquisitely sensitive, and she arched back against him with a muffled sound. "Didn't he do this for you?" he whispered in her ear. "Didn't he know what you liked?" He let his thumb brush against her nipple, using just the right amount of pressure, and she moaned, a deep, sexual sound.

"You should have told him," he murmured. "Most men can't figure these things out on their own—they need guidance." He flicked his thumb again, and her groan was deeper this time, and she pressed back against him.

"Hold on to the wall," he said, but she didn't seem to hear him. He wished he'd brought her to a mirror—he wanted to see her face when he made her come—but he already knew her well enough to imagine it. He wouldn't need the proof.

He reached down and took her hands, placing them against the smooth, painted wall of the bedroom. And then began unfastening her pants.

She struggled for a frightened moment, pulling her hands away, but he simply placed them back on the wall and finished unzipping her baggy black jeans. "Stop fighting it, Summer," he whispered. "You know what you want. You've wanted it since you first saw me. You've wanted it for years before. Stop fighting."

She said nothing, the tension running through her body as he slid his fingers inside the band of her panties. He wasn't sure what he would have done if she'd said no. But she didn't. She shivered in his arms as his hand slid down between her legs, and she leaned back against him. Tense. Pliant.

She wasn't going to run, and holding her against him was now more of an embrace than a prison. If she was thinking at all she'd know how hard he was, pressed up against her butt, but she probably wasn't thinking about anything but his hand, his fingers, touching her.

"I knew you'd be wet," he whispered, and gave in to temptation, biting her ear. She quivered. "Now I want you to spread you legs for me. Just a little bit. That's right," he crooned in her ear. "That's perfect. You're perfect. Beautiful." He kissed the side of her neck, because he couldn't help it. He wanted his fingers inside her, wanted his cock inside her, but he couldn't have what he wanted. If he turned her, yanked off her pants and pushed her down on the floor he wouldn't stop, and this had to be for her and her alone.

He slid his fingers over her clitoris, and a quick, sweet spasm racked her body. This was going to be even easier than he'd thought. "Yes," he whispered against her skin. "You like that, I know you do. And you want more, don't you? Such sweet, wicked pleasure. Let me give this to you. No one's going to know, just you and me." He pressed her forward, so that her head rested against the wall, her hands splayed out, and it was all he could do to keep from thrusting against her, rubbing his iron-hard, aching cock against her sweet butt. *For her,* he reminded himself. *Only for her.*

She was panting now, shaking, ready to explode, and if he were a good man he would have given it to her then. But he wasn't a good man, and the longer the tension built the more powerful her climax would be. He wanted her weeping, helpless, lost in the response he was drawing from her body.

"Next time it will be my cock," he breathed against her ear. "Inside you, filling you, coming inside you. So hard you can't think, all you can do is feel. It's what you want, what you need. But not this time. This time is just for you."

She was shaking all over, covered in sweat, and he knew he couldn't hold out much longer. And then she said the first word she'd spoken since he'd opened her shirt.

"Please…" Her voice was a raw whisper of pain.

"Please what?"

She was ready, so ready, and he couldn't believe she had any fight left in her.

"Please…don't…"

His body froze, so close to her release. He couldn't let go, he couldn't.

"Please…don't…stop." Her words were a muffled plea, and they were the last barrier. He pushed her over the edge, feeling her shatter in his arms, her long, keening wail of total surrender smashing his last bit of control. He managed to hold her, climax after climax shuddering through her body, until he knew she couldn't stand anymore, and he took his hand away.

He'd finally made her cry. He should have held her. Should have turned her in his arms and held her as she wept.

But he couldn't. Instead he let her sink slowly down onto the carpeted floor of the bedroom, a tangle of arms and legs and pain, and he left her there, walking away.

He shut the bathroom door, staring at himself in the mirror. The King of Death, the Great Seducer. He looked as if he'd been kicked in the head.

He'd been so caught up in her body, her reactions, in prolonging her endless orgasm that he'd paid no attention to his own body. For the first time in his life he'd climaxed without anyone touching him, without him even being aware of what was happening. He was wet, and he stripped out of his pants in fury and disgust. Not at the mess. At his own weakness. He had no idea how it had happened, how he'd managed to lose control when he never, ever lost it.

But somehow she'd managed to break through every last defense he had, and when she'd climaxed in long, shuddering waves, he had, too.

For an endless moment Summer lay curled up on the floor, holding herself, as her body slowly settled back into some semblance of normalcy. She'd stopped crying, wiping the tears from her face in fury. The first thing she needed to do was regain control of her traitorous body. Then she could work on her mind.

The bathroom door opened and he came back into the room, dressed in different clothes, his shirt buttoned, the leather jacket in place. "We're leaving in half an hour. If you want to take a shower you'd better do it now." His voice was flat, cool. The voice of a stranger.

She'd managed to pull herself to a sitting position, leaning against the wall, but hadn't fixed her clothing. "Where are we going?" Although the words were familiar, the body she inhabited, the feelings she felt, were foreign.

"To get the Hayashi Urn, so I can complete my assignment. Don't look at me like that. You know you're a job. You were easier than I expected, but in the end it doesn't make any difference. Everyone's expendable, even your sister."

"My sister?" she echoed through a blind haze of pain.

"The Shirosama has her, and he'll be able to find out what he wants from her very quickly. And not as pleasantly as I did. We need to get to the urn before he does."

"No..." Summer protested, but he simply moved forward, grabbed her arm and hauled her to her feet. "She doesn't know anything."

"The Shirosama won't believe that until there's nothing left of her to prove it. You can take a shower and try to wash away what just happened, or you can go like that," he said. "Either way, we're leaving in another twenty-seven minutes."

"How do I know you'll help her? What if I refuse to go with you?"

He shrugged. So beautiful, so cold. "Then I suppose I'll have to leave you here… I can make it fast and painless—you won't suffer. But I'm not leaving you to talk."

The room was like an ice locker; the chill that emanated from him reached into her bones. If she exhaled she'd probably see her breath. But she couldn't breathe.

"I'll be ready."

He watched her go, staring after her for a long, contemplative moment. He'd told her nothing but the truth. In the long run the pride of one California princess was a small price to pay for the safety of thousands, maybe millions.

Though in truth she wasn't that much of a princess. She might be connected to Hollywood power and status, but there was none of the air of privilege and entitlement he found in most of the beautiful women he met, both American and Japanese.

But then, she wasn't, in fact, a beautiful woman. She was pretty, an odd sort of thing. Pretty eyes, pretty soft mouth that he would have liked to explore, warm skin and gentle curves. Pretty, but unremarkable. The perfect Japanese bride his grandfather had chosen for him would make mincemeat out of her.

But that was a different life, one Taka would deal

with when the time came. For now he was on assignment, and all that mattered was getting what he'd been assigned to get, no matter the price.

He grabbed his small duffel bag he'd found in the closet and headed out into the hall. He could hear her shower running, and he paused, wondering if beneath the steady beat of the water she was crying again. She'd been dry-eyed when he'd come back into the bedroom. Had he done enough to her to make her cry?

He shook his head, moving on down the stairs. She was tougher than that, he reminded himself. She'd pulled the tattered remains of her dignity back around her, shutting out of her mind what he'd just done to her. Right now he had to stop thinking of her as anything but a liability. Did she have any other bombshells hidden? Two kimono and a book. They could just be the last remnants of a life, or something more important. And in a situation where nothing was as it seemed, he was guessing Hana's legacy was more important than Summer thought.

He made fresh coffee, finishing up the sashimi in the refrigerator. He heard her come down the stairs, but he didn't turn, reaching into the refrigerator for the heavy cream. "Do you want some coffee?" he asked in a neutral voice.

"No." Her voice was equally expressionless, and when he glanced at her her face was calm, set. He looked at her, remembered the wild, keening sound she'd made when she came, and shoved that mental door closed a little too firmly.

She was dressed in baggy black jeans and a loose black T-shirt—the same kind of clothes he'd always seen her in. Who would think such a soft, responsive body hid beneath all those layers? Assuming she made it through the next few days alive, she needed to find someone who could take proper care of her. Someone to put her into better clothes and give her the kind of sex she needed.

Sex was no longer an issue, and he had to push it out of his mind. He had no doubt given her the first real orgasm—hell, the first two or three orgasms she'd had in her life. She might hate him for it, but at least now she knew that she could.

She waited until he moved out of the way, then opened the refrigerator and reappeared with one of her pink cans of soda and a tub of yogurt. He thought he'd have to make her eat, but she seemed perfectly calm and collected, finding a spoon and eating the yogurt as she stood in the kitchen as far away from him as she could.

Summer was practical—that was a good thing She wasn't going to weep and wail. She wasn't going to acknowledge what had just happened between them at all. Women everywhere were good at the silent treatment, and it made it easier for him to concentrate on how he was going to get the two of them to Bainbridge Island as fast as he could.

Preferably before the Shirosama broke Summer

Hawthorne's teenage sister into a thousand little pieces that no one could ever put back together again.

So far they'd left her alone. Jilly sat on the narrow cot in her cell, perfectly comfortable despite her overwhelming craving for junk food.

As it was, they kept bringing her cloudy water that she didn't want to drink, and piping the Shirosama's creepy voice into the small room through invisible speakers. Invisible, because if she'd found them she would have smashed them.

She didn't know what they expected from her. The droning voice went on in half a dozen languages, none of which she understood. She was relatively conversational in Spanish, but with the Shirosama's accent the words were almost impossible to decipher, and if they were anything like the English version she didn't want to know what he was saying. Just a bunch of New Age gobbledygook that made her long for the predictability and safety of science. She was pursuing a double major at the university—chemistry and physics—and the kind of pseudo-science mumbo jumbo he was spewing through the tiny speakers was grating on her nerves.

She stretched out on the cot, considering her options. They'd dressed her in the white pajamas that reminded her of a kung-fu mental hospital, given her a handful of granola bars, which she despised, and told her to await the Shirosama's attention. She'd await it, all right. The old gasbag wasn't going to get a thing out of her, and if he thought her parents would sit still for anything happening to their favorite daughter he was in for a rude awakening.

It wasn't fair that she was the favorite, but then, as Summer pointed out to her, life wasn't fair. Ditzy Lianne could get away with a lot in her pursuit of a higher consciousness, but when it came to her second born she could pull her head out of the clouds long enough to be a tigress. And no one should ever want to mess with Ralph Lovitz—he could terrorize the Mafia. One puffed-up, self-deluded cult leader would be child's play for him.

Really, there was nothing to be nervous about. The True Realization brethren were far too interested in where Summer was, but since Jilly could honestly say she had no idea, it shouldn't matter. Though when they started going on about some Japanese urn, her kidnappers lost her completely.

They'd told her this was a retreat, a safe haven for her, and she couldn't dispute that the mysterious Petersens seemed to have been holding her as a drugged hostage. Not a whole hell of a lot different than being trapped in the Shirosama's pajamas, without the benefit of chocolate.

She was in no particular hurry to get out of there; her father would eventually make his holiness wish he'd never been born, and for now she had nowhere else to be. If she was blessed with one thing, apart from her brain, it was her overactive imagination, and she could stretch out on the cot for many happy hours, daydreaming. Waiting for the time that Ralph Lovitz was going to tear his holiness a new one.

In the meantime, though, she'd kill for an Egg McMuffin.

13

The mind was an amazing thing, Summer thought, staring out the window as the sprawling southern California landscape sped by. Her sister was in the clutches of a messianic sociopath, people were dying and yet Summer was able to sit in the car beside her betrayer and not scream. Amazing.

She still didn't know why he'd done it. He'd found out what he needed to know; after, there was nothing to be gained by stripping her down to such an elemental level. Maybe just to prove he could.

And maybe if she survived this she'd eventually have Takashi O'Brien's head on a pike.

If it were up to her she'd give up. But she wasn't going to let anything happen to her baby sister. He'd told her the Shirosama had Jilly, and yet he didn't seem to be interested in doing anything about it.

She refused to look at him. When she did so she was filled with such a stomach-twisting anger she couldn't think clearly, and she needed to be cool and self-controlled. Sometime later she could let go, right now she needed to be as deadly calm as he was.

"My sister," she said, staring out the window.

"What about her?"

"Aren't you going to do anything to help? You kept rescuing me—it's what you're good at."

"My orders were to keep you out of the Shirosama's hands. Your sister isn't my job."

Summer closed her eyes for a moment, picturing Jilly's dear, stubborn face, and tried to think of a plan. They'd traded the SUV for the plain-looking sedan parked in the garage, but beneath its modest exterior it had the engine of a race car.

And Taka had a penchant for fast driving.

At least they weren't on the freeway. They were on a lesser road, heading out toward the countryside. Were she to bail out, she might stand a chance— she didn't give a damn whether he survived. She just needed to get away from him and go after her sister. Give the Shirosama what he wanted, in return for Jilly's freedom.

Summer glanced around her surreptitiously, looking for any kind of weapon. Her bare hands were useless against Taka. Her only chance was taking him by surprise, and he wasn't a man who surprised easily.

"Don't." His voice was flat, cool.

She refused to turn and look at him, keeping her eyes focused on the passing landscape. "Don't what?"

"Don't even think it. I'm not letting you out of my sight."

"What if I have to go to the bathroom?"

"I'll go with you."

"The hell you will."

He said nothing—he didn't have to. He was like an eight hundred pound gorilla; he could do anything he wanted and there was nothing she could do about it.

And she would have accepted that, given up, if her sister's safety wasn't involved. Did he have a gun somewhere in the car? In the last two tumultuous days she realized she hadn't seen him with one—he didn't seem to need one when he killed. Her stomach twisted again at the thought. He hadn't killed to protect her at all. He'd killed to protect the knowledge she held.

She wondered why he was bothering to keep her alive now that he knew where the urn was. Unless he very wisely didn't trust her. She'd tricked him twice with the fakes. Maybe he wasn't going to get rid of her until he was certain he had the real urn.

The one thing she couldn't tell him was where it had come from. Hana had never said a word about its origins; if it had come from some mysterious hidden shrine in Japan that secret had died with her.

Summer glanced around her on the floor of the sedan. Nothing. Maybe if she suddenly slammed her elbow into his face she might distract him—except that he was taller and his face would be hard to reach, plus she was pinned down by the seat belt.

The only thing movable in the front seat of the car was his steel coffee mug and her empty Tab can. Neither would do much damage, but the coffee mug was larger and heavier. If she could just slam it into his face it might force him to take his eyes off the road and his foot off the accelerator, long enough for her to open the door and roll out, with less chance of being totally screwed.

The more she hesitated the worse it was going to get. She reached for the coffee mug, and his hand shot out. She wasn't quite sure how he managed it, but he got both her wrists in his grasp, imprisoning her. It hurt. A lot. She remembered a few short hours ago, when he'd hurt her into telling him the truth…and what he'd done afterward.

"I told you, don't even think about it," he said. He hadn't slowed his speed even the tiniest bit—they were going about eighty. Certain death.

"I just wanted some coffee."

"You don't like coffee."

"Says who? Just because I drink soda in the morning doesn't mean—"

"You had no coffee in your house."

"You don't know everything I had in my house."

"Want to bet? I know everything, including where you stash your porn."

"I don't have porn…."

"Your erotica, then, if you're going to be squeamish. You have a taste for sci-fi sex—interplanetary kinkiness. Tell me, is it better when I did it for you? Am I alien enough for you?"

"I suppose it would be a waste of time to tell you how much I hate you," she said in a tight voice.

"At least you're honest." He let go of her hands, and she pulled away, rubbing her wrists.

He glanced over at her. "And if you're trying to distract me, I can think of more effective ways. You could try going down on me and see if it makes me slow the car enough for you to jump out."

"You are such a rat bastard," she said, sick at the thought. Sick, because she felt his words between her legs, and she wanted to lean over and see exactly what he would do if she tried it. Sick, because that wasn't the reason why she wanted to.

The houses were fewer and farther between, the wide, flat countryside was starting to look desolate. If she somehow managed to get away from him there'd be no place to go, no place to hide. Why was he taking her out to the middle of nowhere?

Silly question. She was now just as expendable as her sister. He was taking her someplace where he could kill her, where no one would hear her scream, where he could hide her body...

"Cut it out."

He'd startled her enough to make her look at him. He was staring straight ahead, concentrating on the almost empty road. "What?" she asked.

"Stop thinking about death. I liked it better when you were thinking about sex."

She didn't bother asking him how he knew what she was thinking. She'd worked long and hard on masking her feelings—it was far too dangerous to be vulnerable when you had a mother like Lianne. But Taka seemed to have the ability to know her inside and out, even before he'd known her body.

"And your likes and dislikes are of primary importance to me because…? And don't say it's because you're the only thing that stands between me and the Shirosama. Right now I'd welcome him with open arms."

"I'm sure you would. It would be a mistake."

"Oh, I forgot. You're so much kinder than he is."

"Kindness has nothing to do with it."

"I noticed."

He'd slowed down again, almost imperceptibly, and turned onto a dirt road. She was toast, she thought. If she jumped out of the car she'd die, saving him the trouble. But then, she wasn't particularly interested in saving him from anything, and if he could look into her eyes and choke the life out of her, then she'd come back to haunt him.

"How are you planning to do it?"

"Planning to do what?" He was barely paying attention to her, concentrating on the barren landscape.

"Kill me. I've never actually seen you kill—just witnessed the aftermath. Are you going to strangle me? Break my neck? Stab me?"

She made the mistake of watching him to gauge his reaction. His eyes met hers, and a faint smile touched his mouth. His beautiful mouth, which she wanted to smash with a two-by-four. "I'll probably cut you up in tiny pieces, boil you and eat you."

"Very funny. Are you telling me you're not planning to kill me?"

His eyes slid away. "Not if I can help it. Not unless you're really annoying."

"Then if you're not driving me out into the middle of nowhere to kill me, why are we here?"

"Use your eyes, Summer."

She didn't like him using her name, but replying "Dr. Hawthorne to you" would be like something out of a Marx Brothers movie. She looked around as he slowed down, and realized the vast, empty field was exactly that. An airfield, and there were several small planes sitting over by a ramshackle metal building.

"I'm not getting on a plane," she said in a tight voice.

"Afraid of flying?"

She was, but that had nothing to do with it. "I'm not leaving my sister. I'm not going anywhere until I know she's safe."

"You're going to do what I tell you to do." He pulled up beside the metal shack and turned off the car.

"You're going to have to kill me first."

He sighed, and for half a second she was certain he was going to do exactly that. "Someone's taking care of your sister," he said finally.

"Who? The Shirosama? I don't think so."

"A colleague is getting her out. You don't need to worry."

"A colleague? A member of the Yakuza is going to waltz right in there and snatch her away?"

"You're forgetting that the True Realization Fellowship started in Japan, and almost a third of its worldwide membership is Japanese. I don't imagine a Yakuza would have any trouble fitting in."

"Unless they saw his tattoos."

"A good proportion of the brethren are criminals from one country or another. A Japanese criminal wouldn't be surprising. Now stop arguing with me. You're still alive, and so is your sister. She'll be fine."

"Why didn't you tell me this before? I would have been less trouble."

"You and trouble are synonymous," he said wearily, unfastening his seatbelt. "Get out of the car, and if you try to run I'll shoot you."

"You don't carry a gun."

"Yes," he said, "I do. And I have no problem using it."

And she didn't doubt him for one minute.

Jilly Lovitz was proving to be a particularly difficult disciple. She refused to drink the sacred water they brought to her, she was somehow able to shut her mind to the True Word as it was piped into the barren little room she was kept in. He had some of the most brilliant young scientists working for him, following his path. Chemists, explosives experts, doctors, engineers, along with the disaffected youth who'd made their lives on the streets. He'd offered them all a path to salvation, and they'd taken it gladly. And yet Jilly Lovitz resisted.

It was hard to believe she'd come from Lianne Lovitz, who had barely a brain in her pretty blond head. She was much more like her older half sister, Summer. Too smart, too cynical, too distrusting. That latter was no doubt due to the mother—Lianne would make a saint doubtful. And there were few real saints in the True Realization Fellowship.

The girl wouldn't eat, either. She'd laughed when they'd brought her chocolate, something he'd been told was her particular weakness. In fact, he'd known very few women anywhere who could resist the siren lure of chocolate, but sixteen-year-old Jilly Lovitz was confounding him on many levels.

In the end it didn't matter. She was in one of the induction cells, with his devoted followers watching her every move, and while anything was possible, he doubted that a woman like Summer Hawthorne would have endangered her baby sister by sharing her secrets. No, the girl was only a bargaining chip. As soon as the woman realized her sister was in jeopardy she would show up with the urn and all her secrets. All he had to do was wait.

Except that the Yakuza was now involved, and he wasn't sure whether to rejoice or lament. Takashi O'Brien was the great nephew of Hiro Matsumoto—

his connections were impressive, and who else would have sent him? It didn't matter the Yakuza had the same goals as he did—Japan as a world power once more. *The* world power, in the new order of things. But the Yakuza were more likely to think of the profit the world could provide, while the Shirosama knew the only real future was to wipe it clean.

They were a concern, but a minor one. Summer Hawthorne had been chosen for a reason. Hana Hayashi would never have entrusted such a treasure to someone who couldn't keep it secure, nor would she have shared her knowledge. It was a great tragedy that he hadn't been able to make the old woman talk, a sin that he'd let anger overtake him and he'd ended her life before he found out what he needed to know.

He'd been much younger then, and only beginning to understand his destiny. It had been ordained since the beginning of time that he would run his aunt over with an automobile before he found the family treasure he was searching for. The treasure that would assure his ascendance and transfiguration.

But it hadn't been his time. At that point he had only a few hundred followers, and his path wasn't as clear to him as it was now.

No, all was unfolding as it was meant to be, and each new hurdle was simply to test his readiness for the coming storm. He would handle each obstacle as he faced it.

The girl had thrown her sacred water at Brother Kenno, a crime of such blasphemy that his holiness was only glad that it hadn't been Brother Heinrich. But then, he'd kept Brother Heinrich far away from the girl. The Shirosama's tools were varied and well honed, but one didn't need to use an ax when a dagger would suffice. At this point there was nothing to be gained from having Jilly Lovitz undergo Heinrich's inventive ministrations.

Perhaps she would be a reward to his faithful follower when all finally came together. Though in fact he'd promised him the older sister. While Heinrich might prefer the softer virgin flesh of the young one, his rage toward the older one would feed his pleasure.

The Shirosama shook his head. Heinrich was still so young, so driven by fleeting gratification that he was unready for the higher purpose in store for him.

But that would change. Events were coming together. The Shirosama could feel the winds of power swirling around his head, and he knew his time as a mortal was short.

The time and day most suited for the reunification ceremony were almost upon them. The True Realization Fellowship would retrieve the true urn. They would find where the ruins of the old temple were. Summer Hawthorne was the only living human being who had the information, passed on by his distrusting aunt, though she seemed not to know she had it.

He would help her remember, once he got the Yakuza off his back and the younger sister to break. And then all would unfold accordingly, and the end of the world would be set in motion. He would ascend, chaos would follow, and then nothing but blessed emptiness.

He folded his hands over his belly, let his eyes drift closed, and meditated happily. All would be as it was written.

If only he could find the rest of the text.

The woman moved through the Spartan halls of the True Realization Fellowship with purposeful strides. She had been brought in from Germany, an acknowledged expert in the gift of eliciting information, with or without pain, and she'd been summoned to Los Angeles at great expense. She carried her Hermes bag with her, the silk-wrapped pouch of tools in the bottom.

The brethren ignored her, as they'd been trained, their belief in the Shirosama's will absolute. Most female followers were devout and plainly dressed, their heads shaved. This one was wearing the requisite white, but if anyone had looked they would have known it was a designer suit, and the sleek chignon of dark hair, the perfectly made-up face, were an affront to their ways.

Even her shoes were an insult—the sharp tap of high heels on tile floors seemed to mock the barefoot followers. She was there for a reason, however, and she must follow the Shirosama's teachings despite her flagrant disregard of modesty.

The brethren turned their heads away, moving on

as the woman stopped by the cell that held the noisy girl. They knew better than to linger—his holiness tolerated no questions, and the girl might cry out. Some of the followers were weak in their resolve, and might instinctively respond to a cry for help. Better that they not be tested.

By the time the woman reached the cell the hallway was deserted. She reached down and unlocked the door. And then she stepped through, her purse at her side, and all was silent in the south wing of the True Realization headquarters.

14

Takashi O'Brien was having to put too much energy into not thinking about his companion. Summer Hawthorne was certainly a minor transgression compared to some of the things he'd done. He'd given her the best partial sex of her life. So why was it eating away at him?

Probably because he was stuck with her. Normally he'd be able to dump people once he'd finished with them, but until he got to her family's house on Bainbridge Island they were shackled together.

It should help that she was ignoring him, clearly pissed as hell. She wasn't as edgy, nervy, frightened as she had been. Maybe she mistakenly thought he'd done everything he wanted to do with her. She was wrong.

Her very control was impressive—Committee-level impressive. Every now and then he felt a stray suspicion that she wasn't quite the innocent bystander she was presumed to be, but then he dismissed it. His life would be a lot easier if she were some hard-core danger, a closet follower of the Shirosama, stringing him along. Then he wouldn't have to feel even the slightest bit of this unfamiliar guilt.

But she wasn't. She was exactly who and what she seemed to be. An ordinary woman in her late twenties, with average looks, an average body, too much education and far too much self-control.

Except when he'd made her come.

He'd made her cry, too, which was cruel and self-indulgent of him. He'd done it because he'd wanted to, even though he'd already found out just what he needed to know.

"I'm not getting in that plane," she said, staring at the small seaplane he was heading for. It wasn't the most impressive looking aircraft, but he knew that, mechanically, it was perfect. He never took chances he didn't have to.

"You don't have any say in the matter," he said over his shoulder, wondering if she'd be fool enough to make a run for it. It was a hot day, even for January, and he wasn't in the mood to run after her.

She halted where she was, ten feet away from the plane. "Do you even have a license?"

"I'm not flying the plane. I'm sitting in the back with you. But yes, I have a license."

"You don't need to keep me company," she said with false sweetness. "In fact, I'd prefer to be alone."

"I'm sure you would," he stated. "But the unfortunate thing is I don't trust you."

She didn't move. "There aren't any seats."

"It's a cargo plane."

She didn't say a word, and he wondered whether he was going to have to put his hands on her. Force her in. He didn't want to. He'd tried not to hurt her more than he had to, but time was running out, and if he had no other choice he could hurt her very badly indeed.

She must have known that. After a moment she climbed into the back of the plane, moving as far away as she could from him, up against the bracing on the side. There were straps hanging from the bars, and he caught one, wrapping it around her wrists and then fastening it to the side of the plane. "I'm not likely to jump," she said.

"It's more in lieu of a seat belt." He sat opposite her, winding the straps around his own wrists and hooking them. A moment later the pilot climbed into the front of the plane. "Sorry about the accommodations," he called back. "Are you both strapped in?"

"Yes," Taka replied.

Summer was looking at him, an odd expression on her face, and he realized their conversation had been in Russian. And then she glanced away, and there was no need to explain.

And no reason why he should want to.

Clinging to the straps, she closed her eyes as they taxied down the rough field. It would have been better if he'd strapped himself in beside her—he could cushion some of the shocks. Distract her. Because it was becoming rapidly clear that Summer Hawthorne was almost as terrified of flying as she was of sex.

Her skin was deathly white, and she was holding on to the ropes so tightly her hands had to be cramping. "Maybe I'd rather jump out, after all," she said in a whisper, and he wondered if she was going to pass out from the fear. Fainting would have been a mercy, but she stayed rigid, clinging to the straps as the plane took off into the sky. He waited to see how long it took her to relax.

He didn't have that much time. Her body was so tense she was shaking, and it was making him nervous. He had to do something for his own sake, not hers. He unclipped the straps that held him and slid across the floor of the plane. She was too panicked to even react to his sudden closeness.

"Is it just small planes?" he asked, half expecting her to ignore him.

But she was past any petty issues like pride or fury. "Any plane." She practically ground out the words from between clenched teeth.

He'd already slid one hand into his pocket as he'd moved across the bucking plane, and the small needle was hidden between his fingers. He reached up and pricked her neck with it, and she had only a moment to try to jerk away before the tranquilizer hit her full force, and she collapsed on the floor.

He caught another of the hanging straps, which he wrapped around his waist, tethering his body to the side of the plane as it bounced ever higher into the windy California sky. And then he pulled Summer's limp form against him, settling her between his outstretched legs, and held her.

He had no choice in the matter, if he left her hanging by the straps she'd end up being banged against the side of the aircraft. Not good for her, not good for the plane's stability. You always fastened down a cargo, you didn't leave it loose in the back of a plane.

That was all he was doing, he told himself putting his arms around her to hold her limp body still, letting her head loll back against his shoulder. Keeping the cargo secure.

It was his own damn fault he was getting hard again.

Summer was being rocked. So gently, wrapped in loving arms, rocking slowly in the velvety darkness. She was dazed and dreaming, in some magic world where there were no battles, no fear, just warmth and love and comfort. Rocking softly, gently, and she wanted to stay in that safe cocoon forever.

She'd been dreaming, a long series of strange, interconnected dreams. Some were terrifying—she kept running to find her sister, but everywhere she looked the spooky brethren turned up in their flowing white robes. She ran some more, and she was crying, crying in her dreams as she never did in real life.

But she had cried, hadn't she? The final betrayal. She felt a hand on the side of her face, brushing away her tears, and she turned into that hand, pressing her lips against it, and the dream became erotic, full of red silk and wicked touches and smooth, golden skin hot beneath her flesh. It frightened her as much as her earlier dream.

But now she was at peace, wrapped in warm, strong arms, safer than she'd ever been in her life. Home, when she'd always felt like a stranger wherever she was. She could rest, and listen to the quiet beat of his heart, feel his breath in her hair, stirring it slightly, feel the plane rock beneath her…

Her eyes flew open, her body suddenly rigid, and for a moment his arms tightened around her before he let her go.

She couldn't go far—her wrists were still wrapped with the strapping—and she fell across his outstretched legs, her face in his lap. She scrambled away, desperate, thankful for the murky darkness that surrounded them. She could get just far enough away not to be touching him, a small blessing.

At least they were no longer in the air. She could feel the plane rocking beneath her, hear the slap of water against the sides, and she suddenly realized things could be a lot worse.

"Did we crash?" Her voice sounded groggy to her own ears. "Are we in the middle of the ocean?"

"We didn't crash, we landed. Several hours ago. This is a seaplane, remember? I've just been waiting for you to wake up."

"Thoughtful of you," she said, rubbing her neck.

Something had stung her. She couldn't remember when, but her neck still hurt.

"Not really. You were out cold. You must have needed the rest."

"I didn't get much sleep last night." The moment the words were out of her mouth she choked, and if she could she would have slapped her hands over her betraying lips. But trying would only bring her closer to him, and she wanted to keep as far away as possible.

"No, you didn't," he said in a neutral voice that was almost worse than a leer. "Are you ready to go?"

"So polite. What if I said I wasn't?"

He was reaching for the straps that bound her. "I would do my best to persuade you otherwise. Come here."

She wasn't moving any closer to him, not if she could help it. "No."

"I can't untie your wrists unless you do."

"I can manage…" She was already trying to work her fingers into the knot when he muttered a curse beneath his breath and she felt the straps begin to pull. It was a simple enough matter to drag her next to him—there wasn't that much play in the rope.

"Stop fighting me," he said, undoing the knot with insulting ease.

"Yeah, like that's going to happen anytime soon," she retorted.

"You weren't fighting this morning."

Silence filled the darkened belly of the plane as it

rocked gently on the water. "Everyone makes mistakes," she said finally.

"Yes," he said. "They do." He moved past her, pushing open the door. It was dark outside, and the smell of the sea was strong. Could she shove him out the door and slam it shut, like Hansel and Gretel tossing the wicked witch into the furnace? He wasn't likely to end up being gingerbread.

"Are we going to swim for it?"

"We're tied up at a dock—you won't even get your feet wet. Come on."

"Lucky me," she muttered, trying to stand. There was just enough room do so, but her knees were wobbly, and there was nothing to hold on to as she felt herself falling.

Nothing but the arm that caught her, wrapped hard around her waist, bringing back the memory of that morning with shocking swiftness. She could even hear his words in her head—soft, seductive words.

"I'd rather you didn't drown," he said, lifting her over the threshold of the plane and setting her on the broad dock. He followed after her before she even had time to consider running.

"That's right, you've already saved me from a watery grave, haven't you?" she said, pulling herself together. "Why?"

"To find the urn."

Ask a stupid question, get the wrong answer. He was still holding her, and if she thought she had a chance in hell of shoving him into the icy-cold waters of Puget Sound she would have tried.

"How far do we have to walk?"

"I have a car."

"Of course you do. Where's the pilot? Did you cut his throat and dump him in the sound?"

"I'd have a hard time finding pilots if I made a practice of doing that."

"Maybe you were just taking out your frustrations on him, since you can't kill me."

Silence, deep and dark like the Pacific night stretched between them, and a light mist began to fall. "I can kill you, Summer. If I have to."

She could see him now. There were no houses around to provide light, an oddity in itself. She would have thought every single inch of waterfront on Bainbridge would have been developed. But a slender quarter moon was out, and she could see his face, as expressionless as his voice. And she had no doubt at all he could do just as he said.

He took her arm, and she didn't bother trying to free herself. He led her up the steep incline to the road, not much more than a narrow dirt track, and she barely looked at the car he bundled her into. The numbness was slowly beginning to recede, the numbness that had taken over her body from the moment he'd let her go in the bedroom, the numbness that had shut her down completely on the small plane. Anger was spiking through, shards of fury splintering the dazed calm. He'd lied about everything: why shouldn't he be lying about her sister, as well? Maybe Jilly was still stuck in the Shirosama's pudgy white claws, and maybe Summer would have to take desperate steps to save her. Steps that would doubtless involve getting on another airplane of her own free will.

She could do it for Jilly. She could do anything for Jilly. Including smashing the son of a bitch beside her unconscious while she ran.

He drove too fast, as always, but by now she was getting used to it. She had no intention of giving him directions to the well-hidden family house, but of course he didn't need any. With calm resignation she watched him turn up their long, overgrown driveway.

No one had been in the house for months. Lianne had forgotten it existed, and Summer was the one who owned it, loved it, cared for it. Even if she hadn't made it back since the fall.

It would serve Taka O'Brien right if someone had broken in and taken the urn and everything else of value. Serve him right if the Shirosama had somehow managed to find this place first.

Her father had died long ago, and even his meager family was gone. But Summer did have the house, even though it was in the name of the trust Summer's grandmother had set up for her before he died. Summer never touched the money, any more than she accepted handouts from her stepfather. But she had taken the house.

Taka pulled the car in front of the old place, hidden by the tall grass and overhanging cedars, and she climbed out, not waiting for him this time. Rain was coming down more heavily now, but she didn't care. She couldn't rid herself of the feeling that she was coming home, despite the upheavals of the last God knew how many hours or days.

She trailed after him up the wide front porch. Leaves were scattered across it, along with some broken twigs, and the curtains were pulled tight. No one had been there looking for a lost Japanese artifact. No one had been there at all.

"Are you going to smash a window or break the lock?" she asked idly.

"I have a key."

She didn't bother asking how—he had an answer for everything. He unlocked the heavy front door and pushed it open, and she froze.

She didn't want to go inside with him. She wasn't afraid of him—she was past such idiocy. He'd already done his worst and she'd survived. But this place was her sanctuary, her haven, even if she got here far too infrequently. And if she went inside with Takashi O'Brien, her home would be permanently tainted.

"I'll just wait here—"

He pushed her into the house, slamming the door behind them, plunging them into darkness. The place smelled like a closed-up house—mothballs and dampness. Someone came in once a month to air the place out, and must be due for a visit, because the air was thick and dusty.

And she was standing alone in the middle of the darkened hallway with the man who'd left her shattered and helpless. Wondering why the hell she wanted him to touch her again.

Jilly didn't bother to look up when the woman walked into her cell. She had found her best defense was ignoring them—ignoring the droning voice that was coming through the speakers, ignoring the milky water they kept bringing her no matter how thirsty she was, ignoring everything. She'd been stuck here for at least a day, though there were no windows, nothing to tell her how many hours had passed. She had a small, windowless bathroom off the cell, with just a shower and a toilet, and for all she knew there was a video camera hidden behind the light, but she didn't care. Growing up with Lianne strutting around partially clothed had given her a skewed sense of modesty, and if the Shirosama's creepy goons wanted to watch her on the toilet then let them.

The door closed behind her new intruder, and Jilly turned her head. It was a woman this time, wearing white, of course, but a designer suit of some sort that even Lianne wouldn't have sneered at. The stranger was flawlessly beautiful, with a perfect face, dark hair in a neat bun at the base of her neck, carrying a white leather case under one arm. Wearing gloves.

Jilly couldn't help the sudden anxious jolt in her

stomach, but she fought it. She wasn't going to let these people terrorize her, not even the dragon lady who'd just walked in.

The woman's smile was cool. "Miss Lovitz, my name is Dr. Wilhelm. I've been brought in to help with your reintegration."

Oh, shit. She had a German accent and was almost a parody of a Nazi torturer from an old black-and-white movie. Jilly sat up, scooting back on the narrow cot.

"I don't need reintegration, thank you very much."

The woman snapped open her bag, drawing out a small pouch and setting it on the metal table beside the bed. It clanked ominously. "We are clouded by the mists of our past lives and our earthly desires," she said. "I can help you to free yourself from all that. If you let me."

For a moment Jilly wondered if there was something beneath the woman's chillingly benign words. Freedom was exactly what she wanted, but she didn't think she was going to get it at the white gloved hands of the Shirosama's enforcer.

"No, thank you."

The woman opened the little satchel, and Jilly braced herself, expecting a scalpel. She wasn't afraid of pain—she had a fairly high tolerance for it, as she'd discovered when she'd broken her leg a few years ago. And she wasn't afraid of scarring, Ralph could hire the best plastic surgeons in the world if they cut her. She wasn't afraid of anything.

Except the hypodermic needle the woman pulled out.

"Oh, shit," Jilly said weakly. And that was the last thing she said for a very long time.

15

Taka hit the light switch, but nothing happened. "The breaker's turned off," Summer said. "I can show you where—"

"Never mind. We're better off in the dark." He reached into his pocket and pulled out something the size of a small pencil, knocked it against the door and was immediately rewarded with a bright beam of light.

"Who the hell are you, James Bond?" she demanded, staring at the little thing in fascination.

"Not quite."

"Why shouldn't we turn on the lights?"

He didn't say anything, and the answer came to her with uncomfortable accuracy. "You think someone might be watching?"

"I think it seldom hurts to be careful," he said. "Where did you hide the urn?"

"So much for small talk," she muttered. "I already told you. It's in the closet in my bedroom."

"And you're going to take me there."

She didn't like the ramifications of that simple statement, but she knew she was being ridiculous. He had no interest in her and bedrooms—he'd already taken care of that. She still wasn't sure why she'd awoken to find him holding her in the plane, but she wasn't about to ask. He'd have some coolly deflating response, and besides, she hadn't wanted him to hold her, to touch her. The moment she'd come to she'd moved away. She didn't want him anywhere near her.

The old cottage had been built in the early part of the last century, along Mission lines, and once she grew used to the damp odor she could smell the comforting, familiar scents of cedar siding and lemon polish as well, mixed with the lingering tang of the ocean. The wonderful smells of her childhood summers spent there with Hana-san for company. Summer had had friends there, too; other families with children her age lived nearby. The Bainbridge house had always been such a safe, welcoming place, and she hated that Takashi O'Brien had invaded it, hated that even worse threats might be lurking outside.

"This way," she said, moving down the narrow, wood-paneled hall to her bedroom. She knew her way in the dark, but the bright light behind her illuminated the space. Her bedroom door was ajar and she pushed it open, not wanting to step inside. Not with him.

"Here you go. The urn is in a small trunk on the top shelf of the closet."

He pushed her inside, blocking her exit. So much for her preferences. He flashed the light around the room, and she tried to look at the place through his eyes.

She was uncomfortably aware of the bed. It was a large one, genuine Stickley, and she'd never shared it with anyone. Then again, she'd never done much bed sharing at all.

But of course he wasn't interested in the bed. The flashlight passed it, over the walls, and paused at the antique kimono hanging there.

The garment was a work of art—hand-painted and embroidered, from the late nineteenth century, and Hana had given it to her for her fourteenth birthday. Lianne had been horrified, of course. Something of such value and beauty belonged in her own closet, not in the possession of her grubby little daughter, but even Lianne was cowed by Hana-san's indomitable nature. Just to be on the safe side they'd hung it in Summer's bedroom, the rich colors glowing and alive.

"I don't just want the urn," he said, shining the light over it. "I want everything else Hana Hayashi gave you."

"I told you—the urn, a book and two kimono."

"I'll take them all."

"You can't—" Foolish protest, and he didn't bother to answer. He could do anything he wanted.

"Do what you want," she said finally, wearily. "I'm going to sit in the living room. The sooner we're out of here the better."

He said nothing, moving aside to let her leave the room. She couldn't imagine ever feeling safe there again; with the kimono gone there'd be nothing left of Hana, replaced by the toxic presence of the man who'd started out rescuing her and ended up her kidnapper. Maybe, eventually, she'd wipe his memory out of the place. Open all the windows to let the sea air blow through, burn the sage sticks that New Agey Micah had given her. He'd loved this place, as well.

She walked into the darkened living room, dragging a heavy oak bench up to the bank of windows so that she could sit. The moon was bright and strong, providing some illumination, and she reached up and opened one of the casements, letting the cool night breeze in, rich with the tang of sea salt and cedar. She sat very still, looking out into the night, trying to shut out the noise from the bedroom. Trying to shut out the noise from her mind.

She ought to run. She had finally given Takashi O'Brien what he wanted, and he was too busy in her bedroom to pay any attention to her. Besides, she was of no value anymore. If she ran he'd probably just let her go.

So why wasn't she running?

He said someone was going to help her sister, who was caught up in the same helpless mess that she was. Could Summer believe him? In fact, he was very good at rescuing—he'd saved her life at least three times, maybe more if you counted the fact that she'd almost electrocuted herself in that über subur-

ban house. A safe house, he'd called it. She'd never
been less safe in her life. Maybe he'd also saved her
by just keeping her away from the Shirosama's
goons. If whoever had gone after Jilly was as efficient, then her sister would be safe.

But Taka might have lied. Although he hadn't actually lied that much to her, he had let her assume
things that weren't true. That he was there to help her.

In truth, he'd told her he was no guardian angel,
no rescuer. She'd just chosen not to believe him.
Idiot.

When this was all over she'd bring Jilly back here,
to the place she loved, and the two of them would
heal. Far away from L.A. and her mother's latest enthusiasm and the Shirosama's goons. Far away from
Little Tokyo and the Sansone Museum and the Santa
Monica Mountains. Far away from anything that
would remind her of Takashi O'Brien.

The trunk itself was a thing of beauty. Taka lifted
it down from the top shelf of Summer's closet very
carefully. It was Chinese, which amused him. Hana
Hayashi must have chosen it on purpose, knowing
how much it would gall her ancestors. He opened it,
and the Hayashi Urn lay there in ice blue glory.

He picked up the treasure carefully, turning it in
his hands. How had he ever mistaken those copies for
the real thing? This glowed with an almost unearthly
light, enough to tempt him to believe in the myths
surrounding it.

In the bottom of the trunk lay the book of haiku, handwritten in kanji. He wondered why Summer had kept it. Had Hana Hayashi told her to? Or had it been out of sentiment?

She'd lied about the kimono on the wall, but then, he'd expected that. It was a beautiful thing, embroidered and painted with chrysanthemums, and he stared at it a long time.

The chrysanthemums were another conundrum, one he couldn't quite fathom. They were the flower of royalty.... Were the ruins of the temple somewhere on land once belonging to the imperial family? So many pieces of the puzzle, so little time to find an answer. He glanced back into Summer's closet, and saw a light silk kimono hanging from a hook. The second kimono. Clearly something she used, something of no antique value. It was a pretty thing, and on a whim he wrapped the urn in it before placing it back in the box. He carried it out to the car, then went back for the antique kimono.

She was sitting in the living room, her back to him. Why the hell didn't she run? He'd made up his mind that if she did, he'd let her go. He'd be taking a risk; if the Shirosama caught her before he knew the urn was gone she would be in for a very bad time. But if Taka kept her with him, then sooner or later he'd have to do what he'd been ordered to do. And he was still fighting it. As long as the Shirosama couldn't get his hands on the urn it didn't matter where the shrine was located. There was nothing Shiro Hayashi, the man who called himself the Shirosama, could do about his planned Armageddon as long as Taka held the urn, and he wasn't going to let go.

"Tell me again what Hana-san has to do with all this?" Summer's voice was quiet, contemplative.

He grimaced. "Your so-called nanny came from one of the oldest, most powerful families in Japan, dating back to feudal times. In the chaos following World War II she was sent to relatives in California in the hope that she would blend in with the people returning from the detention camps, and eventually she would be brought home again when things had settled down. But most of her family was killed, and she was stranded here, safeguarding her secret."

"What secret?"

He hesitated. "You want the long version or the short version?" he asked. "In the early seventeenth century a monk and visionary was born in the mountains of Japan. He was an albino, and he took the name Shiro-sama, or White Lord, and he created his own religion, one that combined Buddhism, Shinto and the worship of Kali the Destroyer. He believed Japan must be destroyed to attain its full power in some kind of post-apocalyptic existence, and he had thousands of followers in a time where very few people questioned the way things were."

"I've never heard of him."

"I wouldn't expect you had. What do you know of Japanese history?"

"I read *Shogun*," she said, with light sarcasm. "Not to mention I have a doctorate in Asian art."

He ignored that. "The original Shiro-sama failed, of course, and was ordered by the emperor to commit ritual suicide in his temple in the mountains. He did, and his followers cremated his body and put his bones in a sacred urn to be guarded until the time he was reborn."

"And that's the Hayashi Urn?" she said. "A funeral jar? And I kept my cookies in it?"

"The bones are presumably in the possession of the current Shirosama. I don't think your cookies were contaminated."

She still didn't look too happy about it. "Why did Hana have it? And why does the Shirosama want it?"

"Hana was a descendant of one of the most powerful followers of the original Shiro-sama, and the original temple was on lands once belonging to her family. No one knows for sure where the ruins are— only she kept the secret—but the True Realization Fellowship have every intention of retrieving the urn and returning it to where it belongs."

"What's wrong with that? You yourself said it was a Japanese treasure that belongs in Japan."

"It belongs to the people of Japan, and a government that can watch over it. Not a group of fanatics who are far more dangerous than anyone realizes."

"What harm can an ancient piece of ceramic do?"

He leaned against the wall. "Don't be naive. The urn is nothing more than a catalyst, a symbol. The current Shirosama and his followers plan to take it back to Japan, find the ruins of the temple and the remains of the original Shiro-sama and reunite the bones and the urn."

"So?"

"And then, according to legend, the new Shirosama will ascend in full power to the universe, Armageddon will follow, and the world will be cleansed by fire and blood."

"So they put the bones in the urn and nothing happens," she said, turning to look at Taka in the shadowy room. "And then everyone goes home disappointed and no harm done. Unless you actually believe in doomsday prophets?"

"The problem with doomsday prophets, particularly the ones we have nowadays, is they don't believe in their destiny enough not to give it a little help. Reuniting the urn and the bones will signal a wave of mass destruction that will be very hard to stop. You know what religious fanatics are capable of—the whole world has been watching what's going on in the Middle East, and trust me, the Japanese have always been more than ready to die in the service of their master."

"So you smash the urn and everyone lives happily ever after. Problem solved."

Easier said than done. Ostensibly, he could kill an innocent young woman if he had to, but he couldn't bring himself to destroy such a singularly beautiful piece of Japanese history. It was a simple fact.

"Could *you* destroy it?" he countered.

Her eyes met his in the darkness, and then she turned away again, facing the window. "I don't suppose I could. And you think I hold the key to where the ancient shrine is located? I've never been to Japan, even though I've wanted to go. It was something I was going to do with Hana, and when she died I just couldn't face the idea of it. Maybe if we'd gone she would have told me, but as it was she never said a thing about her family history. She didn't like to talk about it. The war was too painful."

"Nevertheless, she left the knowledge with you. In the book, the kimono. Somewhere."

Summer swiveled around on the bench, silhouetted against the open window and the moonlight. He couldn't see her face, and he didn't know whether that was good or bad. "And what did they tell *you?*"

"We'll figure it out," he replied enigmatically.

She turned away from him, and he fought back his sudden guilt. If she ran, if the Shirosama caught her, then the cult leader know that he wasn't looking for just the urn and the girl. There were other pieces to the puzzle.

"And then what will you do?"

"Stop him before he can set off a wave of attacks that would make 9/11 look like a minor incident."

"Why doesn't someone just kill him, if he's that dangerous?"

"The only thing worse than a cult leader demigod is a martyr. He has hundreds of thousands of followers around the world and the resources and equipment to create deadly havoc. His murder would signal the start of it all. The death toll might be lower—tens of thousands instead of hundreds of thousands—but it's still unacceptable."

She was silent for a long moment. "How high is the death toll now? There's Micah and the followers you...killed. And then maybe there's me and Jilly. How many will die before he's stopped?"

"I don't know," Taka said simply, not denying it.

She turned back to the window. "Tell me when you're ready to go," she said, dismissing him.

Run, damn it! Get the hell away from me while you can. But she didn't move, and he could see defeat in the line of her body, her narrow shoulders. Didn't she realize she wasn't going anywhere? He didn't need her anymore. He had what he wanted. The safest, smartest thing to do would be to permanently silence her, and he was a safe, smart man.

He left her there, heading back into the bedroom to retrieve the antique kimono. He stripped a sheet off the bed to wrap it in, doing his best to clear his mind of anything but what he had to do. He could picture Summer in that huge old bed, sleeping, her hair loose around her. He still didn't know what his damn problem was—him or her. She was nothing, nobody, merely a part of a difficult job, and yet she got under his skin. Maybe he could blame it on the time he'd spent recovering from his last botched assignment.

Or maybe it was simply that the thought of killing an innocent woman was repugnant. Killing young women wasn't part of his normal duties. It was perfectly natural that he'd feel conflicted.

She was still sitting in the living room, staring out into the night, when he returned from the car. The rain was even heavier, blocking out the moon, and there were deep shadows in the house. Some things were easier to do in darkness. He came up behind her, looking past her, out into the damp forest. It was a chilly night, but she had the window open, and he could hear the sound of night birds, the rustle of the wind through the trees, the soft patter of the rain.

"I love this house," she said, in a quiet voice.

Her words surprised him. She hadn't volunteered much in the way of conversation since they'd left the bedroom in that suburban house.

"It's very beautiful. Very peaceful." He wasn't wearing gloves, but it didn't matter. His fingerprints weren't on file anywhere, and he wasn't going to leave the house standing. He'd already activated the device that he'd taken from the car, so there'd be no trace of anything once it went off. They might not even be able to identify her body.

He'd be on his way to Japan by then—probably even before the smoke cleared. And he wouldn't look back.

Summer wouldn't feel a thing. He had no more excuses, no more reason to delay, and she hadn't moved, leaving him no choice. If he left her alive the brethren could get to her, find out what she knew. Once they did, the Committee would have no way of stopping them. The Shirosama had stockpiles of chemical weapons—enough sarin gas to spread through the subway systems of every major metropolitan transit systems. Biological weapons to take care of the countryside, including trucks that could spread it into the air. They'd done test runs in Nigeria, the Chiba Prefecture of Japan, one of the small Hawaiian islands and the American Southwest. No one had caught on, because of the variety—plague spores in Arizona, hemorrhagic virus in Nigeria, a virulent, fast-moving strain of TB in Hawaii. Only the best scientists worked for the Shirosama, and their results were deadly masterpieces. One small woman was not that great a price to pay to keep the world safe from that kind of disaster.

He came up behind her, putting his hands on her shoulders. He would knock her out before he broke her neck—she would never know what happened—and she'd be in her peaceful, beautiful house on the island. It wasn't her fault that she was in the wrong place at the wrong time. That she'd kept Hana Hayashi's secrets too well.

Summer jumped slightly when his hands touched her, and then she stilled. She was wearing that same baggy black sweatshirt, and he wanted to touch her skin. He wanted to see her in colors, something other than funereal black. But that was the last thing he needed. He could feel the tension shimmering through her, her blood racing.

And then she leaned back. She let her back rest against his legs as he stood behind her, her head against his stomach, releasing all the tension in her body as she sank back against his. She turned her head to look up at him, and in the reemerging moonlight he could see her eyes clearly. Fearless, accepting.

The feel of her body against his shook him to the core. He stared down at her, his hands on her neck, and he did the unthinkable. He leaned down and put his mouth against hers.

He felt her shock vibrate through her, but she didn't pull away. She closed her eyes and let him kiss her, passive, accepting, and he realized in the short, endless time he'd known her he'd never really kissed her. Never more than the brief touch of his mouth against hers.

And suddenly that wasn't enough. It would never be enough. He stopped thinking, pulling her up from the bench and turning her in his arms. He caught her face in his hands and kissed her, full and open-mouthed, and her response was instant, powerful, the compliant woman vanishing. She put her arms around his neck, pulled him down to her and made a low sound of need as his tongue touched hers.

He picked her up, wrapping her arms and legs around him as he carried her across the darkened living room to her bedroom, setting her down on the stripped bed and covering her body with his.

Then he realized what he was doing. He started to pull away, but she clung tightly to him. "No," she whispered. "Stay with me." She tried to reach down between their bodies to touch him, but he grabbed her hand, pulling it away as he rolled off her, collapsing beside her on the bed. He couldn't do this. He didn't even understand why he'd started it, except that he'd been fighting his attraction since he'd left her alone in the bedroom that morning.

She tried to run then, too late, scrambling off the bed. But he caught her before she hit the floor, hauling her back under him, pinning her there. She closed her eyes, averting her face. "Stop it," she said.

"Stop what?"

Her eyes flew open, filled with rage and betrayal. "Stop pretending. You made your point this morning—you don't have anything more to prove. You don't want me, you can make me do anything you wish, and I'll be pathetically grateful for your attention, while you won't feel a thing…"

"You idiot," he said, his voice savage. "How blind are you?"

"Leave me alone."

He pulled her legs apart, pushing between them, fully clothed, the rigid length of his cock pressed up against her. Her eyes widened in shock.

"You can feel that, can't you? It's been like that all day. It's been like that almost since I first touched you. You make me crazy with wanting you, but right now doing what I want could get us both killed."

"No," she said. "You're lying. This morning you didn't—"

He rocked against her, and she shivered in unwilling response. "This morning I was so turned on that I came without touching myself. And five minutes later I was hard again. I need you. I need to be inside you, now, and it's too dangerous." He thrust against her, feeling the tremor of response wash over her, and he knew he couldn't stop, not until he made her come again, over and over...

She kissed him then, full and deep, wrapping her legs around his hips to bring him closer still, and the heavy material between them was maddening. He'd reached down to unzip his pants when he heard the sound of someone moving through the bushes, and he froze.

16

She felt the change instantly. He lifted his mouth from hers, his soft, beautiful mouth, and barely breathed the words. "Someone's out there. Stay very still."

He rolled off her, landing on the floor silently, and her body was hot and aching. Then she heard the sound as well, someone moving through the overgrown shrubbery outside. Someone was coming, and whoever it was would be even more dangerous than Taka.

"Get down!" he said, yanking her off the bed and onto the floor, shielding her body with his as something came crashing through the multipaned window. She could smell smoke, acrid, burning, filling her lungs with fire. She heard him whisper in her ear, "Get out of here!" before he leaped up, away from her.

She tried to sit up, but she couldn't stop coughing, and the smoke was too heavy to see more than a shadow play of violence. Taka moving among them, the battle a silent, deadly dance. She placed her hand on the bed, trying to pull herself to her feet, but her knees buckled beneath her and she went down again. With smoke billowing around her, she began to crawl slowly in the direction of the door.

There was a roaring in her ears, one she couldn't identify, and then she felt hands grab her—rough hands. And though her eyes were streaming from the thick smoke, she looked up and recognized one of the brethren, even dressed in uncustomary black like some bizarre ninja. He was immensely strong, and hurting her, and there was nothing she could do but let him drag her, until suddenly his face went blank, wiped clean of any expression at all, and he released her, unmoving. He collapsed in front of her, and Taka kicked him out of the way, reaching for her.

She wanted to scream. She wanted to cry and howl and run, with death and fire all around her, but instead she simply let him take her hand, pull her from the smoke-filled room, out into the rainy night.

The car was parked where he'd left it, with two men lying in the dirt and mud beside it. They didn't look as if they'd been touched, but they were clearly dead. Taka pointed the mobile phone at the car and the lights came on.

He kicked one man's body out of the way and opened the passenger door, pushing her inside and closing it before he moved around to the driver's side. Smoke was pouring out of her beloved cottage, but none of the intruders was following them. Taka started the car and began to pull away, and she felt the sickening thud as he drove over one of the bodies lying in the road. At the last minute he turned and pointed the cell phone at the house. A second later her cottage exploded in a ball of flames, the noise deafening. And they were speeding down the long, rutted driveway.

As they drove down the main road, they passed police and fire trucks, sirens blaring, lights flashing, paying no attention to the dark, anonymous sedan speeding in the opposite direction. At one point Summer turned back to look, and the flames were shooting high into the sky, taking her childhood with them.

"How many men did you kill today?" Her voice was a dull monotone.

"Three in the house. The two outside were killed by the security system on the car—it was set to electrocute anyone who touched it."

"Isn't that a little drastic for an antitheft device?"

He glanced at her, clearly surprised by her even tone of voice. He knew she was feeling nothing, absolutely nothing, a blessed numbness. One moment she was ready to climax from the simple rub of his clothed body against hers, and in the next there was fire and smoke and death…and numbness.

"Maybe," he said, concentrating on the road.

"Did you get the urn and the other things, or were they lost when you blew up my house?"

"I have them."

"That's good," she said. "I'd hate to go through all this for nothing. So why did you bother bringing me along? Why did you save me again? You could have just left me in the house and I would have been blown to hell along with the others. It would be a lot neater."

He frowned. "I didn't want to hurt you."

She began to laugh then. For some reason she couldn't control it—the absurdity of his reply was so wonderful that she had no choice. She could laugh or she could cry, and she never cried.

"Stop it!" he said sharply.

She couldn't. Didn't he understand the cosmic absurdity of it? That no matter what she did, death followed her like a hungry vulture, and any respite was a lie, just a short delay on this inevitable journey of pain and darkness. Really, all you could do was laugh at such ridiculous—

The pain was blinding, stealing her breath, stopping her heart, shocking her into silence. He took his hand away, placing it back on the wheel, and she stared at him, knowing that all color had leached out of her face.

"That's better," he said evenly. "Things are bad enough—I don't need you losing it, as well."

It took her a moment to breathe, to speak. "'Losing it'?" she echoed. "I've lost everything. My job, my car, my best friend, my legacy from Hana—even the house that I loved. And I'm probably going to lose my sister and my life. I think a little hysteria is in order."

"I can hurt you a lot more than I just did," he said. "I don't want to, but I will. I need to concentrate, and I can't have you flipping out on me."

"I want you to either kill me or let me go. And don't even try to convince me you weren't planning on killing me. I can be blind and stupid for only so long."

"No," he said.

"No, what?" she snapped.

"No, I won't try to convince you of that. Those were my orders. And no, I won't let you go. Or kill you." There was an odd, almost resigned tone in his voice. Strange, when he showed so little emotion.

She felt cold inside. "Then what are you going to do with me?"

"Damned if I know," he said. And reached forward and turned on the radio, drowning out any more questions.

Jilly slept. Dressed in her white pajamas, she floated above the narrow cot, into the starry sky overhead. The walls melted away, the floors and the furniture, and she was free, floating.

She knew she shouldn't feel so peaceful. It was all thanks to the needle from the gorgeous neo-Nazi doctor. She'd tried to fight her, but the woman had been much too strong, much too determined. She'd said something to her in her thick German accent, but

Jilly had already been floating, and she was only dimly aware of the reassuring stroking of the woman's hand on hers.

If she was going to be trapped, she'd be happy enough not to wake up, not until she stood some chance of escape. The woman sat and watched her, making notes in a leather-clad notebook, and every now and then some of the undead would wander in, ask questions and wander out again. Jilly was beginning to emerge from her safe cloud. The doctor was busy with her notes. She hadn't realized her patient was beginning to come out of her drugged state, and Jilly wasn't about to give her that advantage. The only thing that could possibly help her was the element of surprise. If the woman knew she was waking up she'd just come at her with another needle.

It took all her concentration not to react when the door to her cell opened. She willed her muscles to relax, her eyelids to keep from fluttering. Particularly when she recognized the soft voice of his holiness, the Shirosama.

"She still sleeps?"

Jilly remained motionless, listening to what was happening. The good doctor had risen, setting her notebook down, and Jilly thought there was tension in the room. Though it was probably only her own.

"She still sleeps," the woman said in her accented English. "You need to trust me, your holiness. This particular girl is very hard to break, and I'm an expert at what I do. By the time I release her from her sedation she'll be totally free of her past perceptions. She will be open and willing to embrace your guidance, and she will tell you everything you want to know. But the process takes time."

"I'm not sure how much time we have," the Shirosama said in the low, mellow voice that her mother likened to the voice of God and Jilly found creepy. "We haven't been able to rescue her sister from the hands of the Yakuza, and countless members of the Fellowship have given their lives in the attempt. Blessings upon them."

Unmoving, Jilly let his words sink in. Japanese gangsters had her sister, the revolting Shirosama had her, some B-movie Nazi femme fatale was drugging her into submission and even if Jilly was conscious she was being watched too closely to get the hell out of there.

"Blessings upon them," the woman echoed. "I will speed the process as much as I can. One thing that would help would be total darkness, to increase her isolation."

There was a long silence. "Would that not be difficult for you?"

"Not at all. I'm used to working in the dark. But it must be absolute. No lights from security cameras or coming from under the door. Give me twelve hours of complete darkness and she'll be ready for your ministry."

More silence. Jilly wanted to cry out, protest. She didn't want to be trapped in the dark with this crazy

woman, she'd rather take her chances with her
mother's guru. But she was still too drugged to say
a word, trapped in a wall of silence.

"As you wish," he said after a moment. "I have
heard great praise for your methods. I put my trust,
and this poor lost child, in your hands."

"You do me honor."

Jilly wanted to throw up. She couldn't move,
couldn't open her eyes—it would serve the woman
right if she choked to death on her own vomit. She'd
try to do it quietly, just to spite the bitch.

She heard the heavy door close behind the departing Shirosama, heard the locks engage. The woman
was rustling in her bag again, and Jilly knew another
needle was coming, knew there was nothing she
could do about it. Even if she weren't already
drugged, the German woman was stronger than she
was. Jilly hadn't been able to stop her the first time,
when she'd had all her strength.

And then the lights went out. Odd how she knew
it, since she couldn't open her eyes. But as she felt
the woman lean over her, the darkness intensified,
becoming a thick, black cocoon, and she waited for
the pinprick in her arm, the return of night.

Instead she felt the weight of the woman as she
knelt on the cot beside her, smelled her perfume as
she leaned close. If the harridan was going to molest
her, Jilly only hoped she was totally out before she
put her hands on her. She could withstand anything,
and this was no time to be squeamish, but she really

wasn't in the mood to have her first sexual experience be at the hands of a torturer…

She felt the woman's lips against her ear. "They won't be able to see anything now, but they can still hear. Do everything I tell you and don't say a word."

Yeah, right, Jilly thought. *I'm going to lie here and let you mess with me, you disgusting…* And then she realized the woman's German accent had disappeared.

She managed to open her eyes, but the darkness was absolute. There was no pinprick in her skin, no unpleasant touches. Just the woman's cool hand on hers.

"Can you sit up yet? Squeeze my fingers if you can."

Jilly tried, but her muscles were still useless.

"Then we'll wait," the woman said. She had a faint British accent, and Jilly wondered if that was just as fake as the German one. Maybe she'd live long enough to find out.

The Nazi bitch was gone, and this woman, whoever she was, seemed determined to help her. And Jilly had no choice but to trust her.

Taka had told her nothing but the truth this time. He wasn't going to kill her. He wasn't sure when he'd finally realized that simple fact—maybe the first time he'd set eyes on her. He'd come close, too many times, but had rescued her more times than that. When he'd sensed the threat in the summer cottage, his first instinct had been to protect her, save her.

He counted on his instincts to keep him alive. He couldn't start ignoring them now and hope to survive. Every intuition kept him protecting Summer Hawthorne, and every time he tried to talk himself into killing her his instincts would take over.

He had enough battles to fight right now without fighting one with himself.

She was going to live. She was going to grow old and fat and have children and live happily ever after, whether she liked it or not, as far away from him as possible. He had every intention of seeing to it.

Once he got her safely stowed he could concentrate on his mission: stopping the deadly doomsday cult before they could put their plans into action. Madame Lambert might give him shit, but in the end she'd trust his judgment. He just had to make certain the Shirosama was stopped, sooner rather than later. That was the only way Summer would be safe.

She wasn't speaking to him now, but staring stone-faced out the window as he drove through the night. Anything was better than her laughter, the eerie sound of her losing control. He'd wanted to stop the car, pull her into his arms and hold her tightly until the hysteria stopped. Crazy notion, when they had to get the hell out of there as fast as they could.

The one good thing in all this was that she hated him with a fiery passion. He'd shamed her, rejected her, destroyed her family home. She even knew he'd planned to kill her. Any tender feelings she might have for him would be burned to a cinder of hatred.

And since, time after time, his crazy instincts had made him save her, he'd save her one more time. He'd save her from him. Then, if there was any mercy in this world, he'd be able to forget about her.

_17_

Jilly woke slowly, drifting into wakefulness in the inky darkness. She could see nothing at all, not even the shape of the woman who was either her guard, her brainwasher or her rescuer, but she knew she wasn't alone. The drugs were wearing off quickly now. She could feel life flowing back into her body, and she tested her muscles, flexing them enough to know they worked, without letting the woman realize a thing. Even her fingers were responding—they were close beside her body, but she could make them move. Now she simply had to decide what to do next. The woman who had drugged her was smaller than she was, but incredibly strong, and if Jilly tried to overpower her she'd probably end up with another syringeful of drugs. The woman hadn't precisely said she was going to help, but anyone who lied to the slimy Shirosama had to be more friend than enemy.

Jilly's body jerked in surprise when she felt the

woman whisper in her ear. "You're ready," she said, and Jilly wondered how she knew. "Do exactly what I tell you and stay calm, no matter what happens."

Not the most reassuring warning, but Jilly sat up anyway, relieved that her head seemed entirely clear. The woman took her hand in the darkness, leading her from the bed. Jilly had a sudden wash of intense paranoia, that this was all part of the plan to brainwash her, to trick her into giving up whatever they thought she had. She had no idea where her sister was right now, and even if she did she wasn't about to tell them. Lianne she would have given up in a heartbeat, much as she loved her feckless mother. Summer was a different matter entirely.

Jilly had no shoes, only the loose white pajamas they'd dressed her in—not good for skulking in the dark. She couldn't see anything, hear anything, but the sudden influx of cool air told her that the woman had managed to open the door to her cell. A moment later they were out, walking silently in the thick darkness, Jilly's hand in the stranger's as she led the way.

It was marginally brighter outside—light pollution from the nearby city—and Jilly got a good look at the woman with her as they stopped in the shadow of the building. She'd lost the glasses she'd worn earlier, but her dark hair was still neatly tucked in a bun at the back of her head. She was wearing heels and somehow managing to be silent in them.

"We're going to have to run for it," she whispered in Jilly's ear. "They won't be expecting anything, but we'll still only have about twenty seconds before they're onto us. Do you see the yellow SUV parked under the tree?"

"Isn't that a little—" The woman slapped a hand over her mouth to silence her. When she removed it, Jilly whispered "—obvious?"

"Trust me. I'm a professional," the woman said, and Jilly wondered how she could sound wry when she barely made any noise. "It's got a remote starter, but the moment I trigger it they'll see us. Wait for my signal and then run for it."

And get a bullet between the shoulder blades, Jilly thought dismally. Not that the Shirosama's goons carried guns. They probably just bored people to death. Still, she didn't have much choice but to obey. She nodded.

The woman beside her was pointing her cell phone at the SUV, and damn if the thing didn't start. "Run!"

Jilly took off, sprinting across the field in her bare feet, feeling like a target. She could hear shouts in the distance, feel the woman close behind her. She was almost at the car when the woman behind her went down.

Jilly looked back. "Keep going!" the woman called out. "Get out of here!"

The SUV was within reach, already running, but Jilly didn't hesitate. She could see the white-robed brethren converging at the edge of the field, she sprinted back, grabbing the woman who lay sprawled in the grass, and hoisting her up.

"Let go of me. Run!" the woman shouted.

Jilly ignored her. She put her arm around the woman's small waist and half dragged her to the SUV, dumping her inside before she jumped into the driver's seat. A moment later she tore out of the parking lot, heading straight for the bright lights of Los Angeles.

She heard a popping sound and the crinkle of breaking glass. So the holy ones had guns, after all... She glanced at the woman beside her. She was pale, and the dark hair was a wig—it had fallen in her lap, exposing silver-blond hair. There was no sign of blood on her white suit, just mud and grass stains, and she was missing one high-heeled shoe.

The woman was swearing under her breath, some really impressive cursing that Jilly hoped she'd remember in the future. Astonishing that such an elegant creature could use words that would make a rapper blush.

"Are you okay?" Jilly asked.

"I think I broke my ankle," the woman muttered, letting out another stream of invective. "Head for the freeway south and drive as fast as you can. If we get picked up for speeding it'll keep the Shirosama's zombies from getting to us."

"Among other things," Jilly said. "I don't have a driver's license."

The woman leaned her head back against the seat and moaned. "I thought everyone in California could drive," she said. The accent was definitely British, and she was younger than Jilly had first thought.

"I can drive very well," she assured her. "I got my license last year. Unfortunately, I didn't keep it for too long. I like to speed."

"Well, in this case it's a good thing," the woman said. "Do you know how to find LAX from here?"

"Yes."

"Then get there as fast you can. I'm getting both of us out of here."

"Not that I'm ungrateful, but you want to tell me who you are?" Jilly asked, pulling onto the freeway at a speed that would have turned her father pale beneath his cultivated tan.

"Call me Isobel," the woman said. "That's all you need to know for now. Just drive."

Jilly wasn't in the mood to argue. Her mouth tasted like sawdust—probably the aftereffect of whatever Isobel had injected her with—and adrenaline was pumping through her body. She was probably a fool to trust the stranger, but anyone was preferable to the Shirosama, and her instincts about people had always been good. For the moment all she needed to do was concentrate on driving like a bat out of hell, and the rest would take care of itself.

Taka picked up his cell phone, answering it by stating a number. Summer hadn't heard it ring, but something must have alerted him to the call.

Taka's replies were monosyllables, and she had no idea whether he was responding to good news or bad until he turned to look at her.

"Your sister's safe."

The relief was so swift and unexpected that it made Summer light-headed. She hadn't dared to even think about Jilly, too terrified to even consider it, and now that that terror was over she felt sick. "Where is she?"

"My boss got her out. They'll be meeting you at the Oceana Air terminal at Sea-Tac. Madame Lambert is going to take you to a safe house outside of London until we can contain the Shirosama."

"I'm supposed to trust you?"

"No," he said. He picked up the phone. "Put her sister on." A second later he handed the small silver device to her.

Summer felt a second of panic—after all, this tiny piece of metal and circuitry unlocked doors, turned off death traps and blew up houses. God knows what would happen if she pushed the wrong button. And then she heard Jilly's voice coming faintly from the other end of the line, and she no longer gave a shit.

"Are you all right?" she demanded. "Did that son of a bitch hurt you?"

"I'm fine, Summer." Her sister sounded as unflappable and in control as always. It amazed Summer that a not-quite-seventeen-year-old could be so calmly self-possessed, but it had always been that way. Jilly had been born an old soul. "I've been playing James Bond, but Isobel got me out in time, with a hail of bullets following us. It was very cool."

And Summer felt very sick. "Where are you now?"

"Driving around L.A. Isobel sprained her ankle and can't drive, but I'm used to the roads, and besides, it's the middle of the night and there's no traffic. Did you hear we're going to England?"

"Yes, I—" The phone was plucked out of her hand.

"Let me speak to Madame Lambert." Summer could just imagine Jilly's reaction to Taka's cool demand, and if she'd had even an ounce of energy she would have placed a bet with herself on how long it would take Jilly to comply. But right now she was too shaken with relief to think much of anything else. Jilly was safe, and they were going to get her the hell out of the country and the reach of that crazy man.

No, they were going to get *both* of them out of the country. She was never going to have to see Takashi O'Brien again, a fact that should almost begin to make up for the loss of her home. She wasn't even going to consider the other losses.

To her surprise, Jilly appeared to have handed over the telephone and a moment later Taka ended the call. No, maybe it shouldn't surprise her. Jilly would have resisted bullying, but Taka's calm control was very…seductive.

"What about my passport? If your boss is taking us to England, what's she going to do about passports? Jilly's father has hers in his safe."

"Phony passports are child's play," he said. "And Madame Lambert tends to travel with diplomatic immunity. No one is going to look too closely at her companions, particularly if they're pretty, young and innocent."

"Yeah, that takes care of Jilly, but what about me?" Summer couldn't believe she'd actually said such a thing out loud. Begging for compliments, reassurances, none of which she needed, thank you very much.

He laughed. She hadn't heard him laugh often, and the sound was soft, momentarily beguiling. Until she remembered she hated him.

"That's right, you're ugly, old and jaded," he murmured. "How could I forget?"

"If I had a gun I would kill you," she said bitterly.

A moment later he reached under the car seat, pulling out a small, nasty-looking handgun, and put it in her lap. "It works very simply. You need to cock it first, then just point and shoot. If I were you I'd wait until we get off the highway. If you shoot me at these speeds you'll probably end up dying as well, and I thought you were past adolescent suicide attempts. Unless you have some romantic notion of a murder-suicide."

She picked up the gun. It was small, cold in her hand. "If you're trying to talk me out of it you're doing a piss-poor job."

"I can pull off on the shoulder if you'd like. That way you could just shove me out and drive on. It'd make a bit of a mess…"

"Just stop it!" She moved to drop the gun into his lap, but his hand shot out and caught her wrist. She let go of the gun, and it fell on the floor at his side. He kicked it under his seat without slowing his speed, but kept hold of her hand. She curled it into a fist, but didn't try to break free. Even when he brought it to his mouth and kissed the back of her wrist.

"You're going to be rid of me in just a few more hours," he said gently. "And then you can forget I ever existed. It would be better that way. Madame Lambert even has drugs that will help you, so that after a while it will all seem like nothing more than a bad dream."

"And how am I going to think of the cottage you blew up?" Why wasn't she pulling away? Why was the touch of his mouth on her skin making heat pool deep between her legs?

"As a necessary loss," he said. He released her hand back in her own lap. "Sometimes you give up what you love to stay alive."

"Have you ever had to do that?"

He turned his head to look at her for so long it should have been dangerous, but he seemed to have a sixth sense when it came to the road. "It's coming," he said.

And he turned away, driving into the slowly dawning day.

18

Dawn couldn't come soon enough. He had to get her out of his life as quickly as possible. It was becoming the most important thing—more important than breathing, living. He needed to get away from her, fast. Because he didn't want to let her go.

Taka had absolutely no idea what kind of insanity had decided to land on his head. He'd almost gotten them killed back on Bainbridge, all because he couldn't keep his hands off her. He could come up with a million excuses, all plausible, all lies. Everything boiled down to one simple thing. He wanted to be inside her. He wanted to make her cry again. He wanted her, maddening though she was, and the moment he let her go it would be forever.

Had he ever given up something he loved in order to stay alive? Destroyed it? What had made her ask that question, and what had made him come up with the instant answer that he'd somehow managed to silence? It was her.

She'd shut herself off again, and as the morning light filled the car he let himself watch her. She was pale and drawn, with violet patches beneath her eyes, the scattering of golden freckles across her nose. She'd managed to braid her long hair again, but it was coming loose, tangling on her shoulders. He wanted to untie her hair and bury his face in it, breathe in the smell of it.

Hell, it probably smelled of smoke and ashes from the explosion they'd just barely managed to outrun. Her skin would smell of fear. But he wanted to drown in it anyway.

He was insane. Out of his fucking mind, and she had no idea. He'd prefer to keep it that way. He just needed a little space to put his head back together again. Once he got away from her, he'd forget all about her.

And that moment couldn't come a second too soon for her. He could see the iron tension in her body, her averted profile, the stubborn set to her mouth. He'd never had the chance to really appreciate her mouth and what it could do. At least he could be thankful for small favors.

The plan was all set. Madame Lambert would take Summer and her sister to England, stash them with Peter and his wife, while Taka headed in the opposite direction, to Japan. To place the goddamn urn into the hands of the Japanese government, through the kindly services of his great-uncle Hiro. That would stop the Shirosama's forward momentum, give them enough time to find the site of the temple and destroy whatever was left there. Give them time to find where the cache of weapons was, the biological and chemical plagues that the brethren's Ministry of Science had been compiling. Time enough to save the world.

He could only hope Madame Lambert would dispense some of those drugs that were so effective in wiping out unpleasant memories to her. Summer didn't need to know she'd ever seen him, and if, in the future, she was illogically repulsed by Asian men, she'd never guess why.

There were enough flights leaving Sea-Tac at the crack of dawn to make the traffic heavy, enough police that he slowed down to the legal speed limit. Taka could have waved one of his many aliases in front of any cop and gotten away with a disapproving look, but there was no need to complicate matters. Though he no longer worried about Summer saying anything. She wouldn't do a thing that would keep her in his company a moment longer than necessary. She wanted her sister, she wanted to get away from him, she wanted safety and quiet, and Isobel Lambert would present just the right sort of nononsense presence. He imagined his boss could put on a maternal front if she wanted to; she could do just about anything.

Summer and her sister would be safe, secure and eventually happy. And he would stop thinking about her the moment he turned his back and walked away.

He had become very good at walking away from things, people.

She didn't say a word when he pulled into the underground parking garage reserved for VIPs, and she followed him out of the car. In the bright artificial light of the garage she looked washed out. She had a smudge of dirt across her cheekbone, and he raised a hand for a moment to brush it away, then dropped it. He wasn't going to touch her again unless he had to.

"Don't look so woebegone," he said under his breath. "You're about to escape me. This should be the happiest day of your life."

She didn't rise to the bait. It would have been easier if she sniped at him, but all the fight seemed to have gone out of her. She'd won—Madame Lambert hadn't voiced any objection when he'd told her flat out during their last communiqué that he wasn't going to kill Summer. Just another few minutes and he could walk away.

He took her arm as they walked into the lower level of the terminal, and after an initial start she didn't try to pull away, instead letting him lead her through the almost empty corridors, up into the busier sections. She remained quiet when he took her through the security gate reserved for workers, and after one glance at his ID none of the TSA workers said a word, ignoring her and waving them through. She kept up with him, mute and seemingly miserable, and he thought he could probably let go of her arm.

But he didn't. He wanted to touch her, sick bastard that he was. Until the last possible moment, he wanted to hold on to her.

They reached gate 11. The man Isobel Lambert had arranged for, Crosby, was waiting for them, dressed in the uniform of a maintenance worker, cap pulled low on his head, pushing a bucket and mop. Taka could just imagine what kind of firepower was in that bucket if anyone came near Summer. No one would—they'd covered their tracks too well this time, but it was reassuring that he was there.

There were just the right number of people in the terminal—enough to keep things safe, not too many that they'd interfere or cause problems. Gate 11 was deserted—the next flight out was five hours later—and Taka pushed her into one of the hard plastic seats facing the walkway. He could have stashed her in one of the VIP lounges, but that's where the Shirosama's buddies would be looking for her. Better to be out in the open. Madame Lambert had picked this place, and she knew as well as anyone the best possible spot for a pickup.

Taka finally let go of Summer, because he had no more reason to touch her. He glanced at his watch, needing to walk away, fast.

"Madame Lambert will be here in forty-five minutes. In the meantime Crosby's over there with the mop, and he'll be looking out for you. No one will bother you. If anyone tries, just scream as loud as you can."

Summer gazed up at him, and for a moment he froze. "Why are you looking at me like that? You're about to get everything you want. Your sister, safety—and you'll never have to see me again. Why are you looking stricken?"

"You wouldn't understand," she said, lowering her eyes.

He couldn't stop himself; he caught her chin and tilted her face back up to his. "All right, so your house is destroyed, your best friend killed and you've lost a sentimental cookie jar and an antique kimono. But you're alive, your sister's alive and you're both going to stay that way. Plus, I'm out of here. You're going to England, I'm going to Japan, and if you ask, Madame Lambert will make sure you forget you ever met me. Even if you don't ask she'll probably see to it. So you only have a little while longer to hate me."

"I don't hate you."

Oh, Christ. He looked down into her blue eyes, those eyes that never cried, and he could see tears there. Impossible, but there was no mistaking the lost, broken expression. "Stop it," he said roughly.

"Stop what?"

"Stop looking at me like that, or I'll…"

"Or you'll what?"

He really didn't know what he'd do. Kiss her. Shoot her. She was making him crazy, and he couldn't afford to let that happen. "What do you want from me?" he demanded in a harsh undertone. Crosby would be listening to every word, probably taping it.

She didn't answer, and Taka didn't expect her to. She didn't know what she wanted, and right then she was just too worn-out and confused to even begin to guess. He was the only constant in her life right now, and she was afraid to let him go. He could understand that. It had nothing to do with him, more a case of better the devil you know than the devil you don't. So he said nothing more than "Goodbye," and walked away without a backward glance, nodding at Crosby as he went.

Takashi moved through the crowds swiftly, heading back toward the car. His contact, Ella Fancher, was waiting, dressed as a flight attendant, and he handed her the keys. "Pack everything and get it on my plane," he muttered. "I don't know what's important and what's not."

She nodded, handing him the packet of materials he'd requested. New passport, e-ticket to Narita Airport, new credit cards. "Where'd you leave the girl?"

"What makes you think I didn't finish her?"

He'd known Ella for a good five years—they'd even been lovers for a short time, and they'd remained friends. "Because I know you, Taka. It would take more than Isobel Lambert's orders to make you kill an innocent. She knows that, as well. That's why she chose you for this particular assignment."

"She chose me because of my background," he replied. "And 'the girl' is sitting up at the gate, waiting for Lambert to pick her up. Crosby's keeping an eye on her to make sure no one bothers her."

"Crosby?" Ella's face turned pale. "Crosby's dead."

He could feel the blood freeze in his veins. "What do you mean?"

"Crosby was killed in that shootout up at Lake Arrowhead. Who told you Crosby was going to be there?"

"Text message from Madame Lambert," he said tersely, shoving the papers in his pocket.

"Not from Lambert," Ella said grimly. "You'd better go…"

He was already gone. Racing back through the empty halls, his heart slamming against his chest. He'd left her, so determined to escape that he hadn't taken the time to make sure the situation was secure. Summer was going to die because of his own stupid weakness. He'd been afraid he wouldn't be able to leave her at all, so he'd abandoned her.

And because of that, she was going to die. And he wasn't sure he could live with that.

Summer sat in the uncomfortable plastic chair, watching the nearly empty terminal. The man who was guarding her seemed busy washing the floors, ignoring her as he moved closer. It should have been a relief—someone else to keep her safe, someone ordinary. Not an exotic, beautiful, cruel creature like Taka.

How the hell had she gotten to this point? She'd looked up at him when he left her, and it was all she could do not to beg him to take her with him. Why? He was going to Japan, and yes, she'd always wanted to go there—ever since Hana-san had told her the stories of her childhood—but not at the side of a Yakuza hit man in the midst of some world-saving quest.

And since when was organized crime interested in saving the world? Shouldn't he be more concerned with selling the urn to the highest bidder, not returning it to the Japanese government?

For that matter, who said he was a Yakuza hit man? She'd jumped to the very logical conclusion that Taka was a gangster by the number of people he'd killed since he'd pulled her out of the trunk of the limousine, and by the tattoos that covered his back. But in fact, he'd only killed to protect her.

Who and what was the committee he'd mentioned in passing? And who was this Madame Lambert she was supposed to meet, the one who was taking both her and Jilly to England?

Summer needed to be with her sister, someplace safe, far away from the Shirosama and his goons. Right now her longing to run back to Taka was just a case of temporary insanity. Of wanting to see how it ended between them. *Idiot,* she thought. It—they—had already ended.

But there was no reason to feel like crying. Because once she started crying she'd never stop, and she couldn't afford to risk that. Not until she was safely out of here.

She glanced over at her guardian angel, but he was nowhere in sight. His cart, however, was still parked against one of the walls. A sudden icy panic began to spike through her, until she heard his voice directly behind her.

"Miss Hawthorne?"

She spun around, filled with relief, and looked up at the face of her bodyguard. At the bald head beneath the cap, the blank eyes. The gun in his hand.

"We need to do this discreetly," he murmured in some kind of accent, one she couldn't place. "If I have to shoot you, then other people will get hurt, and you wouldn't want to be responsible for that, would you? Not after you've already caused so many deaths?"

"I didn't cause any deaths."

"You refused the protection of his holiness, and the man you've been with is nothing more than an assassin, one who kills without mercy. You need to come with me, away from this place, so that he doesn't kill anyone else."

"He's already gone. He doesn't care where I am—you can just leave me here—"

"The woman who's coming for you is just as dangerous. She's already killed your sister, and she'll kill you, as well."

"So you're threatening to shoot me in order to keep her from killing me?" Summer said, calm and frozen. She wasn't going to believe his hideous words. "That doesn't make sense."

"There's a silencer on this gun, and no one will notice. I'll just curl you up in the seat as if you're sleeping, and no one will notice until blood pools underneath your seat."

She rose slowly, knowing he meant what he'd said. "Where are you taking me?"

"Where you belong. Under the protection of his holiness."

"I don't have the urn," she said. "It's out of my hands. I don't have anything the Shirosama wants."

"That is up to his holiness to determine. Walk very slowly and don't make the mistake of trying to attract anyone's attention. My master's orders are explicit. Bring you to his care if possible, but do not let the forces of darkness take you again."

"The forces of darkness?" she echoed, wishing she could be amused at his melodrama. "I'm not going anywhere. And I don't for one moment believe that my sister is dead. I'd know it. I'd feel it."

Instead she felt the gun poking into her ribs. "You will come with me, Miss Hawthorne, and stop arguing."

She glanced around her. The terminal was still marginally empty—no sign of security guards in this security-laden age. Just a few aimless travelers, clearly way too early for their flights.

"This way," he said, prodding her with the gun, and she had no choice but to precede him farther into the terminal, heading down a cement ramp marked Authorized Personnel Only. Maybe he was going to take her to the Shirosama, but more likely he was going to put a bullet in her head and leave her in the dark passageway. It was too late to scream, which Taka had told her to do. Too late to run.

"Stop right there," the man said when they reached the bottom of the ramp. They were in a narrow, dimly lit corridor of closed doors.

Summer leaned against the wall, knowing what was coming. At least Jilly was safe—she was absolutely certain of that despite the man's sinister words. And Taka was safe as well, on his way to Japan with the urn and the kimono, and he might never hear what happened to her. Part of her wanted him to remember, to feel a least a trace of guilt or regret. But he wasn't the kind of man to feel guilt, and besides, he'd done his best for her. Her luck had just finally run out.

She looked at the bald man fearlessly. In the darkened ramp beyond him she thought she could see another silhouette. The goons probably worked in pairs.

"Is the Shirosama trundling his fat butt down here to meet me?" she drawled.

A spasm of pure rage crossed the man's pale face. "How dare you defame the master?"

"The master's not going to show his creepy self, is he? You were never planning to take me to him, you're just going to kill me. So why don't you get it over with?" She managed to sound bored.

"I'm supposed to kill you if you don't cooperate."

He was clutching the gun tightly in his fleshy hands. The gun was bigger than she'd first thought—large enough to blow a good-size hole in her.

"But you and I both know it doesn't really matter, right? You've got the excuse to kill me, and you're going to do it. You'll just tell his sliminess that I tried to escape."

"You'll be going to a purer place." The gun was trembling slightly as he spoke. "You should bless the Shirosama for his mercy."

"Killing me is merciful?" she scoffed. The shadow behind him moved, but she kept her eyes focused on Taka's handpicked maintenance man.

"You'll be removed from sin and worldly cares, moving to a higher plane of consciousness."

"I like this plane of consciousness, thank you," she said. Who was looming behind him? Was it rescue, or a more certain defeat? Was she going to die? Death seemed likely, all without ever seeing Taka again. Which was just as well. If she saw him she'd probably make a fool of herself, because he was all she could think of, even when her life was about to end. She could only hope that Lianne would feel damn guilty about her death.

"You deserve to die," the man said. "For your lack of respect, if nothing else."

"Don't you think you ought to check with the Shirosama before you do this? I gather he doesn't like to have his orders crossed." Whatever she'd seen on the ramp behind the man was gone; nothing was moving at all. No rescue, no deus ex machina. No Taka.

It was up to her, and if she tried to rush him, he'd just shoot her.

"I'll take my chances," the man said, raising the gun and pointing it in the middle of her forehead. A third eye, she thought, feeling a little giddy. Maybe she'd find enlightenment, after all.

19

She heard the popping, the slick, familiar sound of a silenced gun going off, a sound she'd heard so many times on TV and in the movies. Summer felt nothing, but she'd read enough to know that you don't feel anything for a while. You go into shock. Though if he shot her in the head she'd already be dead, wouldn't she? And if she wasn't, wouldn't she feel blood on her face…?

"You can stop playing the virgin sacrifice now. He's not going to kill you."

Her eyes flew open to find Taka in the darkened hallway. She glanced down at the body sprawled at her feet—she hadn't even felt him fall—then back up at Taka's calm face.

"What took you so long?" Her voice didn't even shake.

"I was in such a hurry to get rid of you I wasn't paying close enough attention," he said, his voice cool and emotionless. "I guess you're stuck with me for a bit longer."

For a moment she couldn't move. She was afraid that if she did, she'd throw herself into his arms and start crying. *Can't do that*, she reminded herself.

"I thought you'd resigned as my guardian angel?"

"And I thought I'd told you I never was that?"

So he had. He'd told her a great many things that weren't true. He'd certainly been there to snatch her from the jaws of death again and again. She just hadn't thought he'd really get here this time, and she needed the wall behind her to keep her up.

"He said they killed my sister."

"They didn't. I checked my messages while I was heading back here. Your sister's fine, but they're flying straight to England. Without you."

"You were coming back to rescue me from the killer you accidentally dumped me with, and you took time to read your messages?" Blood was beginning to flow through her body again, hot and furious.

"I can do more than one thing at a time. Are you ready to let go of that wall or do you need me to carry you?"

She jerked her head up, then pushed away from the wall. "You put one hand on me and you're toast."

"Then start moving. Our plane leaves in less than an hour and a half."

"What plane? I'm not going anywhere with you."

"I'm going to Japan, and obviously you aren't safe left behind," he said wearily. "Let's go."

"You're going to get me a fake passport and a

ticket in that amount of time? And what happened to the urn?"

"The urn is already on the plane. The papers will be at the Oceana Air desk when we get there."

"That fast?"

"That fast. They'll probably be there before we are. Are you ready?"

She wasn't going to fall down, nor was she going to give him an excuse to touch her when that was probably the last thing he wanted to do. She stiffened her spine, lifting her head regally. "I've always wanted to see Japan," she said, stepping over the body at her feet.

"Don't count on it," he muttered. "I'm keeping you stashed at my uncle's while I dump the urn, and then you're heading straight back to L.A. No one will want you then."

Bad choice of words. "I don't think anyone wants me now," she said in a breezy tone. She glanced down at the body. "How many people have you killed since you met me?"

"He's not dead."

The relief that washed through her was irrational and undeniable. The man had been about to blow a hole through her skull—he deserved to die. But not at Taka's already bloody hands. "Good," she said. She pushed her hair back from her face, knowing she looked like hell, knowing she needed a bathroom, knowing none of that mattered to Takashi O'Brien. "Then let's go."

* * *

He'd stopped shaking. He couldn't remember ever shaking in his life, but in his rush to get to Summer, with the adrenaline spiking through his body, he'd been positively quaking by the time he saw them disappearing down the rampway. Quaking both with relief and fury.

It had been a close thing. If he'd been clumsy, or too fast, the man would have shot instinctively, and there would be two bodies lying on the ground in that deserted corridor. If Taka had been too slow it would have been too late, as well. As it was, he picked his moment perfectly, and the Brother had gone limp as the bullet nicked his spine.

He'd probably die, a fact that bothered Taka not one bit, but he'd lied to Summer, anyway. She'd had just about more than she could take, and another corpse might send her into hysterics, when he had to get her onto the plane as calmly and discreetly as possible.

So much for his idea of a shower and clean clothes. They were going to be stuck on a jet for thirteen hours smelling like smoke and chemicals, and there wasn't anything he could do about it.

For once Summer was silent and obedient, keeping up with his long strides as he headed for the Oceana Air terminal. He didn't even blink when Ella bumped into him, passing him the new papers before moving on, trundling her little suitcase behind her. Good thing Ella liked to fly; her current cover as a flight attendant was extremely useful.

"This way," he said when Summer started to veer toward security. She followed him to the private elevator, and he pushed the button to close the doors before anyone could get on, then stopped it between floors, using one of the buttons programmed into his mobile unit. Very useful little gadget, and no one would notice the lift was out of commission for an hour, longer than he needed.

"What are you doing?" she demanded. She was as far away from him in the tiny elevator as possible, which wasn't far at all.

"Checking the papers," he said calmly.

"Where did you get them?"

"Trade secret."

He pulled out the pack of documents Ella had given him and opened it up. Two passports, one Japanese, one American.

He looked at his likeness in the Japanese one. Hitoshi Komoru, age thirty-two. Complete with business cards from the Santoru Corporation—someone's idea of a joke. Santoru's was owned by his grandfather, who considered him a mongrel stain on the family honor. Takashi wasn't amused.

He opened the American passport, trying not to show his dismay. They'd made it for Susan Elizabeth Komoru, his twenty-six-year-old wife, and in the photo Summer was smiling. He stared at it a moment, distracted. He hadn't seen her smile the entire time they'd been together. Not surprising—he hadn't given her much to smile about.

"What's wrong?"

He handed her the passport. She stared down at it. "How'd they get that picture?" she said finally.

"I never ask. Does it matter?"

She said nothing for a moment. "Who's Susan Komoru?"

"My wife."

She looked as if she'd been punched in the stomach. "You're married?"

An odd reaction for someone who hated him. "I mean you're posing as my wife. I'm Hitoshi Komoru, you're my American wife."

She just stared at him, as if all this was too much too assimilate. He turned his attention back to the papers as he stuffed them back in the envelope, so she wouldn't see his eyes. Not that she'd be able to read them—she seemed completely clueless as far as he was concerned.

He wanted to cross the tiny elevator and pull her into his arms, press her head against his shoulder and tell her it would be all right. He wanted to comfort her, when she was trying so hard to pretend that she didn't need comfort.

He never should have kissed her on the island. It had thrown him off his game, when his resolve had already been wavering. He could have gotten the information out of her in other, more unpleasant ways, and while he might be inconvenienced by guilt, it would be nothing worse than the guilt he was already feeling.

Particularly when it had turned out that he wasn't pretending at all.

He switched the elevator on again, and it began to move upward with a little jerk. Getting her on the plane would be simple, and once they were in the air he could finally relax. For twelve hours he wouldn't have to think about who he was or what he was doing. For twelve hours she'd be completely safe. For twelve hours he could sleep.

First class on Oceana Air was about as good as it got. Free-flowing booze, seats that turned into beds, in-flight massage therapists. He got Summer planted in her seat, a glass of Scotch in her hand, and stood over her until she drank it all and accepted a second, grimacing as she did. He didn't want to drug her with an audience around them, even though the flight attendants were the epitome of discretion.

Besides, he'd miscalculated the last time, when they'd flown to Bainbridge, leaving him stuck with her in his arms for long hours until she came to. Long hours as the plane rocked on the water and he held her close. Hours to think, when that was always a danger. He didn't want to take that risk again. When they landed at Narita they needed to be ready to move. The Shirosama had more followers in Japan than anywhere else, and they'd all be looking for them.

No, he just wanted her calm and docile for the flight across the Pacific. And maybe he could let himself sleep, as well.

She was trying to stay calm, but even with the whiskey in her belly he could see that her fear of flying was kicking in.

It made no sense—she'd faced death countless times in the last few days, and flying in a well-maintained jet in calm weather should have been the least of her worries.

But he'd already figured out that Summer Hawthorne wasn't the most logical creature. She'd watched her world shatter around her, he'd invaded her soul and her body, and he'd seen the look in her eyes as he'd walked away from her.

Crazy woman.

She was getting confused as to who were the good guys and who were the bad guys. No wonder. Sometimes he wasn't sure there was any difference at all. He might be keeping her alive, but apart from that he was the worst thing that had ever happened to her. And the only thing he could do was move straight ahead with the mission with single-minded purpose, bringing it to a safe conclusion. He'd do his best to make sure she survived along the way—he'd reluctantly accepted that much.

He strapped in beside her, trying to ignore her, trying to shut her out of his mind. He glanced over at her as they began taxiing down the runway, and found her eyes shut, her face pale, her hands were clenched tightly in her lap as she endured her fear. She was good at that. No matter what he or life threw at her, she endured.

Taka reached over and put his hand on hers as the plane began to climb. She didn't look his way, didn't open her eyes, but her hand turned beneath his and caught his fingers, entwining them with hers. Until they were high in the sky over the Pacific and she fell asleep and her hand loosened in his.

And still he held it. Until he, too, fell asleep, for the first time in seventy-two hours.

The darkness was like a velvet shroud, pressing down around her. Summer woke with a start, blinking to try and orient herself. She felt strange, disconnected, floating, and then she realized to her horror that she literally was floating. She *was* trapped in a jet plane somewhere over the Pacific Ocean.

She couldn't breathe. A demon was sitting on her chest, pressing the air out of her lungs, and there were shadows all around. She could barely make out shapes in the dim light. Even the perky flight attendants seemed to have disappeared, and all around her people were sleeping like corpses, including Taka. And she still couldn't breathe.

Summer unfastened her seat belt, trying to be silent, but her hands were shaking so hard she rattled the buckle anyway. Taka stirred beside her, stretched out in his reclining chair, but then slept on as she scrambled from her own skyborne prison.

There was a bathroom directly behind their seats, unoccupied, and she fled toward it, trying to catch her breath. She shoved the door closed and held on to the sink, staring at the crazy woman in the mirror, the one who couldn't breathe.

No, she had to be breathing—she could hear the sound of her tight, rapid gasps as she struggled. She splashed water on her face from the tiny sink, but it changed nothing. She could feel the walls closing in, and knew she was going to either pass out or start screaming, and didn't know what was worse. Or whether she'd have any say in the matter.

No screaming. Screaming would bring Taka, and would endanger both of them. She shoved her fist in her mouth, trying to silence her struggles for air, but that only made things worse. She could hear the tiny whimpers that were beginning to escape from her mouth.

Usually she could control her panic attacks. She'd spent a great deal of time and money working on curing her phobia, and she knew how to go to her peaceful place in her head, to breathe in the serenity around her. But her peaceful place had disappeared in an explosion hours ago.

She had no idea what time it was, and she was past caring. If she could just breathe she'd be all right, but her throat had closed up and the panic was clawing at her.

And someone was pushing at the door, trying to get in.

Her brain wasn't working any better than her lungs. "*Occupado,*" she said, using the first language she could come up with. She'd latched the door, hadn't she? She didn't want anyone seeing her like this—she was barely keeping it together, and in another moment she was going to start screaming…

She'd forgotten that locked doors were nothing to her companion. The bathroom was tiny, though compared to the usual cubicles in coach class it was practically palatial, and he pushed his way in, locking the door behind him and putting his hands on her.

"I can't…" she gasped, hiccupping. "I can't breathe…."

He pulled her into his arms, slapping his hand over her mouth, and she wanted to tell him that wasn't helping matters, but couldn't manage to do so. She could feel the scream of panic bubbling up in her throat. They were going to crash, and the two of them would be locked together in this tiny little space, incinerated, the fire eating her lungs and—

Without a word he picked her up and set her on the shallow edge of the sink, shocking her into silence. With one hand he yanked off her pants and underwear, and she heard the rasp of his zipper, and then he was inside her, pushing against her so hard that her back slammed up against the mirror.

He looked almost brutal in the dim light, and when he took his hand from her mouth, he kissed her, breathing into her. Moving, pushing deep inside her, and her response shocking, immediate.

Instinctively, she grasped the edge of the tiny sink to brace herself when he pulled her legs up around his hips. But then she let go, holding on to him instead, letting him fuck her, not caring, taking in deep, sweet gasps of air as her lungs opened and the hammering of her heart beat in time with the hammering of his cock.

He pulled almost all the way out, and she whimpered, reaching for his hips, trying to pull him back inside her, more, now. She needed the full thrust of him, needed the oblivion, needed not to think, just to feel him, throbbing, pushing, and her legs tightened around him.

"Don't scream," he said in her ear, a hot, hungry whisper. He said other things, words she didn't understand, but she only climbed higher. "Don't make a sound."

He lifted her off the sink, pulling her down onto him, and she felt her body explode, every muscle and cell expanding into fiery pleasure. She opened her mouth and made no sound at all as she came, just an endless, arching silence, until he followed, spilling inside her, and only then a faint whimper escaped from her throat.

He pulled out of her, setting her down on the tiny patch of flooring, and she trembled, feeling the dampness on her thighs. She didn't want to look at him, but if she turned away she'd have to see herself in the mirror, and that was even worse. She leaned against the bulkhead and closed her eyes, shivering.

She expected him to leave her. She heard the zip of his pants, and expected him to step away from her, leave her alone in the bathroom to pull herself to-

gether. Instead, his hands were very gentle as he
moved her out of the way, running water into the tiny
sink.

And then his hands were between her legs, and he
was washing her, and she was too shocked to do anything more than let him. He tossed the paper towels,
then took her discarded clothes from the floor and
put them on her, waiting patiently as she lifted one
foot, then the other. She was trembling, weak, totally
compliant, and when he finished he wet another
paper towel and washed her face with it, gently, like
a lover.

She stared up at him, her eyes numb in disbelief.
"We're landing in two more hours," he said. "Come
back to your seat and try to sleep."

She couldn't say a word. She wanted to scream at
him. Why had he done that? Why had she let him?
In truth, she hadn't been in any shape to stop him,
and now she could breathe again.

She just wasn't sure she wanted to.

Everyone was still asleep when he opened the
bathroom door, and though she had to hold on to the
wall to keep from falling, she made it back into her
own seat in one piece. And then she couldn't move.
She did nothing when he leaned over and fastened
her seat belt. Did nothing when he kissed her, a deep,
drugging, openmouthed kiss. "It was just a fuck,
Summer," he whispered. "To take your mind off
things."

She stared up into his dark, merciless eyes, and for

a moment she thought she saw something else in their black depths. Something human.

But that was impossible. And even more impossible, she closed her eyes and slept.

20

When Summer opened her eyes again the plane was already on the ground. She hadn't worn a watch in days, and she felt as if her brain was stuffed with cotton candy—sticky and impenetrable. Maybe the stress of the last few days had caught up with her; maybe it was just the worst case of jet lag known to man. Her eyes focused on Taka, who was holding her hand, looking calm and beautiful, despite the fact that he needed a shave. As if nothing had happened in the bathroom. Had she dreamed it?

She jerked her hand away, and he let it go easily enough, turning to look at her. "You're awake," he said, the faintest hint of a smile on his face. "You slept well, after all."

She didn't want to think about why. "What time is it?" Her voice was stiff.

"Does it matter? Local time is two in the afternoon. You slept almost ten hours altogether. You were having nightmares, so I held your hand until you calmed down."

Was he going to pretend they hadn't had sex? And why was he making excuses about holding her hand? Had she really just dreamed it? "Did you sleep?"

"Yes."

"Then maybe you'll be less likely to kill someone," she managed to mutter.

A faint shadow crossed his face. "Some people do speak English here," he murmured. "You need to watch what you say."

"They won't think I'm serious," she said. And then she looked at him. He was still and beautiful in the artificial light of the jet as it taxied toward the terminal, but there was an almost predatory air about him. Many people might think he was harmless. They would be wrong. She'd seen his face in the dim light of the tiny bathroom, seen the darkness in his eyes. She could still feel him between her legs, proof that she hadn't been dreaming. But if he wanted to pretend it never happened, that would make life easier for her, as well. She was adept at playing games—she was Lianne's daughter, after all.

"What next?" She changed the subject.

If he was surprised she was just letting it go, he didn't show it. "Next we go through customs and you keep your mouth shut, nice obedient wife that you are. Then we'll pick up our luggage—"

"What luggage?" she interrupted. "You mean the—?" She stopped before the words came out, startled by the blaze in his dark eyes. "Sorry," she muttered.

"Maybe I'd just better talk and you listen," he said. "It's safer that way. We'll pick up the luggage, which includes your suitcase, mine and my golf clubs, which will be packed very carefully because they're extremely valuable. From there we'll go to the Oceana Air first class lounge and shower and change before my cousin Reno arrives to take us into Tokyo. Understood?"

"Yes," she said with unexpected meekness. "I'll behave myself."

His faint snort was oddly elegant. "Just do what I tell you, keep your face down and your mouth shut, and we'll be fine."

She could hear the liquid flow of Japanese around her, and she felt a sudden wave of such intense, nostalgic longing that she felt a burning in her eyes. Hana used to speak to her Japanese, sing her songs, comfort her when she'd hurt herself. Such an odd language, able to sound so harsh and angry and so soft and lyrical. Words were coming back to her, words she'd forgotten she knew.

"*Hai*," she said. "*Wakarimasu*. I understand."

He stared at her in complete horror. "You speak Japanese?"

She shook her head. "No. Only a little from when Hana lived with us."

"And you just decided to tell me that now?"

"I'd forgotten."

"Forget again."

"Wouldn't your wife know some Japanese?" she countered. "I would think—"

"Don't think, don't talk. You're my American wife, we live in Seattle and this is your first trip to Japan. You know nothing of the language except for a few kinky things I've said to you when we have sex."

She could feel the color flood her face. She wanted to hit him, but presumably American wives didn't hit their Japanese husbands, any more than they talked or thought. "Yes, dear," she said in her snottiest voice.

He ignored her sarcasm, unfastening his seat belt, reaching over to unfasten hers when she didn't move. She batted at his hands and unclasped the buckle herself, pushing out of her seat. For a moment she felt dizzy, disoriented. But then, that had become the norm for her. She was half a world away from everything she'd ever known, and whatever lay back there was in ruins. At least her sister was safe. Summer needed to hold on to that fact, like some kind of beacon.

The flight attendants were hovering, and for the first time she could see how they fluttered around Taka. Did Japanese wives get jealous? Was flirting expected?

Apparently not. Taka turned to her, sliding his arm around her waist, and it felt strong and warm, so wonderful that for a moment she forgot the other time he'd held her with his arm around her waist, touched her, and she just wanted to lean her head against him. "Come along, darling," he said in a voice pitched just loud enough for those around him to hear. "Time to meet your new family."

She looked up at him, startled. There was a brief, bitter look in his eyes that was quickly masked. "They'll love you just as I do," he added with only slightly exaggerated fondness.

Which meant she was toast. "I'm looking forward to it," she replied sweetly. "Taka-chan," she added, using the affectionate term.

The flight attendants made soft, approving noises, as Taka glared at her. He leaned down and whispered in her ear in Japanese, something people close to them could hear. The giggles were louder now as he pulled away, and Summer smiled fondly up at him, wishing she was wearing high heels that she could tromp on his instep. She had no idea what he'd said, but whatever it was was clearly smutty.

"Let's go, *darling,*" she said through gritted teeth. And she let him lead her off the plane, into a new world that was hardly more foreign than the life she'd been living for the last few days.

He was waiting for her in the first class lounge when she finally emerged from the changing room, and he didn't look up. It gave her a moment to watch him, unobserved. He looked different. He'd showered and shaved, and his long hair was tied neatly in the back. He was wearing a dark suit, possibly the best looking suit she'd ever seen. He appeared remote and elegant, as if in entering his native country he'd absorbed it, becoming more of a stranger than ever.

The hard-shell golf case was beside him, the treasures of the Hayashi family safe inside such a mundane container, and he was reading a Japanese newspaper, looking like any normal man waiting patiently for his wife. If you didn't look into his dark, merciless eyes.

He folded the newspaper and looked up. Of course he'd known she'd been watching him—he was aware of everything. But that didn't mean she didn't have some surprises in store for him. If she hadn't been looking for it she might not have noticed his reaction, but it was as strong as she'd expected it to be.

Her Italian leather high heels were silent on the thick carpet. For a moment she hadn't been sure whether she should put them on, but the attendants were wearing their shoes, and she assumed that the first class lounge was essentially international territory. And besides, they made her legs look terrific in the stockings that could be nothing less than silk.

Stockings, and lacy underwear that made Victoria's Secret look like Wal-Mart. All fitting perfectly beneath the trim Anna Sui red wool dress. There was even Chanel makeup and perfume in the suitcase provided. Instead of her usual braid, she'd tucked her hair up in a discreet, elegant chignon. She looked as foreign and as beautiful as this unknown country, from the diamond studs in her ears to the diamond ring he'd shoved on her hand just before they'd reached customs. She was Susan Elizabeth Komoru, about to meet her Japanese in-laws for the first time. It was no wonder she was nervous.

He rose, and for once he didn't tower over her. The three-inch heels brought her closer to her baby sister's height, though still a bit shorter than Taka.

The shower had revived her, brought her brain back to life, and with it all her doubts and emotions. She shoved them to the recesses of her mind—she had to deal with this one minute at a time, and the startled look in his eyes, quickly masked, was reward enough.

He stood, staring at her for a long moment. "What?" she demanded in a low voice. "You didn't think I could clean up well?"

He put his hand on the side of her neck, and she didn't jerk away, couldn't. He pressed his beautiful mouth against hers, briefly, and she could feel her body rise to his touch, her lips clinging for a moment.

And then he released her. "My family will love you," he said, the image of sincerity. "Particularly my mother. She's waited so long to be a grandmother." He put his long-fingered hand on Summer's flat stomach, and she jumped, nervous. Aroused.

She didn't know whether he was trying to rattle her or simply lure her into playing the part completely. She didn't like it, though she wasn't quite sure why. Maybe because the reality of it would have been so piercingly sweet.

She gathered the only defense she had left. "I hope so, Taka-chan," she said.

There was an odd gentleness in his smile. "You're far too easy to love, Su-chan." His affectionate name for her was a worthy comeback. Harder to bear, because he made it sound so believable. He stepped back, breaking their contact. "My cousin should be here by now," he added. "If you're ready?"

He couldn't hold on to her, the hard-shell golf case and his own suitcase. She could run when they reached the main part of the terminal, and he'd have to choose between the Hayashi treasure or her.

But she'd accepted the fact that she wasn't going to run. She was trapped in a foreign land with a man who killed, but he was still her best chance at staying alive. Besides, where would she go? She had the fake passport, credit cards and a wad of paper money in the Coach handbag that was part of what she could only think of as a disguise. She had a minimal knowledge of the language, and even in the U.S., where she had all her resources, she had been helpless when she came up against Takashi and the Shirosama.

Here, in their own country, it would be even worse. She had no choice but to play out this hand. It didn't help that she could still feel Taka's soft lips against hers.

"I should warn you about my cousin," he said just before they headed out into the winter afternoon.

"Is he anything like you?"

"Reno is like no one else on this earth. He doesn't care much for Americans."

"That hardly makes him unique. We're not terribly popular, and for good reason."

"His are a bit more…personal. Just don't let him get to you, and I'll make him behave."

Not the words to instill confidence, she thought, stepping through the automatic doors and taking her first breath of fresh air in God knows how long. She could smell the sea. She stood for a moment, breathing it in, when Taka spoke.

"There he is."

She turned, and the first thing she saw was the white limo—just like the ones used by the Shirosama and his crew. Summer froze, ready to make a run for it, when she caught sight of the figure leaning against the side of the car.

Not one of the Shirosama's brethren. He was dressed entirely in black leather, sunglasses covering most of his face, and he had red hair. Bright crimson, a shade not found in nature, and as he pushed away from the car she could see the hair hanging down past his waist.

He pushed his sunglasses up in a gesture of supreme arrogance, taking in Summer from head to toe, and she could see the tattoos around his eyes. Teardrops, but they were red. Like tears of blood.

He obviously wasn't impressed with what he saw. He dropped the sunglasses, turned to Taka and embraced him, still looking at Summer as if she were an unpleasant annoyance.

"How's Uncle?" Taka asked in English.

Reno shrugged, answering him in Japanese, and leaned over to pick up the golf case. Taka stopped him. "I'll keep this with me. You can give my wife a hand with her suitcase."

Reno's mouth curved in a smirk, and he muttered something no doubt highly unflattering. Taka compounded it by laughing, and Summer started thinking she might prefer the Shirosama, after all. Then Taka turned to her.

"Su-chan, this is my disreputable cousin Reno, grandson of my great-uncle Hiro. Reno has no manners, but I'm sure he welcomes you to the family."

She assumed Reno didn't speak English, but he made a universally derisive sound. He picked up her suitcase and strolled around to the back of the limo. The trunk popped open, seemingly of its own accord, and Summer glanced around for the übermobile phone that seemed to serve as a remote control for the world. It was nowhere in sight, and then she realized someone was sitting in driver's seat of the limo, barely visible behind the smoked windows. A chauffeur who stayed in the car and didn't help with luggage was peculiar indeed, and visions of the Shirosama began intruding once more. She glanced at Taka. If he was going to turn her over to His Sliminess he would have done so in the U.S. He wouldn't have brought her all this way to do it.

Besides, there was no way the brethren would include an exotic creature like the disapproving Reno.

The interior of the limo was huge, and Summer climbed in, trying to deal with the short dress and the high heels as she scrambled to the far corner. She didn't even see the man sitting across from her until Taka, following her inside, greeted him, knuckles together, bowing low as he sat on the leather bench seat beside her.

"Uncle," he murmured.

"Welcome home, Great-nephew," the man said. Dressed with the same impeccable care as Taka, he was very old, with wrinkles creasing his face, and almost bald. His perfectly manicured hands were missing two fingers.

Yakuza. A Japanese godfather, for all his benevolent smile. He gave Reno a fondly disapproving look when he climbed in and closed the limo door, and Summer took a surreptitious look at his fingers. Black fingernail polish, but all his digits intact. Which, according to Taka, just meant he hadn't screwed up yet.

She would have thought his appearance alone would be worth a thumb at least—he was a far cry from the Yakuza dress code, if Taka and his great-uncle were any indication. But that was not her concern.

"And you must be Dr. Hawthorne," the old man said pleasantly. "Welcome to our country. I hope my nephew hasn't been giving you too much trouble."

Summer cast a nervous glance at Taka. Trouble was the least of it. "He's been very kind," she said, automatically polite.

She felt Taka start beside her. "I've kept her alive, Uncle. Apart from that, kindness hasn't been foremost on my mind."

Reno leaned back against the side bench of the limo, and even behind the sunglasses, she could imagine the contempt in his eyes. He said something to his grandfather, clearly disparaging, but the old man replied in English. "It's rude to speak Japanese in front of a visitor, Grandson. We will speak English."

Apparently the old man even managed to cow Reno. He said nothing, crossing his arms across his chest in silent disdain.

"Taka-san, we have a problem," the old man said. "I hesitate to discuss business in front of your friend, but I'm afraid I cannot take you back to my house. People are watching."

She could feel the sudden tension in Taka's body. He was sitting closer to her than he needed to—the interior of the limo was huge, with his uncle at the far end, Reno lounging on the side, and the entire back seat for the two of them. But he was next to her, not actually touching, yet close enough so that she could feel his body heat, feel his reactions. Feel a certain irrational comfort from him, her one ally.

"Our contact in the Japanese government has informed me that they've decided not to have anything to do with the entire Hayashi affair. Things are too volatile with the new religions, and there's been a lot of criticism about recent crackdowns. They've decided that the threat is exaggerated, and that the followers of the Shirosama are just harmless fanatics."

"And how many people will have to die on the Tokyo subways this time for them to change their minds, Uncle?"

The old man shook his head. "They and I both know that no one will die. You and the people you work for will see to it, and our government need never get involved. For that matter, the Japanese people will never know how close they came to a major disaster."

"Not just the Japanese people this time, Uncle. The Shirosama is planning attacks on all the major transportations systems in world."

"Then your friends will have to stop him, won't they? I know they can—I am one of the few people who know how close we came to disaster last year with Van Dorn. You were able to foil his plans, so you can the Shirosama's, as well."

"You give me too much credit, Uncle. I had nothing to do with stopping him."

"There is no shame in being tricked by an evil man, Nephew. I am only happy you survived."

What the hell was going on? Evil men, employers, saving the world? Beside her, Taka said nothing.

"Have you not explained to your friend? She seems confused."

"I've told her what she needs to know."

"I would suspect, Nephew, that she needs to know more. Particularly when I see how you look at her."

Taka gave another sudden start, but didn't turn. What did his uncle see when he looked at her? Murderous tendencies? Vast annoyance? Or something else?

"And she looks at you the same way," the old man added, and it was Summer's turn to jump. Definitely vast annoyance, then. And something else.

"You'll need to take the urn to the site itself," he continued, as if he hadn't veered into private territory. "The government refuses to accept responsibility for it, and our people can't get involved."

"I don't know where the site of the temple is, Uncle."

The old man's lizardlike eyes moved to Summer. "She will tell you."

Summer frowned. "Me? I don't know where the site is, either. Trust me, if I did I would have told him long ago."

"Nevertheless, you will be the one to tell him. I feel this."

Taka turned to gaze at her, enigmatic as always. "My honored uncle has been known to see things that others don't. If he says it will be that way, it will."

"But I don't know where it is!" she cried in frustration. "Why won't you believe me? What are you going to do—try to torture it out of me?"

"There's no need," Taka said. "You will tell me, as you did before."

She could feel the heat rush through her body. If his uncle did indeed "see" things, then he'd know exactly what Taka was referring to. How could anyone not? She turned her face away, staring at the Tokyo suburbs as they sped by.

"She isn't lying to you, Taka-san," the old man said gently.

"I know that," Taka said.

Small comfort, Summer thought bitterly.

"I'll drop you both by your apartment. Reno will take the golf case and repack the treasures, and you can make arrangements to pick them up."

Summer expected Taka to protest, but he merely nodded. Everyone fell silent, and it wasn't until the car stopped that the old man spoke once more.

"I hope we meet again, Dr. Hawthorne, next time under more auspicious circumstances. I am certain we will."

Instinctively, Summer bowed her head, ignoring Reno's laugh. His grandfather's sharp reprimand stopped him, and she could just imagine the glare from behind those mirrored sunglasses.

Taka slid out of the car, holding a hand for her, and a moment later they were standing on a busy Tokyo sidewalk as the car slid away.

"They took the suitcases," she said after a moment.

"We don't need them." He was still distracted.

"Do you trust your cousin with the…golf clubs?"

This caught his attention. He looked at her, his dark eyes intense. "I trust him with my life."

"Then why did you warn me about him?" she countered.

"I don't trust him with yours."

For a moment she froze, as people moved all around her, everyone politely ignoring the stranger in a strange land. "Does it matter?"

Taka said nothing. It was very cold, as if there was snow in the air. Summer had never thought of Japan as a cold place, but in mid-January it was freezing, and they hadn't included a coat as part of her disguise.

She looked up into Taka's deep, dark eyes, and for a moment she felt oddly light-headed. She could drown in his eyes, she thought. Just fall into them, slide up against his body and…

His hands caught her arms, steadying her. "Come on," he said.

"We're going to your apartment?" Good. She was feeling almost drunk. If she got him alone she was going to wrap herself around him until she got warm, was going to—

"No. It's not safe. I'm taking you to get something to eat."

"Eat?" she echoed, trying to banish her odd, inappropriately erotic thoughts.

"I don't remember when I last fed you. You'll feel better when you get something to eat, and then we need to find somewhere safe to spend the night."

"I feel fine," she said dreamily. So she was hungry. Maybe so hungry she couldn't stand properly. And he was just so damn beautiful, and right now, for a short while, she was beautiful, too, and she could float against him, feel his arm around her waist, his breath on her cheek, as he steered her down the street. Right now she was going to do anything she wanted, since she had an excuse.

And then she'd behave herself, because despite what his nameless uncle had said, there was nothing in the way Taka looked at her that meant anything at all.

The old man had been far too right about her. She looked at Taka and felt rage, frustration, fear and a weird kind of gratitude. And something else, something overpowering, which she flatly refused to put a name to. Lust, maybe. Insanity. It didn't matter. She'd eat, she'd feel better and they'd move on.

In the meantime she could feel his heart beat through the exquisite suit as he led her down the street. She let go of all the tension of the last few days, and curved her lips in a smile.

21

His holiness the blessed Shirosama was in a state of rare excitation. Other people might call it rage, but such karmic emotions were long gone from his cleansed soul. He felt no lust when he trained the young renunciants who joined the Fellowship, he felt no vengeance when those who were out to harm him were sent to their next stage. He felt no anger when his plans were contravened, or when a stranger infiltrated the very heart of his religion in the western world and snatched an important convert from under the eyes of his most diligent followers. That those directly responsible for that monumental blunder had moved on to the joy of their karmic destiny gave him no satisfaction. Harm was done, and the Lunar New Year, his ancestor's preordained time of ascension, was fast approaching. If he couldn't find the Hayashi Urn he would simply have to figure something else out.

Brother Sammo had been too precipitate in

smashing the fake when they'd broken into the museum, but then, that particular disciple hadn't yet risen above his emotions, which had been running high after he'd eliminated the two guards. The forgery had been good enough to fool the Shirosama himself at the museum reception, it could fool everyone else. After all, he had kept the bones and ashes of his ancestor safe—was the original urn all that important? Could he not ascend just as well with a reasonable facsimile?

It would work, as it was meant to happen, except for two annoying people: Takashi O'Brien and his aunt's surrogate daughter, who had the urn.

If he could get his hands on her, the girl could lead the Shirosama to the ruins of the ancient temple, the site of his ascension. As soon as he found out where it was, his followers were poised to transport his stockpile of biological and chemical weapons to the ruins, the perfect place to unleash them on the world and bring about the destruction that would generate new life.

O'Brien had too many friends, however—the shadow organization he worked for, the Yakuza, the Japanese government. Alone, none was any match for the Shirosama's vision and the devotion of his followers. Combined, they could prove to be a problem.

Takashi had taken her to Japan, not a good sign, but they were in Tokyo, so for now things were safe. Two more days to the Lunar New Year and all would reveal itself as it was meant to be.

And Takashi O'Brien and his American whore would no longer pose a threat.

Takashi sat and watched as the exquisite stranger opposite him tucked into her oyakudon with a deftness that was both unexpected and unnerving. He'd steered her toward a little street corner restaurant, planning on giving her a simplistic explanation of the vending machine, but Summer had gone straight for the chicken and egg dish and the miso soup. It should have come as no surprise—with Hana Hayashi as her nanny, miso soup would be as common as chicken soup, and oyakudon was the Japanese equivalent of comfort food. Still, it made him uneasy, particularly when she thanked the cook with just the right intonation of *"arigato gozaimasu."* The cook had beamed at her, and Taka had glowered at him.

Her color was better. For a moment there on the street he'd been afraid she was going to pass out, not a good way to avoid unwanted attention. They had two days until the Lunar New Year, and the Shirosama's noose was drawing tighter. Taka didn't have time to spend scooping her up off the sidewalk or explaining to helpful policemen what was wrong with his American wife.

He shouldn't have brought her to Japan—he knew that now. He could have found someplace safe to stash her if he'd just tried a little harder. He was making mistakes right and left, a dangerous thing for someone in his position. At any other time he never would have trusted the man he thought was Crosby—all his instincts would have been alerted.

But Summer Hawthorne had managed to block his radar, and he'd abandoned her without the necessary precautions. And she'd almost died because of it.

He'd been so damn crazy with fear that he hadn't stopped to consider other choices; he'd just dragged her onto the plane with him, figuring he'd find somewhere to stash her once he got home.

Wrong. His uncle's place was out, his own apartment was far too dangerous to go near, and there were members of the Fellowship working at all the major hotels.

Takashi had known the moment she'd bolted out of her seat on the plane in the middle of the night that his reasons for bringing her had nothing to do with necessity and more to do with choice. He had known that when he got up and followed her into the first class lavatory, shutting the door behind them.

He knew when he fucked her into compliance—telling himself it was to calm her, screw her into oblivion—that it was his own oblivion he craved.

He had two choices—a ryokan or Reno's place. Reno's was probably the best choice, though the hostility was coming off his little cousin in waves. It wasn't Taka's place to tell Summer why Reno hated Americans—she could just assume it was casual racism. A ryokan was probably a bad idea; the traditional inns were one of the last remnants of the old

Japan that the Shirosama was so eager to bring back and he'd likely have moles strategically placed.

Taka was going to have to wait a little longer for his bath. In the meantime Reno's place would have to do. And he was going to have to ignore the fact that it was the height of Tokyo luxury—two very tiny rooms crammed with things, including Reno's beloved Harley.

"You ready?"

Summer was chasing the last grain of rice with her chopsticks, and doing it with surprising deftness. She probably knew how to pour sake and arrange ikebana, he thought sourly.

The food had made her feistier. Her deep blue eyes were flinty as she looked at him across the table. She hadn't forgotten what had happened in the bathroom—even if she wished she could. "Where are we going?"

"To Reno's. Safest place I can think of," he said in a low voice.

"That's not saying much. He doesn't like me."

He shrugged. "I told you, he doesn't like Americans. He'll put us up. His place his small, though. We'll share a futon."

Her face froze. "No, we won't."

Taka leaned across the table. "Just because you joined the mile high club doesn't mean I can't keep my hands off you. I'm not going to fuck you with my cousin five feet away." His voice was little more than a whisper, and the color in her face flamed.

"You're not going to fuck me at all," she snapped. "Ever again. I'll kill you if you try."

He laughed softly, even though he knew it would outrage her. She was stronger when she was mad, and he needed her strong. "I'm a hard man to kill," he said. "And, by the way, I didn't hear you saying no on the plane."

It was a good thing she had chopsticks instead of a fork—she probably would have stabbed his hand. As it was she withdrew into herself, the dignified Dr. Hawthorne, her silence making her disdain clear.

"Good," he said, clearing the dishes. "Next time, if you don't want it, say no."

Her face was perfectly composed when they stepped out onto the crowded streets. It was getting dark already, and he'd put his hand on her arm, to steer her out of the way of a salaryman on an early drunk when she stumbled against him and her spiked heel dug into his instep.

He jumped, cursing at the unexpected pain, only to meet her smug smile. *"Sumimasen,"* she said with exaggerated sweetness. "I can be so clumsy."

He stared at her in shock. No one had managed to catch him off guard, inflict pain on him, in a long, long time. More proof that he needed to get the hell away from Summer Hawthorne. She made him dangerously vulnerable, and he couldn't afford that, for her sake as well as his own.

She wouldn't be used to the high heels or the time difference, so he walked her the long way to Reno's place, crossing and recrossing the pedestrian bridges that stretched over the busy streets. He was waiting for her to complain, but she didn't, not even when they passed Tokyo Tower for the second time. His cousin lived in the Roppongi district, among the high-rise hotels and the strip clubs, the better to oversee his grandfather's many and varied financial interests. Even now he was probably out prowling in some pachinko parlor, but it didn't matter if he wasn't home; Reno didn't need to lock his doors. No one would be fool enough to mess with the Oyabun's grandson.

She made it up the three flights of stairs without complaint—she'd probably cut out her tongue before she'd admit weakness. Taka pushed open the door, waiting for her to precede him, watching as she automatically slipped off her shoes before stepping inside. She was really beginning to piss him off. He didn't want her to be comfortable in his world. He wanted her to be an interloper, a gaijin, and he wanted her gone.

The golf case was there, open and empty, leaning up against one corner in the crammed apartment. Reno had draped the heavy antique kimono across the table with consummate care, and he'd pulled out the spare futon, leaving the rest of the treasure, including the urn and the cheap modern kimono, on top. He must have known they'd be coming, which was both annoying and reassuring.

Summer's outrage was enough to get her talking

again. "He just left it here? After all we've been through, he just put the urn on the mattress and walked away without locking the doors?"

"No one would dare come in."

"The Shirosama and his zombies would dare anything."

"Yes, but they don't know we're here. Yet."

"Yet," she echoed. She sank down on the mattress next to the urn, staring at it, and he could see the exhaustion in her face. Yet he wanted nothing more than to kick the priceless treasure out of the way and cover her body with his. Strip off the expensive clothes that made her look like a beautiful stranger, strip everything away from her.

Yeah, and have Reno walk in on them while he was doing it? Not likely.

Nor could Taka stay here with her, watching her temptingly yawn and stretch like a sleepy kitten. "I'm going to find Reno," he said abruptly. "We need to figure out what we're going to do next. Why don't you change out of those clothes and try to get some sleep? I don't know when we'll be back, or where we're going when we do."

"Change into what? I don't think Reno's clothes would suit me and there wasn't much besides underwear in the suitcase someone packed for me. The Japanese end of your little organization wasn't nearly as efficient as the one in California."

He nodded toward the old kimono on the bed beside her, the one in which Taka had wrapped the urn.

"Wear that. At least it's yours. Or hell, put the antique kimono on—I don't give a damn."

"It doesn't fit me. I tried when I was younger. It's made for a midget."

"Japanese women tend to be very small."

"And I'm not," she said.

He shouldn't have let her see his amusement. She was so sensitive about her body, her soft, erotic curves. She didn't believe the affect she had on him, and he was just as glad she didn't. He was already having enough trouble around her. The moment they found the site of the old temple and the Shirosama was stopped, Taka was sending her straight to London, to Isobel Lambert's tender mercies and the troublesome baby sister.

Then he could concentrate on doing what his grandfather wanted. This was first and only time the old man had ever asked anything of his despised grandchild. He'd provided the perfect Japanese bride; it was up to Taka to fulfill the bargain.

"I'll lock the door. Don't let anyone in."

"You really think I'm stupid, don't you?"

No, he thought she was too smart, except when it came to him and his sudden weakness for soft American women. One woman in particular, who was making him crazy and stupid.

He didn't answer. "The bathroom's behind you. Don't let the toilet scare you."

"Reno's got a scary toilet?"

"Reno's got the most pimped-out toilet known to

man. You're not used to Japanese ingenuity in the bathroom."

"I wouldn't say that," she muttered under her breath. The silence that stretched between them was deafening. And then he was gone, locking the door behind him, taking the stairs two at a time. Fast. So he wouldn't be tempted to go back.

"Bastard," Summer said out loud, liking the sound of it. "Pimping rat pig bastard." Somehow it didn't have quite the lilt she would have liked, but she'd work on it. She was alone, completely alone, for the first time that she could remember. For the first time since she'd run away from the hotel in Little Tokyo, straight into the Shirosama's arms.

She wasn't going to run again, even though she was tempted. She'd just say no. Over and over again. "No," she said out loud, savoring the word. It certainly sounded believable. She thought of Taka's hands on her, his beautiful mouth on her skin. "No," she said again, but her voice sounded less convincing.

"Rat pig bastard," she muttered, scrambling to her feet to make her way to Reno's frightening bathroom. Taka was right—the toilet could do everything, probably make toast as well as sing an aria, but she used it anyway, stripping off her clothes and folding them neatly before pulling on the kimono Hanasan had made for her.

It was worthless, Hana-san had told her, but made

with love. She'd hand-painted the scene on the back in the traditional manner. The jagged peaks of the mountain to one side, the white crane flying low. Summer let soft silk settle around her skin, and she suddenly felt stronger, safer. This was who she was, not the frightened woman on the run, not the sophisticated creature who dazzled Taka. This was Summer, or what was left of her.

She took the pins out of her hair, shaking it loose over her shoulders and washed the makeup off. It was cold in the apartment, and she shivered as she wandered back into the main room, looking for some kind of blanket to wrap around herself.

The place was crammed with things, including a Harley motorcycle taking up far too much room. There were books everywhere, manga, of course, and thicker, more scholarly looking ones, piled on every surface. Ancient swords hung on the wall, their value considerable, and Reno had an original Hokusai woodblock. Not to mention a stack of porn magazines.

She picked one up, staring at it. Bondage and butt-sex, from the looks of the cover. An improbably endowed Asian girl was tied up and being serviced by a bad-tempered looking man. Summer glanced through the pages, wondering if anything more pleasant was going to happen to the poor girl, when she suddenly realized she wasn't alone.

Reno was standing not two feet away from her. She hadn't heard him come in—he'd taken off his boots, of course, and he just stood looking at her with that thinly veiled hostility.

All of her Japanese disappeared. There were any number of ways to apologize—was *sumimasen* the "I'm sorry I spilled sake on the floor" or the "I'm sorry I killed your mother" one?

"Sorry," would have to do, as she held out the magazine to him.

He moved closer, taking it from her hand. He looked down at the picture, then at her for a long, considering moment. Then back at the picture, as if to judge her worthiness for such kinky activities. She felt a knot form in the pit of her stomach. Taka had warned her, and now he'd left her alone with his cousin.

He glanced back up at her, then shrugged, tossing the magazine back on the table before he headed into the corner of the room that served as a kitchen. The refrigerator was tiny, and he grabbed a bottle of beer and a glass before settling in a chair opposite her, watching her.

She could have done with a drink herself—he was making her nervous. She sat down on the futon, holding the kimono around her, and was rewarded with a derisive snort, as if he was asking why she should bother? *Baby rat pig bastard*, she thought.

"Taka?" His voice startled her. It was the first thing he'd addressed to her.

"He went looking for you."

His smile was slow and evil. He had to be in his

mid-twenties—younger than she was. Too young to be so scary. "I'm not going to touch you."

She jumped. "You speak English?"

"When I'm in the mood." He took off his sunglasses and set them on the table beside him, next to the porn. His eyes were extraordinary, the red tattooed teardrops accentuating them. And she realized with a shock that his eyes were a clear, brilliant green, an almost unearthly color.

"Contact lenses," he said, unnerving her even more.

"You read minds like your cousin?"

"You're…what's the word? Transparent. Why did Taka bring you here?"

"He thought we'd be safe here."

"No, I mean why did he bring you to Japan? His grandfather isn't going to be happy about it. Neither is his wife."

Why did Summer feel as if she'd been kicked in the stomach? Lying about being married was hardly the worst of his crimes.

"His wife has nothing to worry about."

Reno tilted his head sideways. "True enough, but I'm not sure she'll see it that way. My grandfather had a hard enough time arranging the marriage, and she'd probably use any excuse not to go through with it. Taka's got tainted blood."

"I thought you said she was his wife?"

"Sooner or later. As long as Taka does what his grandfather asks him to. And in the meantime you're in the way. So why don't you tell me where the temple ruins are and I'll get you on a plane back to your own country?"

"I told you, I have no idea where the temple is. Hana-san used to tell me stories about northern Honshu. Have you thought to look there?"

"That doesn't narrow it down very much. Maybe I can help you remember."

"You can't help me remember what I don't know," she said nervously. Where the hell was Taka? Why had he left her with this junior psycho?

Reno's smile was chilling. He had a stunning face—not as elegant as Taka's, but younger, more impish. Except that there was absolutely nothing playful about him.

"I'm very good at helping people remember what they think they never knew. Taka might have foolish scruples about inflicting pain, but I'm not so troubled by manners." Reno ran his eyes over her again. "I don't think it would take long at all. The problem is, I'm not as experienced as Taka, and I'd leave marks. I might even make a mistake, go too far, and then we'd have a problem."

"Getting rid of the body?" she countered, rallying.

He shook his head. "I have plenty of people to help me with that kind of work. No, the problem is that Taka wouldn't like it."

"You sound disappointed."

"I am. I don't like you. I don't like what you've done to my cousin, and I'd be very happy to hurt you because of it."

"I haven't done anything to your cousin!"

He poured the beer into the glass and held it toward her in a mocking toast. *"Kampei,"* he said. "And you've fucked him." He laughed. "Don't look so shocked. I don't mean literally. Of course he fucked you—you're pretty enough in a conventional American way, and Taka has a soft heart."

"A soft heart? Do you even know your cousin?"

"A softer heart than mine," he amended. "If he hadn't been squeamish he probably could have found out what he needed to know from you days ago."

"I don't know where the temple is."

Reno rose from the table, pushing the chair away. "Let me see if I can help you remember," he said, starting toward her.

"Get away from her!" Taka's sharp voice stopped him.

Reno turned, smiling innocently, answering in Japanese. Taka was standing in the doorway, and suddenly Reno looked like a naughty child compared to the chilling menace in his older cousin.

"You can speak English, since you already have," he snapped. "What do you think you're doing?"

"Trying to scare her into telling us what she knows. Time is running out, cousin, and you've tried everything else, haven't you?"

"She doesn't know."

"How can you be sure of that?"

"Sex can be as good a way of finding out information as torture, little cousin," Taka said briefly, kicking off his shoes and closing the door behind him.

"Hey!" Summer protested weakly.

"Then maybe we should both have a go at her, just to see if there's something she's forgotten. She's not my type, but I can put aside my standards…"

Taka hit him. The blow was so fast, so shocking that Reno had no time to duck. The rage in the room was palpable, and Summer dived to cover the urn, afraid the room was about to erupt into violence.

But Reno just stood there, blood dripping from his split lip. "Okay, cousin, she's yours," he said easily. "I've never known you to be so possessive before. You want some beer?"

Taka was breathing heavily, and for a moment Summer wondered whether he'd hit Reno again. And wondered why her reaction to the sudden violence had been so visceral. It had been primal, possessive. And incredibly erotic. And then his shoulders relaxed. "Yes. What about you, Su-chan?"

For a moment the entire room froze. Taka's use of the affectionate name had been instinctive, shocking all three of them. Reno went to the cupboard and brought out two more glasses. He sat down and poured the drinks, one for Taka, one for Summer, and set the bottle back down.

Summer rose from the futon, holding the kimono around as she walked to the table. Instead of taking the glass of beer Taka held out for her, she picked up the bottle instead, handing Reno his glass and then refilling it for him. He blinked those extraordinary fake green eyes, and then a faint smile curved his mouth. "*Kampei*," he said again, toasting her. And this time most of the mockery was gone.

She took her glass of beer and turned back to the futon, when Taka's sudden hiss of breath stopped her. "Holy motherfucker!" Reno said in a tone of wonder.

She whirled around, almost splashing some of the beer on her kimono. "What's wrong?"

Taka handed her glass to Reno, took her shoulders in his strong hands and turned her around again. "I'm an idiot," he said in a low voice. "It was the wrong kimono."

"What are you talking about?"

His hands were on her, impersonal, tracing the painting on the back of the garment. "It's been there all the time." His touch followed the curve of her hip, and she shivered. "That's White Crane Mountain." His hand cupped the side of her butt. "There's the torii that would lead to the temple, and there's even a white bird. Do you have a map?"

"Of course," Reno said, pushing away from the table.

"Take off the kimono, Summer," Taka said, grabbing at the shoulders to pull it from her.

She grabbed back. "I'm not wearing anything underneath it!" she protested.

"Americans," Reno muttered under his breath, stomping from the room. A moment later he was back, tossing a cotton *yukata* at her. "Put this on and I'll find your boyfriend a map."

She grabbed the blue-and-white cotton and started for the bathroom, but Taka's hands were still on her shoulders. "You can change here."

"I'm not—!" But he'd already slipped the kimono off her shoulders, and with a shriek she pulled Reno's over her nude body.

Reno laughed, saying something in Japanese, doubtless another insult, Summer thought as she tied the sash around her waist.

"I told you, hands off," Taka said in English.

Well, maybe it hadn't been that insulting, Summer thought, turning around. Reno had tossed the priceless antique kimono to the floor and Taka laid out Hana-san's present in its place. The familiar painting, one Summer had known most of her life, suddenly took on new meaning as Taka spread a map beside it.

"Grandfather was right," Reno said. "She did tell you where it was."

"And I was right. She didn't know," Taka retorted. "Look at this, Summer. The mountain Hana-san painted is right there—" he pointed at the map "—and the torii gate is lower down, just outside the town of Tonazumi. The ruins of the shrine must be somewhere between."

"Good thing it's not been that bad a winter. There can be snow in the mountains," Reno said.

"You think a little snow will stop someone like the Shirosama?"

"That crazy old coot? He's harmless."

"No," Summer said. "He's not."

Reno looked at her for a long, contemplative moment, then back at Taka. "I'm going out," he said abruptly. "I'll be back in the morning. We can work out the details then." He was already at the door, shoving his feet back into his boots, putting the sunglasses down over his extraordinary eyes. "You can use my bed," he added with a grin, and then he was gone, the door closing behind him.

22

"I'll use Reno's bed," Taka said absently, still staring at the kimono. "You can take the futon."

"Why? Is his bed as scary as his toilet?"

He turned to look at her. Her encounter with Reno didn't seem to have daunted her, but then, she wasn't easily daunted. He didn't like to see her wrapped in Reno's *yukata*. More of that irrational macho bullshit that was running through his veins recently. He still couldn't believe he'd hit his cousin, for suggesting something they'd actually done when they were younger. But that had just been sex with a willing young woman, and Taka understood sex very well. He just didn't understand what was going on between him and Summer Hawthorne.

He could blame his mysterious American father for it, he supposed. His Japanese side was much more pragmatic; sex was healthy, athletic, not to be confused with practicalities like marriage and business and the important things in life. He preferred his sex undiluted with emotions, feelings, and up until now he'd managed that very well.

His future wife would be perfect for that. She was exquisite, graceful, controlled and athletic in bed. They would have the perfect marriage, and his grandfather, if he couldn't accept Taka, might finally accept his children.

Unfortunately, his grandfather could go fuck himself, as Taka had politely suggested just an hour ago. The old man had connections, including his brother, Great-uncle Hiro, and once he knew Taka had returned to Japan, he'd tracked down his cell phone number, an impressive feat. A mistake, however. Taka had been too concerned with catching Reno before he came home to find Summer in his apartment, and demands about marriage contracts weren't on the top of his priority list. Or his grandfather's long-withheld approval, he'd realized. The wedding was off, and his reluctant bride would breathe a sigh of relief.

There was something liberating about finally letting go of the old man. Finally figuring out what it was Taka himself wanted. Summer was standing in the room, wearing Reno's *yukata*, and if she had a knife she'd probably stab him. His kind of woman.

"What are you smiling about?" she demanded.

"Nothing," he said. "Why don't you change? I wouldn't trust anything Reno wore next to his body."

"Eww…" she said. "What am I supposed to wear?"

He tossed the silk kimono at her. "It's told me everything I need to know. You can have it now." Taka had a flashing memory of her standing naked in the middle of the room when he'd snatched the kimono off her. He shouldn't have even noticed, should have been too busy looking at the missing clue. But he had noticed, and so had his cousin.

"Am I allowed to go into the bathroom this time?" She didn't wait for an answer, which was just as well. Taka would have told her no, and he had no good reason for it, other than their track record with bathrooms.

By the time she emerged again he'd found her a pillow and quilt for the futon. Reno's bed would have probably been more comfortable for her American bones, but his decor would be a little…off-putting.

She glanced down at the futon and the one pillow, and was probably thinking *Thank God*. She didn't look happy, but that was wishful thinking on his part. He had no excuse to touch her, no excuse to want her. He just did.

"I'll be in there." He jerked his head in the direction of Reno's tiny bedroom. "Call me if you need anything. I've got work to do."

"I won't."

No, she wouldn't. There were no doors between the rooms, but the futon was out of sight, at least. Reno's large American bed filled the room, and the walls held a peculiar melange of posters from gory movies, animated porn and classic woodblocks, and even one of the video game villain Reno had taken his name from. He had a blow-up doll in one corner that he tended to tie up in strange positions, to his own amusement, but Reno's strange tastes were probably a bit much for someone already suffering severe emotional overload.

Taka was going to get her out of here as fast as he could. There had to be some way to keep her safe until they trapped the Shirosama. Some way to get her away from him before he screwed things up any more.

He stripped off his clothes, climbing into the pristine bed. He'd been teasing Summer earlier; in fact, Reno was fastidiously clean. Taka just hadn't wanted her in his cousin's clothes.

He wanted her in Reno's bed, now, beneath him, but that was an impossibility. Things had gone too far. He could have verbally calmed and soothed her in the bathroom on the plane. Instead he'd acted on instinct, and those actions had silenced her, stopped her before her hysterics could alert the entire plane. Very noble of him. He wasn't going to make that move again. Unless he could come up with any lame excuse.

His mobile unit was beginning to run low on juice, despite its state-of-the-art battery, and he hadn't been able to recharge it on the airplane. He had just enough power to text Madame Lambert, but her reply was cut off midsentence, and he had no idea how much had gotten through. He could rummage around

the apartment, find any of a number of cell phones
Reno kept around, but Taka would have a hard time
getting access to the Committee's network, and his
attempts could be easily intercepted by anyone with
the proper skills. And the Shirosama had an army of
people with the proper skills.

Taka would simply have to hope for the best, and
assume that completing the mission was up to him,
and him alone.

The Shirosama was back in the country, following a little close on their heels for Taka's comfort.
He'd only glanced at the newspaper on his hunt for
Reno, but it appeared that his holiness was planning
a major celebration for the Lunar New Year, combined with a great announcement. Taka could just
imagine.

Now that he knew where they were going he had
a pretty good idea what would happen. In ancient
times, the Lunar New Year celebration had begun on
the second new moon after Winter Solstice and ended
fifteen days later, when the moon was full. Time
enough for Hayashi to send his cache of weapons to
the far corners of the earth with his faithful followers. Time enough for Armageddon.

Taka set the dead mobile unit on the table, lean-
ing back to stare at the poster on the wall. *Battle
Royale*—dead teenagers and a bloodbath. Just
Reno's style.

Taka turned off the light. There was enough neon
in the streets outside to fill the room with an un-

earthly glow through the slatted shutters, but he could make himself sleep in any situation, and his instincts told him a few hours rest was acceptable right now. Not actual sleep, but he could close his eyes.

And open them again, as he heard her move in the next room. She was restless and he knew why.

Summer had never done anything so insane in her entire, careful life. She had spent years avoiding pain, avoiding betrayal, avoiding everything that could rip her soul apart.

And she had been wise. At the age of twenty-one she'd chosen the safest, most gentle, least threatening lover, to prove to herself that there were no lingering shadows. She had three months of gentle lovemaking, all of it pleasant, all of it forgettable. And when Scott had left, knowing she could never love him, she'd had no interest in repeating the experience. It was enough to know that she could.

Instead, she'd filled her life with friends who wanted nothing from her and kept a watchful eye on her alarmingly bright little sister.

But Summer's careful life had been shattered, invaded, body and soul, by the mesmerizing man who lay asleep in the next room. The man who'd showed her what her body was capable of, when she'd been better off not knowing. The man who'd saved her, threatened her, destroyed what she loved and taken the rest. The man who thought of her as a mission and nothing more, who used sex as a weapon, who killed without remorse. The man who would send her away tomorrow and never think of her again.

If she let him. It was the fastest, surest way back to some semblance of her safe life. She would never work at the museum again. She couldn't leave L.A. as long as Jilly was there, but she could find something, anything else—some way to earn a living.

She could be a coward, and who would blame her? She'd faced death half a dozen times in the last few crazy days—surely she had the right to take the easy way out and just hide in her safe little world. She would know whether he'd managed to stop the Shirosama; either the world would descend into chaos or the cult would quietly disappear.

Takashi O'Brien might die and she'd never be told. He lived a dangerous life, and he had no regard for his own safety. He could die, and the only way she'd know would be from the hollow, aching wound inside her that never healed.

Maybe she'd lost her mind. Jet lag, lack of sleep, the stress of having people try to kill her had all combined to make her snap.

Except she didn't feel weak or lost, but stronger and more sure of herself than she ever had.

She rose from the mattress on the floor, knotting the belt of the silk gown around her waist. The final message, from Hana-san's hands. Would her beloved nanny have left it, and the urn, if she'd known the kind of trouble it would bring? The danger that would follow?

Summer knew the answer. Hana had protected her as a child and would have given her life for her. But she'd also made Summer the strong woman she was. Hana Hayashi had protected her heritage; she would have expected Summer to do the same, with no excuses.

What would she have thought of the man lying in that bed? Would she have approved? Approved of the crazy, inescapable fact that Summer had fallen stupidly in love with a man who could kill her? Or would Hana have given her a sharp pinch and told her to stop fussing? That was more like Hana-san— never one for sentiment when common sense would do. Never one for hiding from unfortunate truths.

And the unfortunate truth was that Summer had fallen in love with the wrong man. Not the tender, almost worshipful Scott, the man with the cruel hands and the mouth of an angel. And Summer couldn't run from that truth any longer. Hana-san had raised her better than that.

The apartment was dark, lit only by the neon that filtered through the shuttered windows, and she moved carefully, avoiding the piles of stuff that littered the place.

Striations of purple, red and yellow danced across the figure in the bed, courtesy of the bright neon signs outside. He lay on his back, unmoving, and for a moment she thought he was asleep. That she could just watch him for a moment and then slink back to her hard mattress on the floor.

Then she saw his eyes were open, watching her with utter stillness. And it wasn't going to be that easy.

"Come here," he said.

Maybe it was going to be easy, after all. She opened her mouth to say something, to argue, but he stopped her. "Come here," he said again, patiently. "You know what you want. All you have to do is say it."

And that was the one thing she couldn't do. She moved closer, because she couldn't resist, but the words seemed to jam in her throat.

He was naked in the bed; he had the sheet pulled up to his waist, but she knew he was wearing nothing underneath. If he would just reach out his hand, pull her onto the bed, cover her mouth with his, then she wouldn't have to say anything at all.

But he didn't move. His hair was loose around his elegant, beautiful face, his skin was like molten gold, and she realized she'd never touched him, never put her mouth on him. And she was afraid.

"You have to tell me," he said, his voice soft and enticing, so deep it reached into her body and pooled between her legs. "I can't give you what you want if you don't tell me."

She could turn and leave. Walk out of the room, away from him, and tomorrow someone would put her on a jet back to the U.S. It was the easy way, the safe way, and he wouldn't stop her.

"What do you want, Summer?" His eyes were dark, clear, steady in the flickering light.

"I want you."

He closed his eyes for a moment, in what almost seemed like relief. But he still wasn't done. "What do you want me to do to you? Do you want me to hold you while you sleep? Do you want me to make you come while you pretend I don't even exist? Do you want to get in my bed and let me show you things you haven't even dreamed of?"

"Yes. No…"

"Which is it? Be brave. Just tell me. I'll do what you want."

No, he wouldn't. He couldn't. He couldn't love her, give her the kind of crazy happy ever after she didn't even believe in.

But he could give her the night. An endless night, blind and forbidden. All she had to do was ask.

She held out her hand. It was trembling, and there was no way she could disguise the fact. "Maybe I'm not so brave, after all," she said in a shaky voice.

"Bravery is being afraid and then doing it anyway." He took her hand and his warmth flowed into her. "Tell me."

The bed was big and high. She climbed up onto it, letting the silk kimono settle around her as she knelt. He didn't move to make room, just watched her, waiting.

Pulling her hand free, she reached down and untied the sash of the robe, letting it fall open. Her hair was loose around her shoulders, and she was vulnerable, totally open to him.

"I want to put my mouth on you," she said, her voice little more than a whisper. "Everywhere. I want to touch you, learn your body, find out what you like, what you need. I want to make you as crazy with wanting as I am. I want you, everything you can give me, everything I can give you, and I want the night to last forever. Can you give me that?"

"Yes," he said. He reached up and pushed the robe from her shoulders so that she was naked. "As for what I want, what I need, it's very simple. It's you."

She wanted to cry, but she didn't. "Then let me learn you," she said. She put her hands on his chest and found his skin smooth, hot to the touch. She ran her fingers over his body, over his flat, dark nipples, the bone and muscle and sinew of him, and he tilted his head back, closing his eyes, letting her.

He had scars. Some of them barely healed, some of them old and faded. He was deceptively lean—she knew how strong he really was. But she didn't know what he tasted like.

She leaned down, her long hair brushing his face, and put her mouth against the side of his neck, letting her teeth rest against the fierce pulse that beat there. It was his life vibrating against her mouth, and she wanted more.

The base of his throat was soft, vulnerable, and she ran her tongue across it, then felt the shiver that ran through his body. She moved down, over the elegantly defined muscle, to one dark nipple, and without thinking she drew it in, sucking it.

He made a muffled sound, and the nub hardened against her tongue, but he didn't touch her. He lay back on the bed, arms at his sides, letting her discover him.

His skin was alive beneath her mouth. He had no hair on his chest, but was sleek, and so exquisitely beautiful she wondered what she was doing in bed with him. Because she was. In bed with him. By her own choice.

Summer nudged the sheet out of the way. A thin line of dark hair dusted his flat belly, arrowing down, and she tasted that, too, letting her tongue play with the silken curls.

His hands were clenched now, she realized with distant satisfaction. He was burning, he was hard, and she pulled the rest of the sheet off him.

He was bigger than she expected, and she felt a moment's doubt, one she ignored. She already knew the parts fit. Now was her time to experiment.

She touched him, her hand cool on his heated cock, and he seemed to grow harder, bigger beneath her delicate grasp. Such a pretty thing, she thought, wondering what she had ever been afraid of. It was for her, the blood pulsing through the thick shaft, the heat and size and power of him. It was for her, and she took it, her tongue tracing the marbled veins, dancing on his skin, touching, tasting, until she wanted more, and she closed her lips over the head of his cock, drawing it into her mouth.

His entire body arched off the bed, and she could feel the sheet beneath her being torn away in his fists.

She should have taken pity on him, but this was too wonderful, the fierce power of having him a slave to her hungry mouth. She wanted more. She could taste the sweetness against her tongue, and she tried to take more of him into her mouth, needing everything he was willing to give her.

And then he let go of the bed, his hands cradling her head, his fingers threading through her hair, and a spasm of delight hit her, strong enough to startle her.

Before she realized what he was doing he'd pulled her away, flipping her over so that she was on her back, a frenzied protest on her lips, a protest he silenced with his mouth, his tongue where his cock had been, and she took the substitute with heady delight.

He was leaning over her, breathing deeply, his eyes hooded. "You're a fast learner, but you're not quite ready for that."

"Yes, I am," she said, trying to push him back. "I want to. I want…"

"What do you want, Su-chan?" Now it was his turn to touch her, taste her. Another small climax shook her body when he closed his mouth over her nipple, and with each deep, sucking pull of his lips the fluttering contractions grew stronger.

"I want you," she said. "I want you inside me. I want to feel you…"

"Say it. You want to feel me come inside you again. That's what you want, isn't it? You want my cock?"

"Yes," she gasped.

He smiled down at her. "Good girl," he said. "But not yet."

Her cry of protest was swallowed in a great gasp of breath as he slid down her body, pushed her trembling legs apart and put his mouth against her.

She lifted her hands to try to shove him away, then dropped them onto the torn-up sheet, arching her body, lifting her hips so he could use his wicked, wicked tongue on her, sliding his fingers inside her as she trembled, touching her, teasing her, pushing her deeper into a strange dark place filled with stars.

She knew he moved away, but her body kept convulsing, over and over, an endless wave of climaxes that left her limp, weak and breathless. He wiped his mouth on the sheet and then rolled onto his side, pulling her to face him, lifting one of her legs over his. She could feel the head of his cock against her, just touching her, and she went wild with need.

"Please," she said.

He pushed into her, and she could feel her body clenching, trying to draw him in deeper, but he was maddeningly distant.

"More?" he asked, his voice low and hypnotic.

"More," she said. He pushed in just a little more, pulling out again, a gentle, shallow rhythm that was worse than no penetration at all.

"More," she said breathlessly, clutching his narrow hips, trying to rush him. But he was stronger than she was, and he only gave her a little bit more.

She wanted to scream, to beat at his chest. "More," she repeated, and he pushed in farther, half of him sheathed inside her.

And out again, almost completely, and she moaned in despair. "More," she said. "Please, God, more. More. More."

With each cry he pushed in farther, until he filled her, thrusting deep, and she was clinging to him, her fingers digging into his arms as she sobbed in relief and need. It felt as if she'd been empty all her life, and now she was filled, complete, and she wanted it to last forever. She needed to get closer still, to sink into his very bones. She could feel the power building, taking over her body, and she tried to fight it, tried to make it last. He suddenly turned her under him, slamming deeper still inside her, deeper than she thought possible, and then everything was gone, just his sweat slick body in her arms, his cock filling her, spilling into her as she shattered, broken, lost.

And found, as she sobbed against his pounding heart, his arms around her, his hands stroking her, his lips against her tear-streaked face, while he whispered to her in the language she trusted, soft, loving, praise-filled words.

She was almost asleep when she said it, every single defense and inhibition stripped from her. She didn't know what words he was whispering as he held her, but she answered the only way she could.

"I love you," she said, as she drifted into a deep, sex-drugged sleep. For a moment she thought she felt his body tense, and then everything vanished, and she was asleep.

23

Taka was gone when she finally woke, and Summer was almost glad. She wasn't quite sure how she could face him after the endless night they'd spent.

She woke, instinctively wary, with the real fear that something was wrong. Had she been stupid enough to tell him she loved him? Had she felt him freeze in sudden rejection?

No, she had to have dreamed it. Because he'd woken her again and again, taking her to dark, unexpected places where nothing was forbidden, until her entire body ached, her flesh shivered and either she'd slept or passed out, she wasn't sure.

But now she was alone, trying to pull some kind of calm back around her in the bright light of day. There were no defenses left—he'd stripped every one away, and she wouldn't have called them back even if she could.

But neither could she spend the day in bed, waiting for his return.

He was gone, and the urn was missing as well. She wondered where he'd taken it if he'd be back. Of course, he would. And she'd be there, waiting for him.

Even Reno's shower was a bit scary, she thought as she stood under the hot streams of water coming at her from the oddest directions. With his fascination for new technology, he'd done away with a bathtub altogether, a real shame, since right then there was nothing Summer needed more than a long, soothing soak. She ached all over. She could tell herself it was from the long plane ride, but knew perfectly well that had very little to do with it, unless she counted the time spent in the bathroom. She was achy and sore in unexpected places, aware of muscles in her hips and thighs she didn't think she'd ever used, and all she wanted was to luxuriate in hot water for an hour, then start using them again.

Taka would be back, probably with Reno, who'd only get in the way. Despite the endless hours in the darkened bedroom, Taka would likely try to talk her into staying while he went off into the mountains after the Shirosama. But he should know by now that she wasn't going to listen. She was coming with him; she'd gone through too much just to sit behind and wait for news from the front line.

He was perfectly capable of tying her up and locking her in a closet—all for her own good, he'd say. She wouldn't mind being locked in, if he was in the closet with her. She stepped out of the shower, glancing at her reflection in the mirror, and for a moment she was shocked by what she saw.

She looked different. Healthy and glowing, despite the trauma of the last few days. She looked like someone who'd found what she'd been missing all her life.

Okay, so she'd been stupid enough to fall in love with someone who used sex as a weapon. Fallen in love with a man who'd saved her life countless times, protected her, infuriated her, lied to her, seduced her and given her the best sex she'd ever had.

She could find someone else who was as good in bed as he was. Or at least good enough. Someone who'd had enough practice. But the fact of the matter was, Taka's finesse in the sack wasn't just technique. Yes, he knew what to touch, how hard, how soft, how to use his mouth, his hands, his hips, his entire body to bring her shattering pleasure. But deep in her heart she suspected that any man could master any of the same moves and the experience would leave her cold and frustrated. Emotion had nothing to do with sex as far as he was concerned.

Emotion was everything with Summer. And she was enmeshed with Taka, body, mind and soul—addicted to him—and had no idea how she'd ever break away.

There was no way she could change things. She was part of his assignment. She wasn't insecure enough to think he didn't find the same kind of pleasure in her body, but he could probably turn that on and off for anyone. Including the woman he was supposed to marry.

Summer would have to learn to live without him, and soon. And like all addictions, the first step to letting go was admitting the habit.

The next step was to get over it.

She felt very strange dressing in Reno's clothes. She'd lost weight during the last few days, and he liked his jeans as baggy as he liked his leather tight, so she had no trouble pulling them up around her ample American butt. She laughed at the underwear Taka had unearthed—Reno had a secret weakness for tiger stripes and pastels. She put her fancy bra on, wincing slightly at the tenderness in her breasts and then dismissing it as she pulled a T-shirt over her head. It was lime-green, blindingly bright, and said On The Verge Of Destruction. Not exactly her color, but the saying was apt and she didn't fancy pawing through his clothes to find something more suitable.

She even found a pair of orange sneakers—too big on her, of course, but with a couple of pairs of socks and tying the laces tightly, they'd do. She wasn't going to be heading into the mountains in those high heels, no matter how effective a weapon they could be.

Of course, Taka didn't think she'd be heading into the mountains at all. He was about to find out otherwise.

She headed into the kitchen, made herself a bowl of instant miso soup and dished up some rice from the rice cooker. The meal probably wasn't big on nutrition, but at least it was filling.

In a drawer, she found a paring knife. A nasty little thing more suited for street fighting than kitchen work, but it would do very nicely if Taka made the mistake of trying to abandon her. It would cut through rope or duct tape quite handily.

She heard the door open as she was washing the dishes, but she didn't turn. Reno no longer scared her—he was trying too hard. And if it was Taka, he'd come up behind her, press his body against hers, and she could lean back, sinking into the heat and strength of him, letting go...

It happened so fast she didn't have time to react. Something was pressed over her mouth and nose, and she breathed in the stink of it before she could react or lash out. *The knife,* she thought dizzily. She needed to get to the knife.

She felt herself falling, and something was placed over her head, closing out the light, closing out everything, and her last thought was, Wasn't this how the whole damn thing started?

"What are you going to do about her?" his cousin asked. "Not that it's any of my business, but your grandfather will want to know."

"Send her back to America as soon as this is over," Taka said grimly, putting Hitoshi Komoru's credit card down on the pile of outdoor clothing he was buying.

"And you'll be going with her?"

"No. She'll go back to her own life. I'll go on to my next assignment."

"With the Committee? You still think you can save the world, cousin?"

"It's worth trying," Taka replied.

"I'm not convinced of that."

"You're young," Taka said. He was in a foul mood. Considering he'd spent the night fucking his brains out, he ought be feeling a little more even tempered, but right now he wanted to hit something, anything. In a pinch, Reno would do.

"Five years younger than you, you old fart. That just makes you stuffier, not smarter."

Taka stared at Reno haughtily. "And you're so happy working for your grandfather? Overseeing gambling parlors and the sex trade?"

Reno shrugged. "What are you suggesting—that I join your shadow organization and try to save the world, as well? Not exactly my style. Don't you have enough heroes?"

"There's a lot of turnover. It's a little too easy to get killed in my line of work."

Reno grinned. "You tempt me, cousin. Almost. But as long as you're around I'll just concentrate on sex and gambling. Better to stick to the simpler pleasures in life. Besides, Grandfather wouldn't be happy if you lured me away."

"He'd let you go. I asked him."

Reno pushed his sunglasses up, fixing his cousin

with a sharp stare. "You can mind your own fucking business," he said in a low, dangerous voice. "You're the one who's busy screwing up his world by screwing the gaijin."

"You're forgetting, I'm half-gaijin myself."

"I try to overlook that particular failing."

"And you're—"

"Don't even say it," Reno warned.

Takashi had said enough. The cashier handed him the tray with his credit card and receipt, and he took it, shoving it in his back pocket before turning back to the bristling Reno. "Just think about it," he said. Madame Lambert would make mincemeat of his little cousin—something he'd pay good money to see. And with Reno complicating his life, he'd have less time to think about mistakes living in L.A.

Reno responded with an epithet vulgar enough to make the cashier blush, and Taka punched him in the arm. "Behave yourself, cousin."

Reno just snorted, stalking out of the store into the wintry morning air. "I noticed you didn't get any clothes for your girlfriend."

"She's not coming with me."

"She's not staying with me," Reno warned. "I put up with her for your sake, but if you're not around I'd probably strangle her."

"She's harder to kill than you might think," he said.

Reno just looked at him. "Holy motherfucker," he said. "You're in love with the gaijin."

"In love?" Taka echoed, managing a derisive laugh. "You're crazy."

"What's that got to do with anything? And if you've fallen in love with her, then you're the crazy one. Love's a waste of time. Love's like a knife—it'll cut your balls off and stab you in the back."

"And what, little cousin, would you know about love?" he countered softly.

"I keep as far away from it as I can, which I thought you'd be smart enough to do as well. Grandfather found a woman willing to marry you, and sooner or later you could become the good salaryman he always wanted. He could almost forget your parentage, and while he wouldn't leave the company to someone of impure blood, he'd at least leave you a shitload of money and his fancy houses. And Mitsuko has a very nice ass, if you ask me."

"She has a very nice ass," Taka agreed. "But I don't want it. Or the houses, or the company."

"Don't tell me you want the American?"

"No," Taka said, not even considering whether it was a lie or not. "Sooner or later she'd drive me crazy."

"Probably sooner," Reno said. "So where are you going to stash her while we go into the mountains? I don't think there's time to put her on a plane back home, which is where she needs to be."

"We?"

"Don't you remember American television? The line is 'What's this *we*, white man?' I'm going with you. Where do we stash the girl?"

"You're not coming with me," Taka said flatly. "Don't worry, I wouldn't leave her with you. You must know someone who can babysit her. Someone who doesn't understand English, so she won't drive him crazy. Someone who won't get distracted and let her out of his sight."

"Crazy Jumbo might do it. Former sumo wrestler, not too bright. He'd just sit on her if she got too yappy."

"I don't—"

A loud screeching of guitars interrupted him, and Reno dived into his leather jacket for his cell phone. "What?" he snarled. His expression changed, his voice lowered, and he moved off to a less crowded piece of the sidewalk. By the time Taka caught up with him Reno had already finished the conversation and was looking rattled. It took a lot to get Reno rattled.

"That was Grandfather. They've got Su-chan."

Taka didn't even notice Reno's use of the affectionate term. "Who does?" His voice was deadly.

"Who do you think?" Reno said. "They want the urn, or they're going to liberate her to her next karmic level, according to the note Grandfather got. You're supposed to bring them the urn."

Taka's blood had frozen in his veins, like the cold winter wind swirling through the crowded city. "Where?"

"You're kidding, right? You can't give it to them. They'll kill her anyway, and if you give them the relic they'll be able to start their holy war. You can't do it."

Taka dropped his package of clothes, caught Reno's leather jacket in one hand and slammed him against the wall. "Where?"

"Tonight, at the ruins of the temple. Either your girlfriend told them, or they've bugged my apartment. It doesn't matter which—they know where the ancient site is, and they want you there. You're just playing into their hands, Taka-san. They'll kill her and they'll kill you. I don't care how skilled you are, one man against so many is doomed."

"Two men, Reno. You're coming with me."

Reno detached Taka's hand from his jacket, brushing it lazily. "I thought you'd see it my way sooner or later. Let's go."

She felt sick. At least this time she was in the back seat of a car and not in the trunk, for all the good it did her. She still had a bag over her head, but at some point they'd changed her clothes, and she was wearing something loose and light. And cold. Her hands were tied behind her back and something was across her mouth so she couldn't scream. She was curled up in a corner of some kind of vehicle, and the ride was very bumpy, as if they were going over a road of logs and tree stumps. There was a familiar, unpleasant smell in the car, and it took her only a moment to recognize it. The True Realization Fellowship favored a particularly sickly sweet incense, and the scent clung to the followers' clothing. She moved her head down to her shoulder and sniffed the fabric of whatever they'd put her in. The same nasty stuff.

Who else would have gone to all the trouble to grab her? She couldn't figure out why—supposedly the only reason they'd kept her alive was because she could lead them to the ancient shrine. Yet they already seemed to know where it was—she only hoped she hadn't babbled something during some forgotten, drug-induced questioning. They had nothing to gain by kidnapping her, unless they thought she still had the urn.

But if they'd managed to track her down to Reno's apartment, then their information was up-to-the-minute, and they'd know she didn't have the urn; Taka did.

"I believe she's awake, your holiness."

Shit. She shouldn't have moved. She was much better off huddled in the corner being ignored. The bag was pulled from her head, and she blinked at the unexpected brightness of the day. And then focused on her nemesis, sitting in meditative stillness on the scat opposite her, his white hair flowing, his bleached white skin the color of death, his eyes milky.

He turned in her direction. He was almost blind, she realized, wondering if that would do her even a spit of good.

"Remove the covering from her mouth, Brother Heinrich, so that I may hear her thoughts," he said in that singsong voice.

Brother Heinrich ripped the duct tape from her mouth, and she almost screamed. She remembered him—he was one of the men in the alleyway, the one who had gotten away. He had flat, cold eyes of a bright, Germanic blue, thin lips and no hair whatsoever. And he scared the piss out of her.

"Do you want me to untie her as well, your holiness?" he asked, his German accent thick.

"I think not, my son. I doubt we need to worry, even if she becomes violent, but leaving her bound will aid her in the stillness she seeks."

"I'm not seeking stillness and I only become violent when people kidnap me," she said in a husky voice. "What the hell do you think you're doing?"

Brother Heinrich backhanded her across the face, and her head whipped back under the assault. "You will address his holiness with respect."

"Fuck you. And him."

Crack. His fist hit the other side of her face, and through the blinding pain she thought vaguely that at least the bruising would be symmetrical. But then, the Japanese preferred things asymmetrical, and the first and last man she was ever fool enough to love was half-Japanese. He wouldn't like a symmetrical corpse.

"Don't be too hard on the girl, Brother Heinrich," the Shirosama said in his spooky voice. "She has been brainwashed by the man who abducted her, stole her from our care."

"Stole me from your car, you mean. Why was I

dumped in the trunk of your limo if you were so worried about my well-being?"

He nodded benevolently toward her. "My followers were perhaps a bit rash. They merely wanted to get you out of harm's way. They knew the man was watching you, and they were trying to save your life."

"Save my life?" she countered. "You're the one who's been trying to kill me."

"Oh, no, child. We weren't the ones who held you under the water at your house that night. If you think on it, I expect you'll remember other times where you nearly died at O'Brien's hands. Times when you thought he'd saved you. You needn't be ashamed by your foolishness—he's a dangerous, evil man, more than a match for an innocent girl like yourself."

"Hardly a girl," she snapped, even though a cold knot had formed in the pit of her stomach. Taka had told her he wasn't going to kill her, and she hadn't thought any more about it. Had those been his hands holding her under the water in her tub until she passed out?

"You're remembering, aren't you?" the blind man said. "I thought you might. Life is never as simple as it appears to be, and those you think are your enemies can often be your best friends. And those you trust with your life can betray you."

She wouldn't, couldn't, think about that. The Shirosama was trying to manipulate her—persuasion was a cult leader's stock in trade, and she wasn't going to let him affect her. "What do you want from me?"

"I just want to give you safe haven."

"I'll bet. Where are we headed?"

"You are a very wise young woman, Summer. Even your mother admits that much. You would be a great asset to our movement."

"Where are you taking me?"

The Shirosama sighed. "I think you know. I have people everywhere—the moment you discover something, my people find it out as well. We're heading to White Crane Mountain, you should have realized that much. You're not as bright as your little sister, of course. We were hoping she would be open to my teachings, but you know how difficult youth can be. They never listen to the voice of wisdom."

"I guess I'm younger than I thought. You're the voice of bullshit."

She was rewarded with another blow from Heinrich's meaty hands. There, that would keep her face unbalanced.

"Stop hitting her, Brother Heinrich," the Shirosama said in his soft little voice. He was beginning to remind her of a Japanese albino Truman Capote, she thought, suppressing the sudden urge to giggle. She must be getting hysterical, and this time Taka was not around to snap her out of it.

"I haven't given up hope of your sister," the Shirosama said. "The best and the brightest will survive the upcoming conflagration, and she should be one of them. She'll turn to the light by then, if she hasn't already."

"If you mean by 'turn to the light' that she'll think you're anything but a bloated, psychotic charlatan I can tell you it will be a cold day in hell when that happens."

"Heinrich." The Shirosama's soft lisp stopped his henchmen in time. "It's no wonder the poor girl is confused. We've helped many of the lost and deluded to find their way out of this karmic snare. We'll help her, too."

"And just how do you help people out of their karmic snare, your holiness?" Summer asked in a sarcastic voice.

The Shirosama turned his paper-white face toward her and smiled benevolently. "By helping them into their next life, child. How else?"

24

The town of Tonazumi was like a step back into another century. By the time Taka managed to find his way through the twisting, narrow roads it was almost nightfall, and time was running out.

The tiny village at the base of White Crane Mountain shouldn't have been accustomed to tourists, but the townspeople greeted the arrival of two strangers from the city, including one as bizarre as Reno, with polite disinterest. Until the Shirosama was mentioned.

"It's the night of the Lunar New Year," the old man at the noodle shop said. "Much goings-on up there. You don't want to interfere."

"He has a friend of mine with him. I need to get a message to her."

"Not until the celebration is over. There are guards on all the main roads up the mountain—the planned ritual is sacred, and they don't want outsiders watching."

"Then what is a television satellite truck doing here in town?" he responded.

The old man shook his head. "We don't ask questions. The followers of the new religion will do us no harm, and they will bring business to our little village. In return, we must let them do what they wish."

Taka glanced over at the satellite truck. All emotion had left him hours ago—there was no place for it in his life—and his reactions were cool and calculated. The truck was private, belonging to the Fellowship, and if they were bothering with satellites they were clearly planning some kind of live feed. Was it going to be closed circuit to their legions of followers, or had they made arrangements with the Tokyo networks? Worse, were they planning on jamming the airwaves? The Shirosama had followers with the technology to pull this off. Taka had no idea exactly what the Fellowship was planning, but it was sure to signal the beginning of a bloody conflict that would leave the world forever changed. And he wasn't about to let that happen.

He glanced up toward the dark, forbidding mountain. It was a dormant volcano, though in recent years there'd been occasional rumblings. Just the kind of place a melodramatic hack like the Shirosama would want to serve as a backdrop for his ravings.

The question remained, what did he have planned for tonight? He certainly wouldn't hurt Summer in front of a camera—he was far too shrewd a showman. He might have her drugged and compliant,

seemingly a willing participant to whatever ritual he
had lined up. There was always the possibility he'd
brainwashed her in record time. Taka didn't think so;
Summer was far too argumentative to be easily
swayed, particularly by someone she already dis-
trusted. If he knew anything about his unwilling companion of the last few days—and he knew her
well—then the Shirosama would be regretting ever
thinking she'd be a useful bargaining chip. Summer
Hawthorne was simply more trouble than she was
worth. At least as far as anyone with any sense would
realize.

Unfortunately, Taka's common sense seemed to
have deserted him in the last few days.

"If there are guards on all the main roads keeping
unwanted visitors away, then there must be back
roads, not so well guarded," he suggested to the wiz-
ened old man.

"There are."

Taka waited. Reno was stalking around in the
background, fuming. His cousin had never been good
when it came to patience. The old man was going to
reveal the information at his own pace, and a Yakuza
punk from Tokyo wasn't going to get it any faster.

"There's a road heading up past the waterfalls. It
won't take you to the shrine—you'll have to get out
and hike—but it'll get you most of the way there."

Taka didn't ask how he knew about the hidden
shrine—the old man seemed to know everything.
"When did the Shirosama arrive here? Was he alone?"

The man shrugged. "I try not to pay attention. He's not looking for followers like me—he wants them young and smart or old and rich. Someone said they saw his limousine heading into the mountains late this morning, but that's all I know."

Taka bowed low, not making the mistake of insulting the man by offering him money. If the night ended with any kind of success, he'd see that some kind of reward made it into the old man's gnarled hands. Tonazumi was a poor town, and the Shirosama wasn't going to be around long enough to make a difference.

"We'll be climbing partway," he told Reno when he caught up with him. "The main roads are guarded."

"Why don't we just shoot our way through?"

"Because they might kill Summer," Taka said patiently.

His cousin wisely said nothing.

There was an odd glow halfway up the mountain, hidden by the evergreens. Television lights, for the Shirosama's big production.

Fortunately, the Shirosama was missing a major prop. The Hayashi Urn was safely tucked in Taka's leather backpack. Even if the cult leader still had the remains of the original Shirosama, if he didn't have the proper receptacle, then what was the point?

Unless he had a fake urn. The sacred remains were probably a fake, as well. Taka had grave doubts about the condition of bone and ash after almost four hundred years. But if Summer could manage to produce three creditable copies of the urn, then the Shirosama could do just as well faking a pile of ash and some chunks of whitened bone.

In which case, why was he holding Summer hostage for the real urn? Why the hell did it matter? The plans were in motion, the eve of the first full moon of the year was upon them, and the appearance of the real urn tomorrow or the next day would be too late. Tonight was the signal for everything to begin; their intel had been faultless at least that far. The weapons, wherever they were, would be distributed, and in the next few days the subways and train stations would be flooded with toxins, and no color of alert or high level warnings were going to make any difference. There had already been too many false alarms.

For the first time in his life Taka felt absolutely helpless to stop the disaster. Things were in motion, and if the Shirosama had his crazed way, Armageddon would follow.

No, Taka was going to stop it, even if it seemed an impossibility. He was going to put a bullet right between the Shirosama's fat, ruined eyes, and he was going to get Summer the hell out of there to a safe place, where no one could ever put murderous hands on her again.

Including himself.

They ditched the car halfway up the mountain, grabbed their backpacks and began circling around toward the glow of artificial light.

The night was cold, with the sharp promise of snow in the air. For now the ground was dry and bare. If it started snowing, things were going to go from difficult to almost impossible.

Even from a distance, Taka could see the outlines of the ancient torii gate, leading to the temple grounds, and the wide, flat field nearby. A perfect landing strip.

The landing field was an integral part of the Shirosama's crazed doomsday play. Sooner or later a plane was going to show up. In the banked lights of the airstrip Taka could see crate after crate piled high, and he knew with absolute certainty that he'd found the weapons after all. What better place to distribute them than the sacred mountain shrine itself? The Shirosama would send those weapons out into the world with his faithful followers, and it was up to Taka to stop them.

The backpack had more than the well-padded urn inside. There were explosives, firearms—enough firepower to wipe out half the mountain—and Reno was carrying the same. They needed to find cover, wait until the plane landed and take it out. Stop the carnage before it began, with their own rough justice.

But that meant leaving Summer to the Shirosama's tender mercies.

It all came down to this—one woman or the thousands, tens of thousands, maybe hundreds of thousands. Ensuing chaos would raise the death toll higher still.

Takashi had no choice, and he'd always known it. This was one reason he'd tried so hard not to care about anyone, one reason why he'd known immediately just how dangerous Summer Hawthorne could be. Because now she was the one he couldn't sacrifice, couldn't walk away from, no matter how high the stakes. He could die for what he believed in. He just couldn't let her die as well.

Reno was watching him, his expression unreadable in the darkness as Taka made his way silently to his side. "Take out the plane," Taka said. "Kill anyone who tries to board it, anyone who tries to leave. I don't care who they are. We can't let them get away with these weapons."

"You going after her?"

"Yes."

"You got any more guns?"

Taka opened his backpack, pulling out the carefully wrapped urn, then dumped the rest of the contents on the ground in front of his cousin before putting the bowl back in.

"Wait. You're going to need something," Reno protested.

"If I bring a weapon, they'll just take it from me. I have my hands. I know how to use them."

"Crazy motherfucker," his cousin muttered. "Bring her back with you, and we'll all fly out of here."

"I don't see how that's going to happen."

Reno grinned in the dim light. "It'll happen. After

you save the world, my noble cousin. Go off and rescue her. I'll take care of things on this end."

Taka stared at him for a long moment. Reno had been the only brother he'd known, and he'd brought him up here to almost certain death. And he looked to be having the time of his life. Taka hugged him tightly and then headed off into the darkness, leaving the landing field far behind.

Summer was freezing. She considered complaining, but the last time she'd mentioned it Brother Heinrich had slammed her in the ribs. No one really gave a damn whether she froze to death or not, which suggested that she was going to die no matter what. Well, she wasn't going to make it easy for them.

She also had no intention of shutting up, and the nasty Brother Heinrich had forgotten to bring more duct tape up this icy mountain with him. He'd tried slapping the old stuff on, but it didn't stick, and any gag he forced in her mouth she simply spat out again. He'd been getting to the point where she half expected him to shove his fist down her throat in order to keep her quiet, when the Shirosama admonished him, sending him off on some errand or another while Summer hunkered down on the frozen ground, waiting. Waiting for God knows what.

"You shouldn't annoy Brother Heinrich, my child," His Sliminess said in his rich, hypnotic voice. "He has far to go in his search for enlightenment, and I am grieved to say he often falls into his old ways.

It distresses him when anyone fails to show me the proper honor."

"He'll have to get used to it," she retorted with her best approximation of a snarl. "You still haven't told me why you brought me up here. You know I don't have the urn anymore. And any number of people have figured out where this place is. They'll be coming for me."

"That is exactly what I am counting on. Takashi O'Brien will bring me the urn in exchange for your safety, and then the rite of ascension can proceed as predetermined."

"You're crazy," Summer said, not bothering to consider that might not be the wisest thing to say to someone who really was insane. "Taka's not going to trade the urn for me. I'm just part of a job, and that job is protecting the urn. You already pointed out he's been trying to kill me ever since he met me. Why should he suddenly be willing to risk everything just to save me?"

The Shirosama's smile made the temperature drop lower still. "Because I know that he will. It goes against his principles, but he will come for you, and he will bring me the urn, and the Ceremony of Ascension can be performed."

"And you'll let the two of us walk down the mountain to safety, right?" she scoffed. "You think Taka believes that for a moment?"

"Of course not. But he is willing to take the risk for you."

"According to you, the man keeps trying to kill me. He's finally gotten what he's been after for days, and you think he'd throw it all away for me? You're even more deluded than I thought you were."

"Poor child," he said. "I am almost infallible. After tonight I will be infallible."

"And what if Taka ignores your message and doesn't give a shit what you do with me?"

"I am a practical man. You left an excellent forgery behind. We brought the fake with us. On the television no one will be able to tell that it's not the real Hayashi Urn. And I'll let Brother Heinrich finish what he started. A fitting climax to his short life."

"A climax? He's going to dic as well?"

"Miss Hawthorne, we're all going to die."

She stared at him. "Yes, eventually."

"No, tonight. The cleansing will unfold as it was written. People everywhere toil and suffer needlessly, only to die in pain and loss. I am here to free people from that endless wheel of karma and sorrow. And my followers will join me, happily."

"And what about the people who don't follow you? Are they going to join you, too?"

"The only way to save the world is to destroy it."

"You're as crazy as that nut-job who gassed the Tokyo subways."

A faint frown tugged at his mouth. "The Aum Shinrikyo were too rushed, though their vision was correct. The time had not yet come. That time is now."

Summer felt a new chill sweep down her backbone. She tried to rally. "Are you going to be an evil overlord and tell me your plans?"

"I don't understand."

"It's an American joke. The evil overlord, thinking he has the hero at his mercy, tells him his evil plans, and then, when the hero gets free, he's able to thwart those plans."

"Ah, Miss Hawthorne. I am no evil overlord, I am the blessed incarnation of hope for mankind. And you are not the hero—you are simply in the wrong place at the wrong time. Telling you what will happen will make no difference, even if karma decrees that you somehow manage to escape. It's too late to stop it."

"Stop what?"

"In less than an hour a cargo plane will arrive, filled with scientists and soldiers, the best of my disciples. They will take the crates of drugs and gases and fly them out of here. They'll be distributed and shipped to other followers in all corners of the world. Armageddon will commence."

"And what will happen to us? Do we go with them?"

He shook his head, and the white hair floated gently onto his rounded shoulders. "While the cameras are rolling, I will place the ashes and bones of my ancestor back into his ancestral urn. Then I will commit *seppuku*, my blood mixing with his ashes, and be reborn."

"Sounds like a mess to me."

The Shirosama's beatific expression faltered for a moment. "Brother Heinrich will serve as my *kaish-kunin* and release my head from my body, then open the gas canisters. In the open air the toxins will take a bit longer to diffuse than I could have wished, but even as the cameraman falls, the camera will keep filming, and the world will see the lengths the divine are willing to go to in order to ensure the salvation of this world."

"But you'll be dead. How will you know it worked?"

"Death is just another stage on the road of life."

"Oh, please. You'll be dead, the rest of us will be dead, and we'll look like some pathetic mini-Jonestown. In the meantime Taka and whoever he works for will intercept your nasty little shipment and it won't even get out of Japan."

The Shirosama had the most awful smile—the only part about him that wasn't white were his stained, broken teeth. "Perhaps," he allowed. "If that is what is meant to be. But I think your Taka is going to be otherwise engaged, and unable to interfere with my well-structured plans."

"And why do you think that?"

"Because he is here already. I can't see him, but I can sense his presence. Surely you aren't more blind than I am?"

She whipped her head around. She and the Shirosama were sitting in a clearing, surrounded by four small, newly constructed torii gates, a burning fire and banks of lights set up to illuminate the upcoming production. She'd been left alone with him, and if she'd had any sense she would have worked harder to get the paring knife out of her bra. They hadn't found the weapon when they'd changed her clothing; she could still feel it digging into the side of her breast, and in front of a blind man she could have worked on loosening it, cutting her bonds, cutting his throat.

Now it was too late. Three men were approaching, two of them the Shirosama's white-clad goons. And between them was Takashi O'Brien, carrying the Hayashi Urn in his hands.

25

"If you don't want the real urn smashed into a thousand pieces you'll tell your boys to take their hands off me." His voice cool and calm, Taka seemed unmoved by the monks on either side of him. He didn't even glance her way, which was a relief. Summer looked at him and didn't know whether to laugh or to cry.

He'd been trying to kill her. She knew it—somehow she'd always known it—even as she'd kept pushing the thought out of her mind. He was like a poisonous snake, seducing her as he lured her toward death. She had no idea why Taka kept saving her, why he changed his mind. She wasn't even sure it mattered. Those were the beautiful hands that had held her underwater till she began to drown. That had tightened around her throat. The same beautiful hands had touched her, loved her, shattered and redeemed her.

The Shirosama rose to his full height, coming up to Taka's chest, and held out his arms. "Give me the urn," he breathed.

Taka dropped it.

Brother Heinrich dived for the bowl, catching it just before it hit the frozen dirt, and the cult leader stepped back in distaste. "That is not the way to rescue your young woman, Brother Takashi," he intoned, clearly disappointed.

"Don't call me that." Taka's voice was low, deadly.

"Why not? You know as well as I do," the Shirosama replied in that soft, singsong voice, "that you really want to be one of us. But you are afraid to listen to your heart, Brother Takashi. Listen to it now. Join us. It's not too late. Don't waste your time trying to stop me—I'm unstoppable."

Summer couldn't keep from watching Taka's face, his treacherously beautiful visage. "I've brought you the urn," he said. "Now give me the girl and we'll get out of here."

"Do not be foolish, child," he said. "You know I was never going to let you take her. Surely you couldn't have been that naive."

There was no expression in Taka's dark eyes as he stared down at the guru. "Anything is possible," he said. "You might have become a man of your word."

"My word is the sacred word of God," he said.

"And God told you to kidnap a helpless American and murder thousands of people?"

"No one is being murdered. The world is being cleansed. Baptized, if you like. Only the most trusted will accompany me on my final journey."

Taka's eyes narrowed. "What final journey?"

"You don't think I would ask such a sacrifice of my followers if I were not willing to make the same sacrifice, do you?"

"I think you're a lying, devious psychopath who comes up with justifications for everything he does."

"And I think it is time you joined your friend," he replied. "The new moon is upon us, and everything is in place. Do you hear that?"

"The plane? I heard it. I'm assuming more of your goons have come to pick up your little packages of poison to deliver around the world."

"My strongest followers are coming to bring freedom to all corners of the globe."

"The earth is round, your holiness."

"With no place to hide," he murmured. "Tie him up, Brother Heinrich, and let him sit with the woman he tried to kill."

He didn't react. Taka's very lack of guilt was even more telling than a protest. Brother Heinrich bound his arms and legs, roughly, and shoved him down on the ground, against Summer, so that she almost fell over. She scooted away from him quickly, refusing to look at him.

"You see?" the Shirosama murmured. "I told her you were the one who held her under the water, that you were planning to kill her. Even now, you probably believe your best course is to silence her. It doesn't matter. Before long you will both be silenced, and perhaps you'll both do better in the next life."

Taka said nothing, pulling himself into a sitting

position. "You brainwashed her so quickly? I would have thought she'd give you more trouble than that."

"I told her the truth, and she saw it for what it was," he replied. "Brother Heinrich, go to the plane and make certain it's loaded and the disciples are on board. Then return to me with the final packet of medicine. I need to be certain everything is going according to plan before we take the final steps."

Brother Heinrich disappeared into the darkness, but not before glaring at Taka. The Shirosama seemed to have forgotten about both prisoners. He'd begun chanting, some strange mixture of languages that held few words Summer had ever heard, as he sprinkled gray dust on the fire in front of him, followed by the same cloying incense. White-robed brothers began to emerge from the surrounding forest, some carrying weapons, some unarmed. They lay their guns in a pile and moved to form a circle around the Shirosama, taking up the same nonsensical chant.

When Taka had been thrown against Summer the knife had been knocked loose from her bra, and was now beneath her loose shirt. With her hands bound behind her there was no way she could reach it. She would have to count on her would-be murderer.

"Your holiness!" She raised her voice, forcing herself to sound tearful and supplicatory. "If we are to die, would you let me kiss him one last time?"

She half expected Taka to react to her uncharacteristic behavior, but he didn't move, didn't look at her. He was kneeling in the frozen dirt beside her, every inch of him alert, and she was probably the least of his concerns.

"You want to kiss the man who tried to kill you? You are a very foolish young woman," the Shirosama said. "Go ahead."

Taka turned to her, his eyes dark and unreadable, waiting. She reached up, put her mouth against his and whispered, "I have a knife that's fallen down the front of my shirt, you son of a bitch. See if you can get it." The feel of his lips against hers was agony. The sickness deep inside her was that she wanted to kiss him anyway, no matter what he'd done.

A moment later he'd flung himself at her knees, babbling a mixture of contrition and love. Somehow, in the darkness, and even with his hands tied, he managed to reach up under her flowing shirt and grab the knife.

The Shirosama's half-blind eyes were turned in their direction, an expression of distaste on his face. "I misjudged both of you," he said. "You are unworthy of the great honor I chose to give you."

"What great honor?" Summer asked. Taka was still doing a creditable job of being collapsed in grief and hopeless love, and she needed to hold the Shirosama's attention while Taka worked on their bonds.

"The great honor of dying with me, Miss Hawthorne. Your mother would appreciate it and as one of my most generous supporters, she would have had that honor. But someone took her away and I've had more important things to do than try to find her."

"Like kidnap my sister?" Summer shot back. Taka was still now, and she kept waiting for him to lean toward her, to do something about the bonds that were slowly cutting off the circulation in her arms.

But the Shirosama was no longer interested in arguing with her, or anyone. "Drag them out of the circle, Brother Shinya. They can watch from a distance."

Shit, Summer thought, as one of the brethren advanced toward them. He would see that Taka had gotten his hands on a knife, and their last hope of escape would be gone.

But she underestimated the brother's dislike of the unclean, particularly women. He came to stand over them, an expression of disgust on his pale face as if he were enduring a bad smell. "Move back," he ordered them.

With their hands and feet tied, it was a difficult maneuver requiring a crablike effort, but Summer had given up dignity long ago, along with trust, love and the remote possibility of a happy ending. She'd put her faith in a murderer.

They moved back, a good five feet out of the circle, and the brethren took their places, kneeling in a semicircle around the Shirosama. He'd set the urn on the antique kimono, and at another time Summer would have cried out at the sacrilege.

They must have taken it when they'd kidnapped her. If Reno had only left the urn behind this would all be over, for her at least. They would have had everything they wanted and she would probably be dead. If Taka didn't get his shit together she wasn't going to be alive to care about antique kimono or ancient ceramics or anything at all.

For that matter, even if he did, there was no guarantee that he was going to bother to save her.

The Shirosama arranged himself in a meditative position, and then nothing happened. The chanting stopped, and they all just waited, in silence.

A moment later Brother Heinrich reappeared in the firelight. "They're here, your holiness. Brother Neville and his wife have seen to the loading of the plane, and the advance force is already aboard. They wish your blessing before they depart on their holy mission."

"Of course," he said graciously. "Bring them to me, that I may touch them and send them on their way." He turned his face toward Summer and Taka. "Brother Neville is one of England's top scientists, an expert in biochemical weapons, and he allows his wife to assist him. Devoted followers like them assure the success of my vision. Death is nothing more than the gateway to paradise, and my followers embrace that truth. My people are everywhere—there is no way to stop what must happen."

Taka still wasn't saying anything, but he was very still. Either he'd given up on trying to cut his bonds or he'd already managed it and was just choosing his moment to jump up.

Either way, he'd done nothing to release Summer, and clearly he wasn't going to. If Taka was somehow able to stop them before they released the gas, then she might survive. Otherwise she could take small comfort in the fact that at least Jilly was safe. Small comfort that if she was going to die, so would Taka. Slowly and painfully.

The Shirosama's British followers approached silently. One was a tall, bespectacled man, the colorless kind of person who'd disappear in a crowd. The woman with him was similarly nondescript—dull clothes, glasses, dishwater hair, frumpy. Older than her partner. And then Summer realized with horror that they weren't alone—two of the brethren were dragging someone else behind them. Someone with flame-red hair, dressed in black leather. Taka must have brought his cousin up the mountain, for all the good it was doing him.

The British scientist approached the Shirosama first, sinking gingerly to his knees in front of him and bending his tall body in half, so that his forehead almost touched the ground. Beside her, Taka had grown very tense. He must have seen Reno being dragged along behind them.

"Greetings and blessings, holy father," the man said in a perfect upper-class British accent.

"Greetings and blessings, Brother Neville. Greetings to Sister Agnes, too. You have served me well."

"And will continue to do so, your holiness. The world will be cleansed by blood and fire, and a new order will arise in your image."

Summer couldn't keep her mouth shut a moment longer, always her abiding failure. Brother Neville was like some unctuous Dickens character—rail-thin and dependent on a cane, as if he'd recently been sick. His plain older wife would have looked at home as a prison warden, and Summer was damn if she was going to sit silently by while they congratulated themselves on their upcoming Armageddon.

"I thought it was going to be plague and poison, not blood and fire," she called out from her place outside the sacred circle.

Brother Neville lifted his head to look at her, and in the brightness of the fire she could see piercing blue eyes, like chips of ice, glance her way.

"Pay her no attention, Brother Neville," the Shirosama said blandly. "She will soon be in a better place. Who have you brought with you?"

"You cannot see, your holiness?"

"My ascension is almost complete. I have lost most of my sight, becoming one with my ancestor. But I can sense there is someone with you."

Brother Neville's eyes slid to Taka, and for a moment Summer thought she might have imagined a slight nod. Crazy, of course. Unless Taka really was a follower of the Shirosama, and everything had been a lie.

"I think the young man came with your two

guests. We caught him as he was trying to sabotage the airplane. I'm afraid he's dead, but we thought we should bring him here as well, so that he may be joined with you in the ascension. Your mercy and forgiveness know no bounds."

"Indeed," the Shirosama breathed. "Put the body over by his friends. They will join him soon enough in the liberation of their souls."

"I only wish Sister Agnes and I could be here, as well," the man said.

"Your work out in the world is more important, Brother Neville. I'm counting on you to make sure the supplies get dispersed properly."

"It will be as it was ordained," he murmured in a sanctimonious voice. Summer opened her mouth to say something, but Taka managed to nudge her into silence.

Two of the white-robed brethren were dragging Reno's limp body around the outside of the circle, dropping him onto the hard ground beside them, and Summer stared at him, wanting to cry. He despised her, he'd done nothing but razz her, but seeing his body on the ground was somehow the last straw. A small, broken sound escaped from her throat, one of hoarse pain.

Taka glanced at her, face impassive, then back at his beloved cousin. And it was at that moment that Summer realized Reno was still breathing.

As a matter of fact, there was no blood, no sign of injury at all. His eyes were closed, his body still except for the barely discernible rise and fall of his chest. He wasn't dead.

She looked away from him, afraid her expression would be too revealing, and back to the tableau in the center.

"May we stay for the first part of the ceremony, Master?" Brother Neville asked in that oily voice.

"You may. It is time. Brother Heinrich?"

The brother stood up, raising his hands, and the place was suddenly flooded with lights—blinding lights, illuminating the setting. Summer saw the cameramen, two of them dressed in the traditional white robes, focusing in on the Shirosama as he sat in front of the kimono and the sacred, ice blue Hayashi Urn.

He began to intone loudly as he poured what looked like dirt and gravel into the bowl. Belatedly, she realized those were probably the remains of the original Shirosama, and she waited for the next stage, wondering if some kind of genie was going to swirl out of the smoke and ashes, ranting like Robin Williams.

Nothing happened. The bone chips and ashes settled into the bowl, the dust dancing in the firelight, as the Shirosama spoke, again in that crazy mixture of languages. One of the brethren sat to the side of the cult leader, gesturing, and she realized he was interpreting in sign language for the television cameras. Brother Heinrich, his loyal lieutenant, sat at his other side and in the bright light she could see what she'd missed before. The shining silver blade lying on the kimono.

She'd forgotten what the Shirosama had told her. She was going to have the truly forgettable treat of watching the ritual of *seppuku* firsthand, and if she remembered her movies correctly, Heinrich would then decapitate him. Her stomach roiled. Not that she wasn't perfectly happy to have the Shirosama shuffle off this mortal coil, but she really didn't want to watch, and she'd never been big on severed heads. Besides, he was going to get blood all over the priceless kimono.

But she said nothing. Taka was utterly still beside her, next to the supposed corpse of his cousin, but either things had spiraled totally out of his control and they were all going to die, or a lot more was going on beneath the surface and she had a slim chance in hell of surviving.

Either way, there was nothing she could do about it, particularly since Taka seemed to have no interest in cutting through her bonds. She sat back on her heels, figuring she could always close her eyes at the gross part, just like she did with *CSI*.

Other brethren were appearing out of the darkness, forming an outer circle around the kneeling monks, with the Englishman and his mousy wife to one side. As the chanting grew louder the Shirosama began opening his robe, and Summer decided gazing at his soft, pasty body might be even more horrifying than watching him butcher himself. She looked away, meeting Taka's dark, pitiless gaze. Silently, he mouthed something unbelievable. She was sure it was, "I love you."

She was going to die, after all, and he'd taken pity on the love-sick gaijin. She would die with his lie in her heart, and even a lie would bring her some comfort.

She closed her eyes. Then opened them again at the rush of wind as Taka surged to his feet, leaping across the kneeling monks to tackle the Shirosama before he could sink the blade into his belly. Suddenly all was chaos, noise, shouting. Taka was leaner and stronger than the Shirosama, but he wasn't batshit insane, and they rolled on the ground, over the gorgeous kimono, knocking the priceless urn to one side.

Brother Heinrich stood up, but before he could come to the aid of his master, Reno rose from the dead, launching himself at the German. Summer yanked at her bonds furiously, but they wouldn't budge, and she could do nothing but try to scuttle out of the way of what was rapidly becoming a pitched battle. Almost all the combatants were dressed in the white robes of the True Realization Fellowship, though they seemed to be fighting each other and she had no idea who was winning, until Reno fell to one side, his red hair flying out behind him, and lay still.

Taka had managed to straddle the Shirosama, but the cult leader was still struggling, screaming out a mixture of words that Summer couldn't understand;

any connection with sanity seemed to have vanished. Brother Heinrich rose again, and in his hand he held the long, ceremonial katana with the wicked steel blade. For a moment she thought he was going to go for Reno's still body, but then he turned to Taka.

Summer's scream of warning was swallowed up in the noise of the battle, and Taka was too focused on trying to restrain the Shirosama to realize death was coming up behind him.

She screamed again as Heinrich raised the katana, and then he froze. The sword dropped uselessly from his hand while he sank to his knees, then pitched over onto the ground, onto the outstretched kimono, the blood from the hole between his eyes spilling out onto the ancient silk.

The mousy British woman was heading toward her, and Summer tried to scramble farther out of the way until she realized it was her husband, Brother Neville, who'd shot Heinrich. The tall man was now leaning over Reno's fallen body, and he no longer looked like a gray ghost at all.

"Stop squirming, Summer," the woman said in a clipped British accent. "I can't untie you when you fight me."

Summer stopped moving, her gaze focused on Taka, his hands around the Shirosama's neck, squeezing, as the man's pale eyes began to bug out of his bleached face. "He's going to kill him," she said in a hoarse voice.

The woman glanced toward them. "No, he won't.

There's nothing Hayashi would like more than to be a martyr. Taka knows what he's doing."

Summer's hands were free, and even as her shoulders screamed in pain she started for the bonds around her ankles herself. "Who the hell are you?" she demanded.

The battle was already over. She could no longer see Taka and the Shirosama—the silent, defeated brethren were blocking her view. Brother Neville seemed to be directing things, and Summer had the sudden fear that this was simply a religious coup, one crazed guru overthrowing another. Until he headed toward them and she looked up into icy blue eyes and he held out a hand for her.

"Are you all right, Dr. Hawthorne?"

She let him pull her to her feet. "Who the hell are you?" she said again. She still couldn't see Taka past the crowd of silent brethren, and she couldn't fight the clawing panic in her stomach.

"Takashi works for us," he said simply. "That's all you really need to know. We have to get you and Taka's cousin off the mountain. Now. The plane is waiting."

"The plane with the poisons?"

"They've been neutralized," the woman said, rising, suddenly looking a great deal more authoritative. "This young man must get to a hospital, and I think you need to get out of this country and back to your sister."

For a moment Taka was forgotten. "You have Jilly?"

"I'm the one who brought her out of L.A.," the woman said. "She's staying with Peter's wife right now, and they're waiting for you to join them." She nodded toward the tall man. "That's Peter, by the way. Peter Madsen. And I'm Madame Lambert."

"The head of the Committee," Summer said.

The woman did not look pleased. "Takashi has been much too talkative. He's usually more discreet. Just exactly what went on between you two?"

"None of your business, Isobel," Peter Madsen said easily. "Besides, Takashi never gets involved during his missions. He knows how to separate the job from life."

And Summer was the job.

The stunned, defeated brethren had moved enough so that she could see where Taka and the Shirosama had been battling. They were both gone, and only the body of Heinrich, his blood soaking into the kimono, remained.

"Where are they?"

"It doesn't matter," Madame Lambert said in her cool, controlled voice. "It's over, and the sooner you forget about the last few days the better. In the meantime we need to get the boy airlifted to a hospital and take you out of Japan before there are any kind of political repercussions. I'm sure you can't wait to leave here."

Summer glanced around her, at the frozen hillside. One of the ceremonial torii gates had been smashed, and the prized Hayashi Urn lay on its side in the dirt, forgotten. She'd lost track of time long ago, but it seemed as if she'd only just arrived in Japan. And leaving the country would mean leaving Taka forever.

"I can't wait," she echoed in an expressionless voice. Reno was being loaded onto a stretcher by a couple of the white-robed brethren, though they were clearly working with the Committee, not the cult and she felt as if her head was exploding. "Can you tell me just one thing?"

"I doubt it," Isobel Lambert said, taking Summer's arm and leading her up the hillside, skirting the fallen bodies.

"Who are the good guys and who are the bad guys?"

The woman stopped to look back at the fallen bodies, then at Summer. "Shades of gray, Dr. Hawthorne. It's all shades of gray."

26

Post-traumatic stress syndrome, wasn't that what they called it? It didn't matter that she was sitting in the window seat of a beautiful old country house an hour outside of London, and that even in winter the garden outside was calming and beautiful. It didn't matter that her almost-six-foot-tall baby sister seemed completely unscathed by her adventures, and spent her time either in the kitchen with their hostess or foraging through the impenetrable textbooks Peter Madsen had managed to procure for her. Jilly was safe and happy, adjusting. Genevieve was the perfect hostess, warm but not intrusive, and Peter turned out to be absolutely charming. Nothing the slightest bit scary about him, despite Summer's initial doubts.

Madame Lambert had kept away, which suited Summer just fine. Isobel was cold, controlled and completely unemotional, which was what Summer had needed for the numb, endless plane ride to England. But right now her main goal was to keep calm, and Madame Lambert simply reminded her of the horror on the hillside.

The Shirosama was in a Japanese mental hospital, babbling, incoherent, totally insane. Summer would have thought that was a little too convenient if she hadn't seen the blank madness in his eyes as he'd rolled on the ground with Taka. The famed Hayashi Urn was on display in Kyoto, and the True Realization Fellowship was in disarray. And no one seemed to know how close the world had come to total chaos.

She wasn't going to think about Taka. Not for one moment. Peter and his wife never mentioned him, and Jilly must have been warned not to ask her too many questions. Summer would sit in the garden window, looking out over the wintry garden, and learn how to knit.

It seemed a silly thing to do, but it soothed her. While her fingers manipulated the hand-spun wool, her mind began to heal, when she hadn't even realized she was wounded.

She even managed to tolerate Lianne's rushed, abject visit. It was easy enough—most of their mother's guilt centered on Jilly, and she accepted Summer's   calm at face value before taking off to India on her newest quest for spiritual enlightenment. Summer was even able to laugh about her with Jilly. At night, Summer would lie in her big soft bed, dry-eyed, sleepless, her body restless, empty, and she wouldn't even think his name.

"We need to think about going home," she said one morning as Jilly was poring over her physics text. Genevieve was in her office, doing some long distance pro bono legal work, and there were just the two of them at the ancient oak kitchen table.

Jilly looked up. "I'm in no hurry," she said. "I've got my books, and I should be able to jump right in next semester. Besides, I like it here."

Summer looked out at the garden. They'd been in England for almost two months. It was getting warmer now, with a faint blush of color on the trees, in the grass. There were even daffodils out in the sunnier patches. Things were coming alive again. It was time for her to come alive as well.

"I need to find a new job. The Sansone doesn't want to have anything to do with me or the scandal, and I don't really blame them. But there are a lot fewer jobs than there are qualified curators, and the sooner I get started looking the sooner I'll be able to get back to a normal life."

"Is that what you want?"

"Yes," she said. As far as she could remember, it was the first lie she'd ever told her sister.

She didn't want a normal life. She didn't want a job at an L.A. museum; she didn't want to head west. She wanted to go east, back to Japan, find Taka, slam him against the wall and find out why he'd lied to her. Why had he told her he loved her and then disappeared out of her life? She wanted him groveling at her feet for forgiveness. She wanted him on top of her, beneath her, behind her, inside her. She wanted to put out her hands and feel him, solid and warm. She wanted his beautiful mouth against hers, wanted his eyes staring into hers, unguarded and wanting. She wanted to taste his tattoos.

She wanted what she couldn't have. He'd lied. When they were both likely to die he'd lied to her, proving he had at least a kind streak in his cold, beautiful body.

Genevieve breezed into the kitchen, her glasses perched low on her nose. "It's going to be warm today," she announced. "Tea in the garden, I think. Peter will come home early, and he'll probably bring Isobel. We all need frocks."

"Frocks?" Jilly echoed with a laugh. "You're not putting me into Laura Ashley—I'm bigger than you and I fight dirty."

"Isobel's coming?" Summer said in a neutral voice.

"I don't know why you don't like her," Jilly complained. "She saved my life."

And ordered Taka to kill me, Summer could have added, but she kept silent.

"Isobel's okay," Genevieve said, pouring herself a cup of the coffee she still thankfully preferred in the morning. "Just a bit of a cold fish, but she gets the job done."

"I don't think I have a frock," Summer said, trying to summon some enthusiasm.

"I have dozens," Genny replied cheerfully. "And

I'll make scones and serve clotted cream and we'll have a lovely time."

"Lovely," Summer echoed. She'd lost another ten pounds since she'd been there, not because of her hostess's cooking, which was excellent, but because she had no appetite. Any of Genny's Laura Ashleys would hang on her, but she could always sash one in, play English countryside to the best of her ability, just to make Genevieve happy. More pastels—the funny thing was she'd given up wearing black, at a time when her soul was in mourning. It made no sense, but black depressed her, and she was depressed enough.

Tomorrow she'd get on the Internet, book herself a flight back home and put all this behind her.

Because he wasn't coming. She hadn't even realized she'd been waiting for him, watching the winter-dead garden, her fingers busy wrapping yarn around needles.

Genevieve was right, it was a beautiful day, unseasonably warm. She had set a table out in the awakening garden, dripping with country fabrics and beautiful old china, and Summer liked her too much to resent playing dress-up. The pale blue flowered dress she'd borrowed was the very essence of a "frock," flowing, feminine, discreetly ruffled and laced. She even let her hair loose around her shoulders, deciding she, too, could be a British debutante from the 1930s, or whatever fantasy Genevieve was living.

When Summer walked out into the warm air of the garden, she could see that Jilly had been willing to play as well, though there was a certain goth streak to the black sash against the pale lavender flowers of her dress, and her spiky hair was tipped with the same lavender color. She was also wearing her Doc Martens, but she was bubbling and happy, and for a short while that was all that mattered.

Coffee for breakfast, Hu Kwa for afternoon tea. Summer would have preferred something Japanese, she thought, and then mentally slapped herself as she sank into one of the delicate chairs, her knitting in her lap. She really had to get home.

Peter was the first to arrive. He was barely limping by now, and Summer had refrained from asking what had happened to him. She knew enough from Taka to know how dangerous a profession they had, but she didn't want to think about that.

Peter leaned down and kissed Genevieve's cheek, and she looked up at him with such adoration that Summer felt her stomach clench. Not blinding adoration, but a wise, knowing look, as if she'd gazed into the heart of darkness and accepted what was there.

Could Summer do the same? She wasn't going to be given the chance, she thought, concentrating on the complicated pattern between her fingers.

"Isobel will be along soon," Peter said easily, accepting a cup of tea from his wife. "She had to make a couple of stops along the way."

"I can put some more water on," Genevieve said.

"That's all right—you know she likes her tea strong enough to strip wallpaper, and you can just microwave it."

"Blasphemy!" Genevieve said. She was facing the drive, and her eyes narrowed suddenly. "Help me in the kitchen!" she demanded.

"Now? I just got here," he protested.

"Now," she said. "You, too, Jilly. I need some help with the scones."

Jilly was sitting cross-legged in a chair, her textbook in her lap, and she looked up, blinking. "There are plenty."

"I need your help, Jilly," Genevieve said in her most lawyerly voice, and the girl suddenly emerged from her physics-induced stupor and rose.

"Sorry," she said. "Of course. We'll be right back."

"I can help, too..." Summer began, but all three of them said no in unison.

Shit. Was it her birthday? she thought, when they'd disappeared into the house. They had some jolly little surprise planned for her, and she wasn't in the mood. They'd all been watching her for the last few weeks, as if they were expecting her to explode, but she'd gone through her daily life with complete calm; it was only when she was alone in her room that she lay dry-eyed, miserable, sleepless. That she faced the fact that she was being torn apart.

Post-traumatic stress syndrome, she thought again. There was probably some kind of drug for her condition, and L.A. was the place to find any kind of prescription pill you needed. Just pop something twice a day and she'd forget all about him.

No, her birthday was in May. They couldn't be planning any kind of surprise celebration. She could only hope and pray that Lianne hadn't returned to provide some cursory maternal caring. She'd never been that good an actress.

Summer set down her knitting for a moment, and was reaching for her cup of tea when a shadow fell across her. She looked up.

It was Takashi O'Brien. Of course. Standing there, looking at her. And Summer burst into tears.

He pulled the knitting away from her, throwing it in the grass, then sank down on his knees in front of her, wrapping his arms around her waist and burying his head in her lap. He was shaking, she realized, and the tears were pouring down her face, onto him, as she stroked his long, silken hair and cried.

She didn't care what it sounded like—the hiccupping noises, the choking sobs. Her own body was shaking, racked by the final release, and he sat back on his heels and pulled her out of the chair, into his arms, holding her so tightly that a weaker woman might break, whispering to her in Japanese, sweet, loving words, letting her cry.

She was a strong woman, and her tears, so long denied, only made her stronger. His heart was pounding against hers, his hands firm and tender, pushing the hair away from her tear-drenched face. When he kissed her she couldn't breathe, and she didn't care.

"Holy motherfucker." The voice came from behind them, and she jerked her head up, to see Reno standing there, a bandage tied rakishly across his flame-red hair, looking at them with disgust. "Do you have to make such a disgrace of yourselves?"

She'd finally stopped crying. Isobel Lambert was coming up behind Reno's slight figure, impeccably dressed as always. "Hi, Reno," Summer said, her voice raw from her tears.

"Hi, yourself, gaijin. Just so you know, I don't approve of you joining the family. I'm putting up with it, but that doesn't mean I have to like it."

"Behave yourself, Reno," Peter said, emerging from the house, carrying a tray with glasses of champagne. "You're not nearly as tough as you'd like everyone to believe."

"I eat gaijin for breakfast...." His words trailed off as Jilly came out of the house, in her pseudo-frock, her combat boots, her spiky hair and her young, young face. He just stared at her, motionless, as if someone had clubbed him over the head with a mallet.

Jilly froze where she was, staring back at the exotic creature in black leather and bright red hair who'd invaded the garden.

"Stay where you are," Genevieve said to Taka and Summer, handing them both glasses of champagne. "You look too comfortable."

Taka had his arm tightly around her waist, holding her against him, and if her hand shook slightly when she took the glass, so did his.

"To happy endings," Peter said, raising his glass.

"To true love," Genevieve added.

"To my sister," Jilly said, clearly shaken, trying not to stare at Reno.

"Holy motherfucker," Reno muttered, pulling himself together, trying not to stare at Jilly. "You're all crazy."

Summer looked into Taka's dark, beautiful eyes. "Yes," she said, "we are." And he kissed her.

Deadly Secrets
Don't Stay Buried Forever

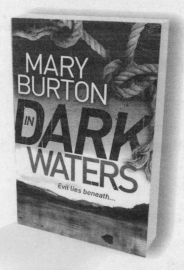

High-flying journalist Kelsey Warren has never forgiven her mother for abandoning her as a teen. Then Donna Warren's long-dead body—and evidence of her cold-blooded murder—resurfaces.

Despite Sheriff Mitch Garret's pleas to leave the case alone, Kelsey swears to find the truth. And as they come closer to uncovering the truth, someone is determined to silence Kelsey—*for good*.

 *Have Your Say*

You've just finished your book.
So what did you think?

We'd love to hear your thoughts on our
'Have your say' online panel
www.millsandboon.co.uk/haveyoursay

- 🌹 Easy to use
- 🌹 Short questionnaire
- 🌹 Chance to win Mills & Boon® goodies